ATROPOS

By the same author

Espionage Novels

Azrael
Snark
Cronus

Matt Cobb Mysteries

Killed in Paradise
Killed on the Ice
Killed with a Passion
Killed in the Act
Killed in the Ratings

Historical Mysteries

Five O'Clock Lightning
The Lunatic Fringe

Mysteries

The Hog Murders
Unholy Moses—originally published as by Philip DeGrave
Keep the Baby, Faith—originally published as by Philip DeGrave

ATROPOS

William L. DeAndrea

THE MYSTERIOUS PRESS
New York • London
Tokyo • Sweden • Milan

Copyright © 1990 by William L. DeAndrea
All rights reserved.

The Mysterious Press, 129 West 56th Street, New York, N.Y. 10019

Printed in the United States of America
First Printing: January 1990

10 9 8 7 6 5 4 3 2 1

Library of Congress Cataloging-in-Publication Data

DeAndrea, William L.
    Atropos / by William L. DeAndrea.
      p.   cm.
    ISBN 0-89296-208-9
    I. Title.
PS3554.E174A94 1990   89-36064
813'.54—dc20   CIP

for Sandy Manilla

ATROPOS

PART ONE
CLOTHO

She who spins the thread of life . . .

Chapter One

August 1974

He had expected it to be horrible—burning the house, burning Pina—but it was really sort of pretty.

He stood in the doorway and watched the flames, orange and yellow and blue, crawl their way across the floor toward her body as the linoleum bubbled beneath. He knew he should leave, knew he shouldn't waste time standing there, watching, but he couldn't bring himself to leave her so abruptly. He had been very fond of Pina. He would miss her.

He himself was in no danger from the flames. The layout of the bungalow was such that a fire might believably start at the space heater near the cheap bedroom curtains and incinerate the bed before ever endangering the front door, and he had set things up just that way.

It occurred to him that Ainley Masters would be proud of him. A problem had come up, and he'd dealt with it without panic. Not just without *visible* panic, but without panic of any sort. He hadn't *shown* panic to anyone outside the family and a few trusted family retainers since he was five years old. Gramps had made it clear that a Van Horn must always be *seen* to be in control, whatever he might be feeling inside. And that old man's cold contempt had been stronger than Hank's terror. Hank Van Horn got back on the horse—though the horse had round, rolling eyes, and big yellow teeth, and made a noise like lightning in his throat—he got back on the horse and rode it until Gramps said he could stop, and then he went home to the room Gramps kept for him in the big house, and he went into his bathroom and threw up until he felt he was going to turn himself inside out.

Since then, Hank Van Horn had felt a lot of strange things inside, but only the chosen few had ever seen them.

But tonight was different. Tonight he'd faced an impossible situation, and *he hadn't panicked at all*. Inside *or* out.

Well, he had, just at first, of course he had, or else Pina wouldn't be dead. But after that first, familiar moment, when the world and his name and History were all crushing in on him, when he couldn't stop his ears from hearing or his hands from doing, he broke through to a garden of peace and calm. He'd known precisely what to do and how to do it. Fire. Fire would conceal. Fire would purify.

Fire had reached the foot of the bed now, climbing the sheet he had artfully left trailing on the floor, playing with Pina's feet and legs, and he knew he should leave now, but he was frozen in the doorway. It was fascinating to him that she didn't try to get herself out of the fire. He knew it was ridiculous to feel that way—of course, she's dead, dead people can't feel anything—but he watched with amazement just the same.

The smoke was getting a little thick now, but the smoke, and the smell of the smoke, really, were no worse than at one of Gramps's famous family barbecues. Gramps had died at the last one. He'd been roasting an ox, and he'd let no one else near the job. In control, as usual. He stood by the coals, watching the carcass darken and drip and sizzle, turning the spit himself more often than not. The doctors said he'd given himself a stroke from the heat and the exertion. But stroke and all, when Gramps had keeled over and fallen into the barbecue pit, he'd tried to get away, clawing at the coals with the unparalyzed arm, trying to push himself free with the leg that could move. Some of the men pulled Gramps out, some of them burning themselves badly in the process, but it was too late. Hank hadn't been among them. He was too busy being seen to be in control. He'd thrown up that night, too. He'd strained his throat, but he had recovered sufficiently to deliver the eulogy at Gramps's funeral. The hoarseness made it seem as if Hank had been choked up with emotion—Ainley Masters said that had probably won Hank another twenty-five thousand votes in that year's election. Not that it made a difference—in that district, the Van Horn name was magic.

The fire had conquered most of the bed now. Hank had left Pina naked—he wondered if he shouldn't have put a nightgown on her or something, if she wouldn't have burned more thoroughly with cloth around her. He shrugged it off. Too late to worry about it.

Hank watched. He watched Pina's long, black hair first crisp, then turn gray-white, then disappear. He watched the fire attack her pretty face, distort it, corrupt it, until it looked just like Gramps's face when the men had pulled him out of the fire.

And suddenly, overwhelmingly, it *was* horrible, and the spell was broken. Hank Van Horn turned and ran for his life.

• • •

He had never meant to kill her. Why in the name of God should he kill her? He liked her. She was a lot of fun. Smart, too. Dedicated. A hard worker. Pina had organized Hank's out-of-state fund-raising phone calls more efficiently than in any of his previous campaigns.

She was even nice to Ella. That was the really amazing thing. Hank Van Horn had dallied with a lot of girls, and all of them but Pina had shown it when they came in contact with his wife. There was always some kind of smirk on their faces, or some icicle-sharpness to their voices when they talked to Ella, as though they were scoring some big points off her.

It wasn't as if Ella *cared* or anything. She had her charities and her tennis and a more than generous allowance from the family coffers; she was happy enough. And she had Mark, their son. Since he'd been born twelve years ago, he seemed to be all the man she needed in her life. Mark looked more like his mother all the time, as though proximity reinforced heredity.

And he was sharp, too. He had already learned, with a lot less pain than Hank had, what it meant to be a Van Horn. Hank was proud of him, when he thought about it. He made it a point to tell the boy whenever their schedules coincided.

This tended to happen less and less frequently these days. Ella seemed to want it that way. They'd be together in the fall, when the campaign heated up. Ella always dropped what she was doing to campaign with him. She was a fair campaigner—she could nod sympathetically when a factory worker held her hand and talked about his problems, even though she'd never seen the inside of a factory before her first campaign stop at one. Her real value, though, was in campaign photographs. Ella always photographed beautifully, and she had a way of looking at Hank that always came across as worshipful respect, whatever emotion it really reflected. The message to all who saw the picture was, "If this classy broad feels this way about him, he must really have something."

It was a big help, and it wasn't something Hank wanted to lose, so he made it a point to change girlfriends whenever they started to try to lord it over his wife.

Pina never did that, so Pina lasted much longer than any of the others, well into her second year, now. She was his Collierville girl, now, the one who got to live in the modest bungalow in the not-too-great section of town. The house had belonged to the family for years, always as a rent-free home for poorly paid campaign workers far from their own apartments. One time, a columnist in a New York paper had suggested it might be a—a "*love nest*" was the phrase he used—but Gramps had persuaded the paper to discourage the fellow from pursuing the point.

So when Hank was in town, he'd frequently drive Pina home from campaign headquarters when they'd work late. And he'd frequently go inside, where he and Pina would discuss campaign strategy, the way Nelson Rockefeller used to work late on a book about modern art.

That's what they'd done tonight. Hank and Pina had discussed campaign strategy in the shower, and again in the bed. He was just catching his breath after the second discussion when Pina told him she was pregnant.

Hank looked at her. "I thought you were taking care of that."

"Hank, darling," she said. "Nothing works all the time. I'm sorry."

She didn't seem sorry.

Then Hank told her she'd have to go somewhere far away, have the abortion under another name. He didn't need the anti-abortion nuts sniping at him because someone on his staff needed to get herself destorked. He told her he'd get Ainley Masters to handle all the details.

Pina went all Catholic on him. No abortion. Under no circumstances. She was going to have their baby.

That pissed Hank off. She hadn't been too Catholic to fuck a married man. She hadn't been too Catholic to suck his dick or ride his toes or do any of the other so-called sinful things they'd done together. She was just too Catholic to keep it from becoming a huge mess because she hadn't been able to keep from getting pregnant. "Sorry, darling."

What *really* infuriated him was that it was so *trite*, like a goddam outtake from *Citizen Kane*. If the press got hold of this, they wouldn't print much of it—the Van Horn name was magic with them, too, and they were having too much fun at the moment with the Nixon impeachment hearings—but there would be a horse laugh in the halls of the Nation's media that would kick up again every time Hank showed up.

And then Hank saw Pina's face, and there it was. The smirk she'd never shown to Ella. The self-satisfied look of someone who thinks she's getting away with something.

Hank could read the future in that face. Pina would make a big deal. She'd insist on marriage, at first. Then she'd settle for money. A lot of money. Or maybe she'd go for money right away, money to go away and have their baby (Hank remembered she hadn't said "*her* baby") and she'd raise it and love it, and she'd always be there for him.

Sure, Hank thought, until she decided she could use a million-dollar book-and-TV-movie deal.

"Give it up," he said. "It's not going to work."

"Hank, what are you talking about?"

"No Van Horn has ever payed blackmail, or ever will." He was quoting Gramps.

"Blackmail? Hank, I *love* you. Don't be silly."

There it was again, that smirk. The bitch was enjoying this.

"We'll work something out," she said.

"Work something out," Hank said. Then he said, "Bitch," and his hands jumped to her throat and started shaking her. He was not aware of wanting to do it. His hands did it, as though they were a pair of staffers who thought they knew more than the elected official they were supposed to serve.

Pina tried to talk, but her voice came out in a series of bubbling noises, like a sound effect in a cartoon. Then her eyes got wide, and her hands came up to try to pull his away. She started to scream. Hank's hands shook her harder, to make her stop. She had a lot of nerve, screaming. *She* was the goddam blackmailer.

She stopped screaming. Her tongue came out, and her head flopped back and forth like the head of a teddy bear, as though it were held on only by stitching on the outside.

"Bitch," Hank said again, and kept shaking for another half minute. When he let go, Pina flopped to the mattress.

"Now let's talk about that abortion," he said. He was panting and sweating. He wasn't so angry anymore.

He nudged her. "Come on," he said. "Don't sulk."

He pushed her hair off her face and rolled her over.

And she was dead. Her face was twisted and blue, and her tongue was out, and strands of her long black hair were clinging to the surface of one staring eye.

He'd strangled her. He hadn't meant to, but he had. The bruises on her throat might have been a tattoo reading CHOKED. He'd been shaking, of course, but he didn't remember *squeezing*. He had no *intention* of squeezing. Of course, he had no intention of shaking her, either—he'd just found himself doing it.

Well, he thought, at least she won't be coming around with a brat making trouble for me. Then he realized what kind of trouble he was in already.

But he didn't panic—he planned. He planned while he got dressed. He planned while he pushed Pina's tongue back in and got the hair out of her eyes and placed her comfortably on her back. Five minutes later, the fire was beginning to crackle.

• • •

It was a shirt-sleeve night, but Hank started shivering as soon as he reached the sidewalk. It was simply, Hank was sure, the contrast between the heat of the fiery room and the relative coolness of normal weather. All he had to do now was reach his car (parked down two blocks and over one) and drive away. He'd call Ainley Masters, and together they'd decide what Hank should say when told of the tragedy.

He heard a sudden explosion and the sound of shattering glass. Hank hit the ground and started crawling for cover, the way the family security experts taught every Van Horn. There was a roaring and a bright light. He looked back at the bungalow and saw what had happened.

The heat built up inside had popped one of the windows. Now the air was rushing in and turning the house into a furnace. The flames spiked up through the roof like bright yellow spears.

Hank allowed himself a small smile. The more heat, the less evidence.

Pina and her little bastard would burn to nonexistence. The less there was, the less there would be to react to for the police and the press.

Hank heard the voices as he was getting to his feet.

"Fire . . . my God!"

". . . Like a bomb, for Christ's sake . . ."

". . . anybody called the fire department?"

The noise and the light of the fire had drawn them, a little excitement for a run-down neighborhood. A crowd for Hank to filter through. A good thing. He worked his way toward his car.

More voices.

". . . hope there was nobody inside."

"Senator?"

". . . and where's the goddam fire department, will somebody tell me that? That fucker could spread!"

"Senator? Senator Van Horn?" The owner of this voice had him by the sleeve. It was a short man with brownish teeth and slicked-back black hair. "Senator, I'm Jack Smael. I'm party coordinator for this neighborhood." He held out his hand to shake. Hank took it automatically. Jack Smael went on to tell Hank how they had met a couple of years ago at the victory party for Congressman Delgado.

Hank's mind was empty. Habit and training brought the proper words to his lips. "Yes," he said. "Of course. Good to see you again. How are you?"

"More to the point, Senator, how are you? You look like you got too close to the fire. You need a doctor?"

All of Hank's resources were devoted to keeping the calm politician's smile on his face. There was nothing left for speech, or action, or thought.

"What are you doing in the neighborhood, Senator?" Jack Smael asked. "Next time, let me know, I'll arrange something. I don't have to tell you how important it is not to let an opportunity to meet the public go to—Oh, I got it. This is Miss Girolamo's house; she's on your staff. Jeez, I hope she's okay."

The smile went away. Hank could feel the muscles fail one by one. His face seemed to hang on him, dead and alien, like fungus on a tree. *I've got to get out of here,* he thought.

Then he heard the sirens, and saw flashes of red and white light on the black smoke billowing from Pina's house. *I've got to get out of here.* He threw Jack Smael's hand away like something dirty. "I've got to get out of here!" he said, and turned and ran.

• • •

Ainley Masters lived alone in an apartment on Lakeside, on the most exclusive block of that exclusive street. He had accumulated the necessary money in the course of serving the Van Horn family throughout his adult life. No one begrudged it to him—he had earned it.

He had earned his share of enemies, too. Hank had to stand on the doorstep for the better part of two minutes before Ainley peeped through all his peepholes and undid all his locks.

"Senator," he said, as he swung the door open. "What the hell happened? Have you been attacked?"

Hank's mistake was trying to tell it so it made sense. It was impossible to relate what had happened to him tonight so that it made sense. A few disconnected phrases made it past Hank's mouth. "Pina's dead . . . fire . . . somebody saw me—lot of people . . . had to get away . . ."

"Stop it."

"Ainley, help me! The police will be after me, I'll go to jail. I didn't mean—"

"Hank, *shut up!*"

The Senator shut up and goggled at him. Ainley, though about ten years older, had *never* called him "Hank."

Hank looked at him, waiting. Ainley was thinking. He had a very good face for thinking—large, dark, sort of sad eyes, long aquiline nose, thin lips, strong chin. He was quite a small man, but he gave an impression of power all the same.

"There's the phone," Ainley said. "Call the fire department. Give your name. Report the fire."

"But, Ainley, the fire department was just getting there when I left. I thought it was the police, that's why I ran, but I realize now—"

"You ran because you were obsessed with calling the fire department," Ainley said. "You're so agitated, you aren't thinking straight."

"That's the truth," Hank said. "Can I have a drink?"

"After you make the call. Maybe. As soon as you call, I'll get the family lawyers busy." Ainley had gone to Harvard Law at Gramps's expense, and had passed the bar years ago, but he had never practiced law. His brain was too valuable to waste in court, or in drawing up documents.

Ainley handed Hank the phone. "Call," he commanded. "Your name, and the address of the fire. Nothing else. Just hang up."

Hank made the call. The dispatcher had tried to ask questions, but Hank pretended not to hear them. He turned to Ainley. "Was that okay?"

"That was fine, Hank, especially with the strain you're under. You know, I can guess exactly what happened tonight."

"I've been trying to tell you."

Ainley was stern. "*Don't* tell me. I'll guess. You and Miss Girolamo and a few others?"

Hank nodded.

Ainley nodded back, as if he'd expected that. "And a few others worked late. You drove Miss Girolamo to the house the campaign has provided for her. You left her there, and headed for your own home. On the way, you realized there was a document you'd forgotten to give her, something to do with the upcoming campaign. You have such a document in your car right now, don't you, Senator?"

"I've got neighborhood income breakdowns, but—"

"Neighborhood income breakdowns. It was important she have them, an important addition to her duties. You turned back to bring them to her. When you got there, you smelled smoke. You went inside—the door was unlocked—and called her name, but there was no answer. The smell of smoke was stronger. You went through the house, fighting flames and smoke, looking for her. It was a terrible risk, but the Van Horns inspire loyalty by giving it.

"You couldn't find Miss Girolamo. You knew the fire department was needed, but by the time you made your way out of the house, you were so dazed by heat and smoke that you were temporarily at a loss as to what to do.

"The approach of the fire department—or at least the sirens and the distant lights, you didn't actually see any fire trucks, did you?"

Hank shook his head.

"Good, good," Ainley said, like a doctor listening to a patient's chest. "The siren and lights, without registering on your conscious mind, reminded you subconsciously of your resolve to call the fire department. In your confused state, it never occurred to you to ask to use a stranger's phone, and you didn't want to take time to find a public phone. So you came here."

Ainley regarded him blandly. "Does that sound about right, Senator?"

Hank took a few seconds to repeat the story to himself. Ainley was amazing. Of course, the image of the Van Horns always being in control was going to be shaken, but Hank was sure Gramps, wherever he was, would look down and forgive him. The alternative was too horrible to contemplate.

"Senator?"

"Yes, Ainley. That's exactly what happened. To the letter."

"It's a talent I have. I can put myself in another person's place. Let me get myself presentable, and we'll go to the fire department and talk to the press. Are you ready?"

"I will be," Hank promised.

"Don't get *too* calm. You've had a terrible experience."

I certainly have, Hank thought.

"And don't get too rattled, either. This is going to be sticky. Most of the press loves you, but they'll latch on to this like a terrier and shake. Be contrite. Mourn her as a worker and a friend. Get indignant over suggestions of anything improper."

"Of course, Ainley." Hank was feeling better already. He could do this. Once someone gave him a program, he could stick to it and look good in the process. He was almost eager to get on with it.

While he was changing, Ainley called from the bedroom. "Oh. And, Senator, you have a talent I admire."

Hank was surprised; it was so rare for Ainley to admit admiring anything. "What's that?"

"Timing. On any other day, this would be the news story of the decade. Now it will get just a corner of the front page."

"Why?" Hank knew it was silly, but he was almost disappointed.

Ainley reappeared, knotting his tie. He smiled sardonically. "I take it back," he said. "It's not your timing I admire, it's your luck. I've got this from Washington, absolutely solid. Nixon's resigning the Presidency at noon tomorrow. Come on, let's go."

Ainley was reaching for the doorknob when Hank grabbed his hand. "Ainley, is this going to work?"

"Why not?" Ainley said. "It's worked before."

• • •

Ainley, as usual, had been right. It *was* sticky. It was a lot worse than sticky. At times, it was agonizing. There was an autopsy (inconclusive—too little soft tissue remained unburned). There was interrogation by fire marshals and policemen. They'd learned the fire had been started by the space heater.

Senator, why would someone be using a space heater on a warm August night?

For one suicidal moment, when a fire marshal first asked him that question, Hank had been tempted to make up an answer. Then he'd realized that this was a matter about which an innocent man would be completely ignorant. He proclaimed his ignorance, indignantly.

But Ainley was also right about his other assertion—the story worked. Eighty percent of the ranking police and fire officials in the state owed something to the Van Horns, as did ninety-five percent of the judges, and a goodly number of the journalists. Most of the rest could see the futility of mixing it up with that kind of power over one little Italian-American social climber. The few remaining were easy to paste a label on—vindictive bastards who were out to smear, not only a Good Man and a dedicated public servant, but worse, an innocent young girl who could no longer defend herself.

A lot of that labeling was done by Mr. and Mrs. Aogostino Girolamo, recently retired from the gray, industrial town of Irondale, downstate from the capital, to a lovely condominium in Boca Raton, Florida, courtesy of a sympathetic Van Horn family. In the expressed opinion of Mrs. Girolamo, Senator Henry Van Horn was "a saint," and their Giuseppina had been blessed to know him.

So while there were some sneers, especially out of state, when the inquest ruled Death by Misadventure in the case of Josephine Ann Girolamo, there was a minimum of harm done. Some said it might have cost the Senator any future chance at the White House, but the Van Horns, unlike some political dynasties, knew the White House was not an essential base of operations for steering the country in the direction you wanted it to go.

After all, Hank was reelected, and continued to be reelected, growing in seniority and power.

Mr. Nixon was long, long gone.

Chapter Two

The Present—January—Kirkester, New York

Trotter hated to stop on an even number. He pressed his back down into the bench, tightened his hands on the grips, and forced the muscles of his legs to lift the weight one more time. It was burning, tearing agony, but it had to be done. When the thirty-pound weight clanked home at the top of the hinge, Trotter was tempted to let go and let the thing crash back down, but he didn't. He eased it down, if anything that took that much effort could have anything to do with "ease."

There, he thought. I should videotape these things. Let the Congressman and all the Agency doctors see he wasn't dodging his rehabilitation. Trotter had even been given to understand that the President himself had been asking after him.

This is what I get, he thought, for going tame.

Trotter sat up, pulling the sweatband off his head as he did so. As always, he held it out at arm's length and squeezed. Liquid oozed from the top of his hand and between his fingers, fat drops of sweat that spatted loudly on the floor. He threw the sweatband across the basement of his new two-bedroom ranch, making a basket in the open top of the washer. He missed maybe one day out of six. He didn't bother to retrieve the ones that went behind the washer.

Trotter said, "Ah," as he stood up. He always said "Ah" when he stood up these days. When the doctors felt like being particularly honest with him, they told him he probably always would make some kind of noise. When they were being brutal about it, they told him he'd probably be in some "discomfort" every waking hour for the rest of his life. Even a doctor being brutal doesn't like to use the word "pain."

"After all," they'd tell him, as if he'd been looking for an argument, "you were hurt very badly."

Yeah, Trotter thought. I remember. I was there. Thirty feet, from the catwalk to the concrete floor of the Hudson Group's press room. Fractured skull. Ten smashed ribs. Broken hip. Three bones broken in his legs. Punctured lung. He knew all about it. That's what he was rehabilitating himself from.

It was even working. He hardly limped at all, now, and he had stopped using the cane weeks ago.

He limped after these goddam workouts, though. He limped now over to the laundry area. Trotter kicked off his sneakers, slid out of his sweatpants and jock, pulled off his shirt. He threw everything but the sneakers into the washer, added soap and softener, and started the machine. When they'd first let him out of the hospital, he used to take a rueful inventory of his surgery scars every time he found himself naked; now he didn't bother. Rehabilitating the mind, too. Trotter said, "Ah," bent down and pulled a towel out of the dryer. He wrapped it around himself and headed upstairs.

Going upstairs was no problem. Trotter had been surprised to discover that. It was going *downstairs* that was the killer, the forcing of muscles and joints to give in to gravity, but only just enough. The only times he missed the cane were when he found himself at the top of a steep flight of stairs.

Trotter padded across the kitchen floor to the cabinet next to the refrigerator. He took out a bottle of Advil, carefully counted out six of them. Then he opened the refrigerator and took out a bottle of Gatorade and a jelly doughnut. He swallowed the pills, washing them down with the Gatorade.

Forget cocaine, he thought. Ibuprofen was the new drug of choice. This dose every six hours kept the "discomfort" to a level he could manage. He could get a prescription for Motrin, which was the same stuff in bigger doses, but why bother? Hell, with his connections, he could get codeine, morphine, Demerol, stuff that would make him forget there was a thing *called* pain.

Trotter didn't want them. It wasn't that he liked the pain. It was that he worried about what *else* the stuff would make him forget. Two many lives depended on the functioning of Trotter's brain for him to mess around with it lightly. That knowledge was with him every waking moment, too. He was beginning to appreciate what the Congressman had gone through all these years.

He caught himself thinking that, and laughed around a mouthful of doughnut. He had spent nearly half his life making vows to himself to die rather than to be like the old man, and now look at him. Things had changed.

A *lot* of things had changed. For instance, he was through as a field agent. Certainly he was done with foreign work. It was very difficult slipping inconspicuously into a country when you had enough pins and plates in your body to set off every metal detector in every airport in the world. The only way he'd been able to get back to Kirkester when he'd left the hospital in Washington was with a note from his doctor and a copy of his X-rays for the benefit of airport security.

But it wasn't only that. There were a lot of things he'd once been able to do that he couldn't do anymore. He couldn't run, for one thing, or climb ropes. He had enough strength and stamina to lift that goddam weight with his legs a hundred times. A hundred and one, rather. But that was all he had. As soon as he finished, he needed pills and Gatorade and jelly doughnuts and a nice hot shower before he even felt like something worth burying.

Trotter trudged to the bathroom. He dropped the towel, started the shower. He looked at himself in the mirror, leaning close to it, so he could see what he looked like without his glasses. He still looked gaunt, older than he ought to be. Bash kept telling him he looked fine, but Trotter wished he could fill out a little. Maybe he'd up it to two jelly doughnuts.

Trotter tested the water, increased the heat a little, and stepped into the shower. He stood there letting the water hit him for a while before he reached for the soap.

Of course, not all the changes had been for the worse. For the first time in his life he had a home, a place he was not likely to have to leave secretly in the middle of the night. He had a job. *Two* jobs. There was his bullshit cover job—Consultant to the Executive Editor of *Worldwatch* magazine, which was just an excuse for him to put the resources of the Hudson Group to work for him—and there was his real job—running the Agency while the Congressman completed his own rehabilitation.

Considering the years he'd spent running *from* the Agency as he would a demon from hell, the job hadn't turned out too badly. So far. Of course, that could change at any moment. He was now a top executive in the dirtiest business humans had come up with yet. The fact that the opposition had been fairly benign over the last couple of months hadn't led him to forget that. Sooner or later, unless the Congressman recovered quickly enough to take back the reins, Trotter knew he was going to face a situation where he'd either have to do something morally repulsive, or put the country in danger. The genius, the benefactor of humanity, who could figure out a way to remove that burden from the backs of those who chose (or were forced) to shoulder it, had yet to publish his findings.

To hell with it, Trotter thought. It was a beautiful winter's day, and the pills and the hot water had drawn a lot of the pain away. He had a home now, and he'd stuck with one name and one face longer than he had for any other period of his adult life. He hadn't had to kill anyone or order anyone killed in over a year. And he was in love.

He'd never been so happy in his life.

Chapter Three

Regina Hudson looked at the numerous items still unticked on her agenda, and sent mental thanks to her mother for having hired such good people over the years. Where was Mother today? Seattle, for the Single Parents Federation Convention? No. That was last week. Today, Petra Hudson would be in Hollywood, conferring with the producer who had bought the film rights to *Living It Over*, Mother's best-selling autobiography. The critics had all called the book "a fantastic story." She wondered what they would have said if they'd known the *whole* story, Allan's part in it, and the clergyman-assassin and the rest.

Anyway, Mother's book had contained enough of the truth to fix it so that no one's life would ever be the same again. My own, for instance, she thought. Regina Hudson, twenty-six, was now Publisher and Chairman of the Board of one of America's most powerful media combines. She owned it. She and her brother did, anyway. Mother had signed it over to them right after she'd gone public with her story. Jimmy, however, had never been very interested in the family business, and the ordeal they'd gone through over the Azrael affair had soured him on it for good. He was living in the Rockies somewhere under an assumed name, brooding, probably. Regina had never been one to brood.

On the other hand, she'd never been much of a big-shot executive, either; though she'd spent her childhood watching her mother wield power, Regina sometimes found herself a little arm-weary when she tried to heft it herself.

Still, here she was, at the head of the big oak table in the publisher's conference room, presiding over ten grizzled journalism veterans at the latest campaign-coverage strategy session.

"Now," Sam Weicker said, "we got papers in all but one of the primary states. I think we ought to coordinate the magazine correspondents with the local papers until the field thins out a little." Weicker was the chief accountant. He was very good at his job—he was doing his job, now, trying to save the company money—but Regina had trouble taking him seriously. He was big and fat and loud and vulgar, and slightly greasy. Regina had a fantasy that when Sam was starting out, he had decided to fulfill a stereotype to the ultimate degree—but had somehow pulled the wrong file, and made himself into the caricature of a sportswriter rather than an accountant.

"I've already had a preliminary talk with the people in Keokuk—"

"No," Regina heard herself say. "Absolutely not."

Ten sets of eyes were leveled at her. She saw resentment in some of them, amusement in others. Surprise in all.

She looked to Sean Murphy for help. Sean was Executive Editor of the Hudson Group, recently promoted from Director of Operations. What all that meant, aside from the pay raise, was that he basically ran the show while he showed Regina the ropes. A lot of people in any business—grizzled veterans, especially—might have used that kind of setup to build an empire, to reduce the young owner, damp behind the ears and a female at that, to a figurehead.

It never crossed Murphy's mind. He was the one who looked like the accountant, bespectacled and slight, with hair edging from gray to white. He was just short of fifty, but his perpetually worried look made him seem older. He was quiet, and seemed shy, except on those rare occasions he took a drink. Then he had the filthiest mouth in the newspaper business.

So the legend said, anyway. Regina had never seen him that way. She'd asked him about it once; he'd simply said he was a lot more serious about being Irish when he was younger.

These days, he was serious about helping Regina learn her job. Now, for instance. Her glance at him had been a request to expand on her refusal to Weicker. Murphy's response was a small smile, and a slight gesture with his hand that said, "No, no, dear lady, after you."

"Sam," she said, "this meeting is about how *Worldwatch* is going to cover the election. The local papers have nothing to do with it. You get back to the people in Keokuk and tell them to forget it."

"Regina," Sam said. "Miss Hudson, I mean."

"Regina is okay," she said, then wondered if it was. What the hell, she decided. He'd known her since she was a little girl. Besides, she'd called him "Sam."

"Regina, we could save millions using those people. It's a big advantage we've got. *Time* and *U.S. News* don't have any papers to help them, and *Newsweek*'s got a lot fewer than we do."

"One of them is the *Washington Post*," someone pointed out.

"Since when is there an important primary in Washington?" Sam retorted.

"That's not the point, Sam," Regina said. She caught herself fiddling with her pencil. She made herself stop and look Sam in the eye. "The Hudson Group is committed to the independent operation of all the local papers. If they serve their communities and make a profit, the people stay on, period. I'm not about to pre-empt or co-opt any of these people. We promised them independence when we hired them, and we're not about to go messing with it."

"Regina," Sam said wearily, "when you've had as much experience as *I* have, you'll find out you've got to make the occasional compromise on things like this."

It was true she didn't have all that much experience. Before becoming Publisher and Chairman of the Board, she'd been the editor of the Kirkester *Chronicle,* a job her mother had given her the way a carpenter would give his kid a piece of wood to play with. But she'd made the job real, the way she'd make this one real. Also, she hated Sam's goddam patronizing attitude.

"That's bullshit, Sam. You're acting as if the company's on the verge of bankruptcy. Unless you're fudging the books you showed me a couple of weeks ago, we're making record profits."

"There's never so much money around you couldn't piss it away by being careless."

"I'm not being careless, I'm sticking with the practices that led us to the record profits in the first place."

"Part of the record profits—forgive me, here, Regina—come from the fact that your mother turned out to be a Russian spy."

Sean Murphy spoke for the first time. "That's really unfair, Sam," he said quietly.

"I'll handle it, Sean," Regina said. Her hands were fists on the table now; she was leaning out over them as though ready to spring.

"Yes," she said. "My mother came to this country as a spy, to infiltrate my father's business and run it to make the Kremlin happy. I won't forget that. Don't you forget that she found herself so in love with this country and this business that when the Russians called on her, she risked her life rather than compromise the Hudson Group."

Sam shrank back. "All right, all right. Don't get so excited."

"I'm sorry," Regina said. She supposed she was, too, but not much. She sat back and took a breath. "Okay," she said. "I know you're doing your job. I also know you tried this local-paper–*Worldwatch* tie-in business on my mother like clockwork every Presidential election since 1964. It didn't work with her, and it's not going to work with me."

She turned to Murphy. "Sean, why don't you take up manpower allocation?"

There, she thought, half-amused and half-proud. Now that I've shown my authority, I can delegate some. Anyway, the small details of manpower allocation bored her silly. The important thing was that the allocation should be made in accordance with their reading of the way the campaign was going to shape up, something she'd already been through in detail with Murphy and her senior people, as well as with independent analysts and pollsters.

It really looked as if November was going to be a formality. The real contest was going to be in July, at the convention of the party in power. It was going to come down to Stephen Abweg of Missouri, House Majority Whip, or Carl Babington, Governor of New Jersey.

The *Worldwatch* bureau editors felt the same way.

"The other guys should all drop out by Super Tuesday."

"Yeah, they'll hold on that far in the hope that us or *Time* or CBS or the Miami *Herald* will turn up with a picture of Mr. A and Mr. B taking turns at the Ayatollah's camel or something."

Laughter. "The Gary Hart syndrome. I can hear it now. 'I wouldn't be the first camel humper to enter the White House.'"

"Do you think the President is going to endorse one of these guys?"

Sean Murphy scratched his head. "They'd love him to. He's a lame duck, and he's made a lot of mistakes the last year or so, but he's still enormously popular. His endorsement this early would swing a lot of weight."

"The new President would owe him a lot," somebody speculated. "Not that he'd especially need it, what with the pension and the lecture possibilities and the books and the rest of the automatic elder-statesman business."

"Oh, he'd like to do it, all right," Murphy said. "But I don't see how he can. Since the Teddy Roosevelt–Taft thing worked out so badly, Presidents have avoided trying to hand-pick their successors. Our incumbent is superconscious of what history thinks. Besides, he can't really pick either of them without looking like an ingrate. Abweg's worked like a dog to get his programs through Congress, and Babington's his oldest friend in politics, the one who talked him into running for office back when he was starting out."

"So the President sits it out."

"Right. Then after the convention, he goes all out for the nominee."

"Well, he'd do that anyway."

"All right, if the President's going to stay out of it, whose endorsement is the big trophy?"

"Van Horn."

"Hank Van Horn?" somebody said, and laughed.

"What's so funny?"

"No, no, you're right. He's got a stranglehold on a state with a lot of votes, he's senior enough to have a lot of juice in the Senate, he's the acknowledged leader of the liberal wing of the Party, and a lot of Americans still see the family halo around him, burnt-up girlfriend and all."

"Campaign associate."

"Yeah. Right."

"Those are all reasons his endorsement *could* make the difference."

"I'm not saying it won't."

"You laughed."

"I laughed because I cover the Senate. I've seen that guy make endorsements in every election since '76. It's hurt him worse than a man with hemorrhoids shitting peach pits. He looks at the White House the way Moses looked at the Promised Land."

"A lot of people think he's lucky not to have gone to jail," Regina said.

"I know what a lot of people think. I was telling you what Hank Van Horn thinks."

"So," Sean Murphy said, "we'll have people with all the candidates, but as they thin out, we'll quietly redeploy to Abweg or Babington."

"What about the other party?"

"It looks like Milton, for them, but it could be anybody."

"Doesn't matter. Whoever it is is meat."

"That doesn't matter, either," Murphy said. "We'll cover them exactly as though they had a chance to win. Strange things can happen in politics."

"Jimmy Carter," someone suggested.

Someone else asked, "Who is *Worldwatch* going to be for?"

"*Worldwatch* has never endorsed candidates," Regina said.

"I know that. I asked who we were going to be *for*."

"We," Regina said, "are going to be impartial."

Silence fell. "My God," someone whispered at last. "An idealist."

"Okay, okay," Sean Murphy said. "Back to business." They talked about travel arrangements and expense accounts, and egos of star reporters, who did not wish to grace with their celebrity candidates of insufficient stature. It went on for a long time. Regina was glad when it was finally over.

She headed back to her office. Sean Murphy caught up with her.

"You did fine," he told her. "Your mother will be proud."

"I knew you were reporting to her."

"I'm not spying on you or anything—"

"Of course not. I wouldn't want Mother to lose all touch with the company."

Murphy grinned at her. "You're going to be fine. Anything you want to talk over?"

"No. Thanks, Sean, but it's—" She looked at her watch. "My God, past eight o'clock already. Of course I'll stay if there's anything we need to go over. Is there?"

"No. I think it's going to be fine." They walked along in silence for a while, then Murphy said, "You're going to see Trotter tonight, aren't you?"

"I think so." Actually, she was damned sure of it. "Why?"

"Be careful about him, okay? Everything about him on the surface is fine, but I've got a feeling . . ."

Regina laughed. "So did I, when I first met him. It's okay, Sean. You'd like Allan, if you could get to know him."

"Then it's unanimous. Your mother tells me not to worry, too."

"Good. But you're sweet to care. Good night."

"Yeah," Murphy said. "Good night."

Chapter Four

Trotter pulled the evening report off the Teletype machine in the locked room next to the study. His "Special Assistant" tag was a convenient excuse for him to *have* a Teletype room in his house, in case anyone noticed. He didn't go around bringing it to anyone's attention. The machine itself was unremarkable, though the circuitry included sophisticated tamper-alarms and the latest in anti-bugging devices, specially installed by Jake Feder, who'd once again come out of a Florida retirement to help the Agency.

Three times a day (more if necessary) the machine brought detailed reports of what the Agency was up to. The reports were compiled by the Washington staff, most of whom thought they were working for a crooked international cartel instead of an independent, hyper-secret agency of the government of the United States. The fact that it was much easier to recruit people to gather intelligence for (supposedly) a group of conscienceless economic royalists that it was to find them willing to do the same for their country was a sign of something unhealthy, Trotter wasn't sure what.

The reports were in code. Code was much safer than cipher. With computers as smart as they were these days, any cipher could be broken, if you got a big-enough sample for it. A code on the other hand, where the word "ELBOW" could have the previously agreed-upon meaning, "Meet the Cuban defector at 9:15 P.M. on the north end of parking lot AA at Kennedy Airport," and the phrase "URGENT NO HITCH IN SARCASM EFFACED—THEY LOOK LIKE BEARS—PLEASE ADVISE" could mean (as it did today) "nothing to report," was practically unbreakable, assuming, of course, the key to the code did not fall into the wrong hands. Since the copy of the book in Washington was as safe as vaults and personnel screening could make it, and Trotter's copy had been memorized and dissolved in acid months ago, he didn't worry about it.

The reports had shown a quiet day. The biggest news was that the operative they had infiltrating a racist skinhead group in Colorado was now a fully accepted member of the gang. There was no sign yet of any foreign influence, should he keep looking? Trotter had sent a ten sentence reply that meant "yes." The afternoon report was all various forms of "nothing to report," which suited Trotter fine. The evening report was more of the same.

Except at the very end, where it said, "BIRDS CLOGGING FEEDER PIPE—SUMMON ELECTRICIAN."

That meant to report to the Congressman. In person. As soon as possible.

• • •

"As soon as possible" in this case meant grabbing a plane tomorrow morning about eight—for years, Trotter had made it a point to memorize all the public transportation schedules of any town he happened to find himself in—which would get him to Washington about ten-thirty or so, which meant he had something like twelve hours to wonder what the hell the old man wanted.

It was, of course, useless to try to guess, so that's what he did. The paper shredder hummed background music as he got rid of the day's reports and speculated.

It could be a personnel problem. Fenton Rines, who had resigned from the FBI and now ran the Agency's Washington operation, had had too much and was packing it in, and the old man wanted his son to come down to talk over a replacement.

Or perhaps Rines had finally recruited the Congressman in his campaign to force Trotter to move to Washington. That was a never-ending battle. Rines's point was that it was inconvenient and time-consuming to send coded reports. Trotter pointed out that the Congressman, when he had been running things day-to-day, had routinely kept up-to-date by means of coded reports.

Trotter, on the other hand, had several good reasons to stay where he was. If the big one came, and Washington got wiped out in a nuclear attack, the Agency wouldn't have to lose a beat—the acting head had his operation set up several hundred miles away in an insignificant little town that was unlikely to be a major target.

Also, it was more secure. The Congressman had designed the Agency in the wake of World War II because he had seen that the soon-to-be formed CIA, even in those relatively untrammeled days, was going to be too bureaucracy-bound to do some of the things that had to be done. He'd picked a small group of men and women and sent them out to do all the dirty little jobs that needed doing in a hurry.

When Watergate and related scandals broke, and it became apparent that Congress was going to have a much bigger say in the running of the country's intelligence operation, the General (as he had been) found an exploitable district in his home state and got himself elected to Congress. A little sophisticated wheeling and dealing, some pressure judiciously applied, and the Congressman now found himself in charge of the committee that was supposed to regulate all the government's intelligence agencies. The Congressman made sure his own Agency remained a deep dark secret from everyone but himself and the President, whoever that happened to be. Over the years, a couple of Presidents, learning of the existence of the Agency on Inauguration Day, had been horrified, and had ordered the Agency disbanded. As General, and later as Congressman, the man in charge of the Agency had aquiesced gracefully, asking only for sixty days to wind things up. No President had been able to function in office for sixty days without finding a use for the Agency, and, Trotter was sure, none ever would.

Maybe that's what it was. Maybe the current President, to spare his successor the necessity of fighting with his conscience, was going to order the Agency out of existence now. Trotter wondered whether he would care. Strategically, it would be a catastrophic mistake—without the Agency, the Kremlin would be running the country, maybe not openly, within twenty years. Personally, Trotter decided he wouldn't give a damn. He'd make an honest woman out of Regina, play at the news business for twenty years, and raise a couple of kids who knew how to survive with a certain degree of dignity in a police state. It could be done. It took a lot of self-control, and a lot of ruthlessness, but those traits can be instilled. A father can teach his child to be ruthless and self-controlled.

After all, Trotter thought, my father taught me.

Miles, names, and lives ago, Allan Trotter had been conceived as one of the General's long-range plans. The General had planted him in the womb of a Soviet agent who thought she was using her sex to prey on the General's weaknesses. Her mistake. The General didn't *have* any weaknesses, at least not that kind. He had seen her, a dedicated, fearless, and successful spy (her capture had been a fluke), as ideal breeding stock with whom to create the perfect agent.

Trotter often wondered how successful the old man thought his plan had been.

Maybe the old man was dying, and he wanted to see his son before the end.

Trotter laughed. No, it wouldn't be that. No sentiment from that old man.

To hell with it. Tomorrow would tell. Bash would be here soon. He dropped the shreds of the day's reports in a stainless-steel tub, opened a medicine bottle, and put one drop from an eyedropper on the paper. There was a flash of fire and the whoosh of a miniature explosion. As always, Trotter looked to make sure it was all gone. As always, it was. Not even a smudge of ash. Science was wonderful. He went to the living room to wait for Regina.

• • •

Regina had a key to Allan's house, but she had only used it once, the time she'd entered a darkened foyer, then stepped into the living room to find Allan behind her, holding a fireplace poker casually in one hand, and apologizing profusely. He had been, he said, raised paranoid, and that was probably never going to go away. After that, she used the doorbell.

Allan let her in, and smiled. "Hello, Bash," he said. He waited until he locked the door before he kissed her. It was worth waiting for.

"Long day," he said.

"I know, I was there for every dismal second of it. The horrible part is, when I was a little girl, this is all I wanted to do when I grew up."

Allan grinned. "Maybe you just haven't grown up yet."

"Maybe that's it," Regina said. "Can I have a glass of wine, or are you going to card me?"

"Nah, I'll trust you. Help yourself. I want to get the steaks on."

"One of these days I'll have to learn how to cook," she said. "I knew there were drawbacks to growing up rich."

"You make a salad. You can tear lettuce, can't you?"

"I could probably be coached through it. Do I have time to change first?"

"Sure."

"I'll be right back," she said. They kissed again. Regina scooted off to the bedroom and switched to some of her hanging-around-Allan's-place clothes, a faded pair of jeans and a Sorbonne sweatshirt. She got rid of her makeup, then went to the kitchen to tear lettuce.

They ate at the small table in the kitchen—Allan's dining room had been turned into a library. The steak was perfect—it crunched, then oozed, then melted as she chewed it. She wondered where Allan had found time to learn to cook. She didn't ask. The way he took questions about his past, no matter how innocuous, varied wildly. He never flared up at her or anything, but he never told her much, either. Sometimes he answered, sometimes he brooded, as if he didn't want to remember the answer himself, sometimes he shrugged it off with a joke. Regina had learned not to ask at all, unless it was something she felt she really had to know.

Allan cleared dishes away, then joined Regina in the living room. She liked it. Growing up, she had lived in rooms wished on her by boarding-school administrators or by her mother's decorators. Everything in Allan's house had been picked by him on the basis of what use he intended to make of it. None of the furniture matched, but it was all comfortable and sturdy. There were books, almost a whole wall of them, at right angles to the windows. Against the opposite wall was a bank of consumer electronics. And other electronics that only very special government-sponsored consumers could get their hands on. It *looked* like a component TV, and a turntable, reel-to-reel and cassette tape players, a CD, a VCR and a laserdisc machine, amps, pre-amps, tuners and speakers, and they were all there. But Regina knew that somewhere behind the dials and lights were components that could send a scrambled radio message around the world, and devices that notified Allan the minute anyone stepped within twenty yards of his house.

When Allan had told her all this, Regina had been surprised to learn there was no electronic security *inside* the house. "It's supposed to be secret in here," Allan had said.

Regina was just as glad. She was keeping a secret, herself. From Allan. She had trouble deciding whether the thought frightened her or made her want to giggle.

"Do you want to watch TV or anything?" Allan asked.

"No, I just want to sit awhile."

"Suits me," he said. For a split second, Allan's control slipped and Regina could see the weariness in him. Sometimes, he hid it so well that Regina could almost forget how badly he'd been hurt. Almost. Because she could never forget what she'd seen that day as she looked over the edge of the catwalk. The ocean of blood. The pieces of the man who'd been going to kill her, sliced apart by the wicked edge of newsprint traveling two hundred miles an hour through a printing press.

And she'd seen Allan, with his left lower leg pointed back up toward his head, his right arm invisible underneath him, shards of bone poking up to make an obscene circus tent of blood-soaked clothing. She'd nearly turned herself inside out being sick when she first saw it. Even now, it made her shiver.

Allan put his arm around her. "Cold?"

She smiled. "No, I'm fine. Just tired."

"I have to go out of town tomorrow."

"What for?"

"I don't know. I've been summoned."

Regina looked at him. "You're supposed to be running that outfit, aren't you? How can *you* be summoned?"

Allan smiled. "That's the thing. I'm *supposed* to be running it. As it is, I'm really part of a troika with Rines and the old boss."

Not for the first time, Regina wondered just who this "old boss" was, and why he seemed to have such a hold on Allan, even after he'd given up his job. She did not ask.

Instead, she said, "When are you leaving?"

"I'll have to get out of here by seven."

"A.M.?"

"Right."

"Yuck."

"I couldn't have put it better myself."

Regina put her head against his shoulder. They were silent for a few minutes.

"Well, look," she said. "I've had a long day and I'm kind of tired; you're *going* to have a long day tomorrow . . ."

"Yes?"

"Whatever are we doing," she demanded, "out of bed?"

Allan smiled sadly. "There was a time," he said, "when I would now grab you and carry you upstairs."

"I don't mind."

"Now it's all I can do to get up them myself without limping."

"Carrying would take too long anyway. I'll run up and meet you there."

Allan laughed. "Right. And if I'm not there in ten minutes, start without me."

"I'll wait," she said. She leaned over and kissed him hard. "That ought to energize you," she told him. She giggled and ran upstairs.

She was amazed to hear him running up the stairs after her. He caught her at the bedroom door, grabbing her around the waist and lifting her from the floor. "That's what this exercise program needs," he said. "A little *incentive*." Still holding her, he walked to the bed and fell on it.

They rolled around together, laughing, kissing, laughing, kissing, kissing, kissing. She loved the feel of his hands on her, his strength used only for gentleness.

"Here," he said, "let me—"

"Mmm. And I'll—"

Clothes flew to the corners of the room. There was some more laughter now, the whispered mirth of happy secrets. Then they were quiet for a while.

Allan said, "Now?"

Regina said, "Mmm. Me on top, okay?"

"Pushy woman. I'm not a complete cripple, you know."

"I *like* to be on top."

"Oh. Well, in *that* case . . ." He grabbed her and rolled her on top of him. She smothered his laugh, pinning him to the pillow with a kiss. She sat up and guided him inside her. She began to move. Allan's strong hands held her hips, sometimes gliding up and down her body, sometimes moving forward to cup her breasts. This was the only time she ever wished she had larger breasts, breasts she could lean forward and brush his face with. Allan had never complained or anything, it was just something she wished she could do.

After more than a year of practice, their rhythm was perfect. As always, Regina was amazed that *this* was the use she'd found for all the expensive horseback-riding lessons her mother had forced her to take years ago.

It was almost time. She increased her speed; Allan held her tighter.

Closer, closer. Here it was. She threw her head back and let it shudder through her. Then she bent forward and met Allan's mouth in a kiss that caught fresh fire with each aftershock. Finally, Allan was there, too, and Regina collapsed against him. There was one more twinge of pleasure as she rolled free of him. They lay together in each other's arms, waiting for the fire to come back.

And as Regina looked into Allan's dark eyes and played with the hair on his chest, one thing kept running through her mind. *Let it work,* she thought. *Let it work.*

• • •

Trotter killed the alarm before it could wake Regina up. For a few seconds, he sat staring at it, marveling at the fact that he needed it at all, that he had actually been asleep. Because until Bash had come along, the man who now called himself Allan Trotter had never slept in the presence of another human being. To be asleep is to be vulnerable. To sleep with someone else around is to show that someone a level of trust that Trotter, raised as he had been raised and trained as he had been trained, considered tantamount to suicide. But here he was, sharing his life with a woman, loving her, sleeping in her arms like a normal man. It was quite a wonderful feeling, all the more wonderful because he'd been convinced he could never experience it.

He was still holding the clock. The digits changed. Trotter saw he'd better get moving, if he expected to make the plane. Still, there was a little time. Should he wake Bash and tell her what he was thinking? No, he'd write her a note. Regina had brought her purse upstairs, and Trotter knew she always carried a notebook and pencil in it. She was a reporter, after all; notebook and pencil for her were like rosary and prayer book would be for a nun.

He looked through the purse, but he stopped before he found writing material. He had found something else.

• • •

"Bash?"

Regina had been having a pleasant dream. Allan's voice blended in nicely with it. She smiled in her sleep.

"Bash, wake up."

He was shaking her shoulder now. She woke up. "Morning," she said.

"Good morning."

"You leaving now?" She was squinting against the sunshine, but she could still see Allan had the strangest look on his face.

"Soon. Wake up."

"I'm awake, I'm awake," she said. It was practically the truth. "Kiss me good-bye."

"I'm not leaving yet." But he kissed her, anyway.

She rubbed her eyes and sat up. "Okay. I'm awake now."

"When did you stop taking your pill?"

She'd tried to tell herself that Allan wouldn't find out until it was too late, but she'd never really believed it. "A-About three weeks ago."

"Why didn't you tell me?"

Regina looked at him. She'd expected him to be angry, and the thought of his anger had frightened her. Not enough to keep her on the pill, but plenty.

But Allan showed no anger at all. If his expression could be believed (and, though he'd never done it to her, she knew Allan could lie as skillfully with his face as with his tongue) what he was feeling now was a combination of happiness and worry.

"I didn't tell you because I was afraid you'd stop me."

"I— Well, I would have tried to talk you out of it."

"I thought so. Every time I mentioned having a baby, you went into a shell. You wouldn't even go so far as to say it was a bad idea. You just didn't talk about it."

"I'm hardly ideal parent material."

"Who is? There's something wrong with *everybody's* parents. People get by. *I want a baby*!" To her own amazement, Regina found herself angry. "*Your* baby, damn it!"

Allan kissed her gently on the forehead. "What were you going to do, say you found it on a doorstep? Or that you got pregnant by the milkman?"

"I thought that once it was well under way, you'd accept it."

"You're really not going to be happy without a baby?"

"I'm happy with you, Allan, I just—" How could she tell him? It didn't make complete sense to Regina herself. It was just that her own birth had to do with lies and plots and treachery and death, and while Mother had ultimately redeemed herself, it still made Regina uncomfortable to think about it. Somehow, having a baby of her own, because she loved a man and wanted to love a baby, would break the cycle and make things right again.

"I just—"

"You just want one. All right. That answers my question. Two things."

"Yes?"

"We've been going at this kind of hit-and-miss. Unless you're pregnant already."

"I don't think so."

"Well, assuming we're both fully equipped, if we do it every day for a month, we ought to connect."

"Allan, do you mean—?"

"Yes," he said. "I mean. I'm scared to death, but I mean. You have become indispensable, and I want you happy."

She threw her arms around him and hugged.

"One other thing."

"Uh-huh," Regina said, nodding seriously.

"If we're going to do this, we might as well get married. I've got nothing against bastards, but why add complications to a kid's life?"

"That easy, huh? I'm probably going to wake up in a few minutes and find out I dreamed this."

"No dream. I'd better get moving if I'm going to make the plane. We'll talk about details when I get back. I love you, Bash."

CHAPTER FIVE

Washington, D.C.

Ainley Masters watched the door of his apartment close behind Stephen Abweg. Congressman Abweg's staff had spirited him out of an Iowa Howard Johnson's Motor Lodge, and had flown him to D.C. for a meeting with Senator Van Horn. Since all concerned wanted to keep the press from any premature drooling over the matter, it had been arranged that the meeting would take place at Ainley's Washington digs. The theory was that while reporters certainly had Abweg staked out, and possibly had Senator Van Horn's office and home covered, the home of the Senator's top aide just might be safe.

That was the theory in the Abweg camp, anyway. Ainley had made it clear, in setting up this business, that the onus of security was on them. If there was any premature word of a possible endorsement from the Senator, that endorsement would not come. It was the same agreement he had with the Babington camp—that meeting was scheduled for a few weeks from now.

So Abweg and his people had come and gone, and Ainley Masters was confused. He did not like to be confused. He looked at Hank Van Horn in open wonderment.

"If I gave a damn," Ainley said, "I'd feel cheated on."

Hank was sitting quietly, drinking a brandy, looking pleased with himself. "What do you mean, Ainley?"

"Why do you ask me for advice, Senator? I said to be noncommittal, that we've still got to talk with the other people, and not to say too much."

"Well, I didn't, did I?"

"Yes, you did. 'I think I can see my way clear to backing you' sounds pretty committal to me."

"I can see my way clear to the bathroom, Ainley." He indicated the way with the snifter. "That doesn't mean I'm going there."

"Oh, good," Ainley said. "Someone's taught you sophistry. Listen, Senator. What you did today wasn't a mistake because it was dishonest."

"You'd hardly be the one to complain about that."

Ainley caught his breath, then let it out through a smile. "You know, Senator, you haven't come to an apartment of mine since you showed up at the one I keep back home all those years ago. The night of the fire, you remember."

Then the Senator set the snifter down hard. Brandy spilled on his hand; he didn't seem to notice. "I don't like to talk about the fire, Ainley." His voice was deadly.

Ainley wasn't worried. He knew too much about the Van Horns, and too much of what he knew was written down in places that would come to light if anything happened to him. The worst the Senator could do was fire him, and then only if Ainley wanted to go. Not that being fired would hurt him. Ainley got richer every year. He had a joke among his friends at the club—he didn't pay income tax anymore. He just got the Senator to tell him how much the government needed and wrote a check.

But Ainley wasn't about to let himself be fired. He had no intention of retiring. Serving the Van Horns had started out being a job; it had become a career, then a life.

And the quality of that life would improve greatly in the next couple of years. Because, thank God, Hank was not the last of the Van Horns. There was still Mark. Mark would be ready to make his first run at office before too long, and Ainley awaited the day the way a child awaited Christmas morning.

Comparing Mark with Hank was to contemplate the mysteries of genetics. All the family qualities Hank lacked—the courage, the vision, the ability to enjoy and use his power—Mark had in abundance. Mark's physical inheritance had come from his mother—the slim build, the blond hair and blue eyes—but the inner stuff, the stuff that counted, was pure Van Horn. Mark reminded Ainley of Hank's grandfather, who had built a lumbering and paper-pulp operation from a family business into an empire, and of Hank's father, the first Senator Van Horn, a war hero who had been destined for the White House until he had been assassinated by a fanatical Turk during a fact-finding mission to Cyprus, or Hank's brother, the astronaut, who has died heroically during a training mission.

Hank was still a boy. That was the problem. He was a spoiled, stupid boy with the responsibilities of a powerful man and the sex drive of a rabbit. About the same amount of courage, too. The mysteries of genetics. How could Hank have passed along traits he himself did not possess? Ainley decided not to worry about it. He'd just be grateful for it.

"No," Ainley said, "I don't suppose you do. It's just nice for me to remember, every time you decide to get snotty, how you sat sniveling, begging me to help you."

"That's your job, Ainley," Hank said stiffly.

Ainley sighed. "Yes, it's my job. It's my job to advise you, too, although lately you seem to like someone else's advice better than mine."

Hank had just decided to go back to the brandy. There was a slight tremor in his hand as he brought the snifter to his mouth. "I don't know what you're talking about," Hank said.

"Really, Senator," Ainley said. "I know my job, and part of that job is knowing you. I know you get phone calls you don't log. I know on some nights when you want everyone to think you're over in Georgetown screwing the cello player, you go somewhere else."

"You've had me followed." Hank sounded hurt.

"Occasionally. For a while. Often enough and long enough to know you've had some expert coaching in how to avoid being followed."

"You need a vacation, Ainley."

"All right, do what you want. You'll step in something, eventually, and you'll come crying to me to scrape it off your shoe, and I'll do it because that's my job. But you just watch it, Senator. If you do anything to hurt Mark's chances in politics, I really won't have any reason to look out for you anymore."

"I love my son, Ainley."

"Fine. To continue the lesson. Stringing Abweg and his people along wasn't a mistake because it was dishonest; it was a mistake because it was a *mistake*. If you made no commitments, you could get Abweg and Babington *bidding* for your endorsement. You could name a price. Unlimited pork for the home state. Maybe you could name the next Secretary of State or Treasury."

"Maybe I still can."

Ainley shook his head. Who would have dreamed a Senator with this much seniority, from a powerful political family, would have to hear a lecture in basic politics?

"Stephen Abweg is now convinced that when he needs you, he can call on you for your endorsement. He thinks all he'll owe you for that is what they call in football 'future considerations.' If you decide to go with Babington, Abweg will be furious; and since he'll probably be out of it anyway, he'll do the best he can to screw you. And if he gets the nomination in spite of you, he'll wind up President, and you'll find yourself really inconvenienced."

"You think so?"

"I wouldn't have said it if I didn't think so."

Hank rubbed his chin and looked thoughtful. Ainley wished he knew who the hell Hank had been listening to. Ainley had really only noticed it recently, but once he did, it became apparent that Hank had been taking advice elsewhere since shortly after the fire.

"Have you been talking to some reporter?" Ainley demanded.

Hank jumped.

"It would be like you," Ainley said. "Having some hack work on your memoirs for years at a time, strung along with tips and leaks. And it wouldn't be long before you let him tell you how to behave so the book would come out the best read."

"Ainley, don't be ridiculous."

"It's hard sometimes, considering the kinds of things I have to deal with."

"Ainley, I promise you, I'm not talking to any reporters. I'm not talking to anyone but you."

Ainley looked at him. He used to be able to tell when Hank was lying, but that was getting harder all the time.

Hank smiled. Even Ainley, who knew infinitely better, could feel the charm of that smile. "How's Mark doing?" Hank asked.

That was another thing. Hank loved his son, so he said, but it was Ainley to whom Mark wrote his letters. Hank didn't seem to mind. Since he'd divorced Ella, Hank had no interest in anything but the perks of Senatorial power and fucking. He acted as if his beloved son were a pleasant acquaintance and nothing more.

"He's coming to town in a few days."

"Oh," Hank said. "School over?"

Mark, after a few years of living on the family trust, was now attending Whitten College Law School. Both things were family traditions. He was also *not* attending Whitten College Law School, when his spirit moved him to be someplace else. This was also a family tradition. When Van Horns needed to pass the bar exam, the bar exam was passed. Attendance at classes was a necessity only for lesser mortals.

"He just wants to visit," Ainley said.

"Oh." Hank said. "How nice. I'll have my secretary tell Mrs. Rodriguez to prepare his room."

"He'll stay here with me, Senator," Ainley said.

Hank nodded, as though pondering a question of monumental importance. "That's probably best," he announced. "Lot of committee work coming up, and all the press fallout from Iowa, too."

"Yes, Senator," Ainley said. He forbore to point out that as head man of the Senator's staff, *he'd* be busy too. Part of the idea of the visit was for Mark to get some hands-on experience of the maneuvering at the fringes of a Presidential election.

"I don't know how much I'll be home, anyway."

"Yes, Senator."

"But I want to get together with him." Hank frowned, then brightened.

"I'll have Nancy check the calendar, and any lunch or dinner that isn't spoken for belongs to Mark."

"That's first-class, Senator," Ainley assured him. He showed Hank out. After he was gone, Ainley looked at the door for a few seconds, slowly shaking his head.

CHAPTER SIX

New York, New York

Someone knocked on the door. Arnie ignored it, he was too busy on the phone. Sometimes he wished he had never stopped free-lancing, had never opened Power Dish Communications in the basement of his apartment building in the East Eighties. He was just too damned busy.

Arnie had no idea where they came from. He had deliberately picked a place in a residential neighborhood to keep the clientele down to pros and people he knew. And he didn't put on the dog. The store looked just like his workshop had when he was doing security stuff. Maybe it was the sign Sally had given him as a gag, the black-and-red-and-white painting of a chick in a bikini holding a handful of lightning bolts. She was the "Power Dish."

Arnie shook his head. Maybe he ought to replace it with one that said "A. Gillick, by appointment only," like those diamond places.

He'd done a security check for a place like that in Amsterdam, once. Found a bug, too. Had to be an inside job, because the mini recorder was right there next to it. There must have been the combinations to a lot of loaded safes on that tape, if the relieved look the Dutchman in charge of security gave him meant anything. Of course, Arnie never knew for sure, because it was a point of honor with him never to listen to stuff he collected. He was doing this for clients, after all, not for himself. He didn't need to go stuffing up his brain with other people's secrets. It was just here's the tape, gimme my check, thank you very much, and off somewhere else.

That was all before Sally, of course. Sally was a small brunette he'd seen at a party about two years ago. He decided to do her a favor, since there weren't any worthwhile blondes in the place. What Arnie didn't know was that Sally was a witch, and six months later he would be happily hypnotized into becoming Sally's husband, and stepfather to eleven-year-old Pete.

So the security business, at least on the footing it had been on, was over. All that globe-trotting meant too much time away from Sally.

He had learned, on the other hand, that he didn't want to be under her feet all day, either. Arnie had never been a big spender; he'd done high-risk, high-paying jobs for the challenge, and banked most of the money. But he needed to give Sally a break from his face. So he'd opened the store. He'd noodle around for a while, order out from the deli, close for lunch, noodle around a few more hours, and rejoin his wife about the same time Pete came home from school.

If it weren't for the damn customers, life would be a dream.

They were pounding on the door now.

Arnie put his hand over the mouthpiece. "Go away! Can't you read, for God's sake?" He would go look to make sure he'd put the CLOSED FOR LUNCH, BACK AT 1:30 sign on the door, but then the asshole out there pounding would see him and make things worse.

Arnie turned back to the receiver. "No, I wasn't talking to you. I know you can read, you work for the Encyclopedia Victoria."

A few weeks ago, Arnie had conceived the notion of buying Pete an encyclopedia. Pete was a good kid, and smart. School-smart, which Arnie had never been. Besides, he'd seen the ads on TV about the kid walking through what looked like a goddam monsoon to get to the library. Pete spent a lot of time at the library, and in New York, even in a good neighborhood like this one, there were elements your kid might be exposed to coming home late that should worry you a lot more than the weather.

So when Arnie had seen a coupon in *TV Guide* to request more information, he filled it out and sent it in. What he got back was worthless; an expanded version of the magazine ad. So he'd said to hell with it.

Then today, they'd called him on the phone. A guy with a slight Spanish accent asked him if he was Mr. Arnold Gillick, and when Arnie admitted it, told him he was a Customer Representative for the Encyclopedia Victoria, and that Arnie had sent for their information packet.

"Yeah. The information packet didn't tell me what I wanted to know."

"What might that be, Mr. Gillick?"

"How much does it cost?"

And the guy wouldn't tell him! He launched into a spiel that was word for word exactly what was in the brochure!

"Look," Arnie said, ignoring the first knock at the door, "I know it's the best. I want to know what it costs."

"New members of the Victoria family find Victoria surprisingly affordable." He sounded like Ricardo Montalban on that old car commercial.

"I don't want to be *surprised* I can afford it, I want to *know*."

That was when Arnie had turned away to deal with the door pounder.

"Yeah, yeah. You can read," he told the phone. "Read me the price."

"The Victoria family offers payment plans from as low as five dollars a week."

"How many weeks?"

"The flexibility of Victoria Family payment plans is such that payments can be made at the new member's convenience. In addition—"

"Stop it."

"—when you acquire Victoria—"

"*Stop it.*"

"—or simply preview it in your home, you will receive—"

"*Shut up, goddammit!*"

The Customer Representative seemed shocked. Apparently, the members of the Victoria family had better manners. "Mr. Gillick?"

"If the next word out of your mouth," Arnie said, "is not a number followed by the word 'dollars,' I'm gonna hang up. Hard."

"But the Victoria Family—"

"Good-bye, asshole!" Arnie yelled, and banged the receiver down. Jerks. He wouldn't buy their damned encyclopedia if they put his picture on the cover, now. What the hell kind of way was that to run a business? Afraid to let the customer know the price of the goods until you had him hooked? Especially a supposedly classy business like the Encyclopedia Victoria.

Outside, someone was pounding on the door again.

"Goddammit!" Arnie said again. It was probably somebody from the encyclopedia company, he thought, sent to drag him by the ear into the Victoria Family. Arnie chuckled to himself, and felt a little bit better.

When he got to the door, he saw he was wrong. It wasn't a kidnapper, it was a private eye. Somebody not especially tall, but sturdy, wearing a trench coat with the collar turned up, and a felt hat pulled down low.

"What do you want?" It occurred to Arnie that this was ridiculous. Here he was, a big electronics expert, yelling through a door. He ought to hook up an intercom or something.

"Mr. Arnold Gillick?"

"*Are* you from the encyclopedia?"

The guy in the trench coat tilted his head to the side, puzzled. Arnie still couldn't see his face. "No. No. What?"

"Doesn't matter. Look, it's my lunchtime, can't you come back?"

"This will only take a second. You are Mr. Arnold Gillick, a security consultant?"

"I'm retired from that. I can't help you."

"But you were in the field in, say, 1971?"

"Oh, yeah, I did that kind of stuff from '69 to about eighteen months ago."

"Continuously?"

"Yep. Hardly even took a vacation. Of course, there was a lot of trav——"

The man in the trench coat took his hand out of his pocket and the glass shattered. That was how it seemed to Arnie. He'd never get a chance to correct the impression, because the .357 magnum slug that shattered the window shattered Arnie's head just a split second later.

CHAPTER SEVEN

Washington, D.C.

"So that's why I had to drop everything and come down here. To meet a President who's going to be out of office a year from now."

The old man stopped walking and turned to his son. That meant he was going to say something. The Congressman had made excellent progress in recovering from his stroke, but he still hadn't reached the point where he could ply his walker, breathe and talk all at the same time.

"He wanted to see you. He's still the Commander in Chief, you know." The Congressman faced forward again, plunked the walker a foot or so in front of where it had been, then inched up to it.

He stopped again. "Besides, I think he was beginning to doubt you existed."

"I can't wait until you're well enough to take the Agency back," Trotter said. The Congressman muttered something about hoping he lived that long, and plunked on.

This walk was supposed to be part of the old man's rehabilitation. The doctor (the President had lent the Congressman his own personal physician) had prescribed all the walking the Congressman felt like doing. Trotter reflected that his father had certainly picked a good place for it.

The Capitol Mall will take all the walking you can do, and then some. Trotter was beginning to get a little tired himself, but he was damned if he was going to complain about it to a man who'd had a stroke. He just wished he had a walker of his own to lean on.

The trouble was, the Capitol was so damn big, down there at the end of the road, and the Mall was so damn straight, everything looked closer than it was, easier to get to. The looming museums of the Smithsonian, lining either side, added to the illusion. Trotter reflected that this might be symbolic of what was wrong with Washington—lots of majesty, but lack of perspective.

Trotter walked alongside his father, taking care not to go too fast and leave the old man behind. He was a little peeved that the emergency summons was an audience with a temporary officeholder and a spell as a physical therapist, but what the hell. The government was paying the plane fare. He could be back in Kirkester tonight.

The walker stopped again, in front of the Air and Space Museum. Trotter waited for the Congressman to speak, but nothing happened. Tourists, sparse in the January cold, paid much more attention to the old man who seemingly slipped into suspended animation than they ever had when he was discussing top-secret projects in a public street. Trotter's father had taught him that that would be the case. You can talk about anything in public if you keep your voice normal, don't be too specific, and don't act too interested.

But if you stop, stand in one spot, and stare straight ahead, you're going to attract attention.

Trotter figured *one* of them ought to say something. "What is it? Do you want to go inside and touch a moon rock?"

His father came out of his trance and looked at him. He always spoke out of the corner of his mouth these days, but this time, it seemed especially appropriate. He gave his son a one-eyed scowl and said, "You mockin' the afflicted, boy?"

Then he did a very unusual thing. He laughed. Real, genuine laughter, as though he had actually perceived something as funny. Trotter found it a revelation.

"No, son. I was thinkin' something over. Let's get out of the doorway, and I'll tell you what's on my mind."

The Congressman stopped again about twenty yards farther down the Mall. "All right," he said. "There was another reason for calling you down here." The Congressman's Southern accent had dwindled to practically nothing, a sure sign that he was getting down to business.

"Thank you. As somebody said recently, I'm supposed to be the boss."

"You are, son, you are. People keep secrets from the boss all the time."

"I'm glad you're going to tell me. I'd hate to have to fire you." That raised another chuckle.

"Well, it's a personal thing, too. I got a call from Jake Feder. He wants to talk to me. I told him you were running the show these days, and he said he knew that, but he wanted to talk to me."

"You said okay."

"I said okay. He worked for me for a long time, and he was my friend before he worked for me."

"I have never noticed," Trotter said, "that friendship ever cut a whole lot of ice with you."

"I could never afford it to. And anyway, you know Jake. Doesn't give a fat hairy damn for anything in the world but circuits and his grandchildren."

Trotter nodded. He'd gotten a full load of Jake Feder's grandchildren when Jake had come up to Kirkester to install Trotter's electronics.

The Congressman continued. "Well, he gives a damn about this."

"So talk to him."

"I want you there."

"He asked for you. This might not even be Agency business."

"Right," the old man said. In the old days, he might have spat, but his control over his lips wasn't what it had been. "What are the odds of that?"

"Slim," Trotter admitted.

"So I want you there. People like Jake have to know you're the boss now."

"I'm the boss *for* now. There's a difference."

The old man gave him that half smile. "Whatever you say. Boss."

• • •

For the first forty-plus years of its existence, the Agency had operated like a guerrilla army, disappearing before anyone even started to look. The Congressman had had things arranged so that his headquarters (a couple of secure rooms for privacy, a john, and a linkup with the people who were actually doing the work) could be moved overnight. Things could still be done that way. The Congressman, as Director Emeritus, or on leave of absence, or however he chose to think of it, still had a hideaway in a basement somewhere. It wouldn't do for him to be seen too much at the new, more permanent headquarters.

Today was an exception. Fenton Rines's secretary buzzed him to let him know the Congressman and a Mr. Trotter were here. Rines said, "Send them in," and sat looking at the door, waiting for them.

This door showed him nothing but woodgrain. The one that opened to the eighth-floor corridor outside read simply, FENTON RINES INVESTIGATIONS. The door didn't lie, as far as it went. It just didn't go very far. The Agency was behind that door, and it was a whole lot more than Fenton Rines. And there was a whole lot more going on than investigation, too. Disinformation, espionage, assassination, and things they didn't have names for. Rines reflected that he had come a long way from the crew-cut ex-Marine who'd joined the FBI so many years ago.

It had been a Fenton Rines investigation that had gotten him into all this. Rines had been a staunch and loyal Bureau man. Some said that he might have been in line to be Director someday, if Watergate hadn't happened. Rines didn't know about that, didn't care that much. He liked doing what he was doing.

But he chafed under the post-Watergate reforms. It bothered him that the Bureau should be hampered in its work because of some overzealousness in the past. Overzealousness, it should be added, in which Rines took no part. Still, it was annoying. And it was even worse because Rines's practiced eye could see that *somebody* was doing *something*. Strange operations that looked like nothing a criminal in his right mind would want to do, but too well planned to be the work of a maniac.

When he brought his findings to the Congressional Committee that was supposed to oversee such things, he was patted on the head and sent away. That was when he decided somebody in the government was according somebody privileges that were denied the Bureau.

It all came to a head with the Liz Fane kidnapping. The Congressman had sent Trotter, who was then known as Clifford Driscoll, to straighten things out. Which he proceeded to do in an effective, if unorthodox, fashion. In the process, Rines had learned about the Agency, about the Congressman's role in it, and the fact that Driscoll—now Trotter—was the old man's son. The *President* didn't know that. Jake Feder, who was also supposed to be coming this afternoon, had worked with the Congressman since the War, and *he* didn't know it.

Trotter had arranged for him to learn all this so he might get out of his father's clutches. Which he had, until he'd voluntarily walked back into them. Apparently, the Congressman had been right. The spy business was bred into every cell of Trotter's body. To use the Congressman's homey phrase, "That boy can no more walk away from this business than a buzzard can walk away from meat."

But while Trotter had been freed to make up his own mind, Rines had found himself trapped. Since the old man no longer had any secrets from him, he trusted Rines with *everything,* told him things it scared the FBI man to know.

And he'd started *using* him. The Congressman would get messages to him suggesting that he assign a few Special Agents to investigate this building or that person, and let him know what turned up. Before long, Rines was doing more work for the Agency than he was for the Bureau.

Then the old man had had his stroke. It was obvious that Trotter should take over top position. No one else had the training, experience, and brilliantly twisted brain necessary for the job. For a few mad moments, Trotter had tried to duck the job and wish it onto Rines, but the fall that had smashed up his body had apparently also knocked some sense into his head, and he'd taken the job.

But that had meant a restructuring. It was a radical change, but at the same time it was a perfect demonstration of the Agency's use-everything philosophy. Trotter now had the resources of a huge national and international news-gathering operation to put at the Agency's disposal. Rines, who because of the decentralization would be needed full-time on Agency business, had "retired" from the Bureau and gotten a Private Investigator's license. "Investors" (the Agency) had put up money for him to hire a staff and open these sumptuous offices in Alexandria, Virginia, not far from the Pentagon. Nobody who worked in these offices—except Rines, the top computer people, and the communications technicians who sent Trotter and the Congressman their thrice-daily reports—knew whom they were really working for.

This had a few advantages. For one thing, for an outfit like the Agency, recruiting was always a problem. The Congressman had started with men and women he'd known from OSS days, but they were dead now, or too old to cut it in the field. He'd bred one operative; for the rest, he had to depend on recommendations from the few people he trusted. But with the PI business, Rines hired likely candidates (he paid top money to get top prospects) and actually got to see how they did at the work before trusting them with information they might find too heavy a burden.

Fenton Rines Investigations also put all the information gathered from the straight business (and business was excellent) at the disposal of the Agency. It might not be especially gentlemanly, concerning yourself with the extramarital and/or financial peccadillos of the kind of people in the D.C. area who could afford Rines's rates, but it was of inestimable value in spotting potential security risks, or for putting pressure on when you needed someone to do something.

And the Agency hadn't lost touch with the Bureau when Rines had retired, either. The Azrael operation had made it necessary for a young Special Agent named Joe Albright to be brought in on some of the Agency's secrets. That included the big one—that it existed. He'd shown an aptitude for this extra-special kind of Special Agentry that working for the Congressman—for Trotter, rather—required. Albright also had a girlfriend in Kirkester, someone he'd met during the Azrael thing, so it was perfectly natural to use him as a courier whenever they needed to send anything to Trotter.

The door opened. Rines rose to meet the Congressman and his son.

"Where have you got Jake?" the Congressman asked.

"Not here yet," Rines told him. "How's the President?"

"Seems like a nice guy. At least he's a known quantity. Who knows what the next one's going to be like?"

"Sit down," Rines said. "Claudette will buzz me when Feder gets here."

"As long as we're here, we might as well get a little work done," Trotter said.

"Sure, you want to go over the afternoon report? I was going to suggest that you do that first even if Feder had been here already."

"Why's that?"

"I think it might tell you what he's got on his mind."

• • •

Norman Jones keyed the door of the next car open and backed in, sweeping the platform behind him as he did so. He wasn't in any hurry, but he wasn't dawdling, either. His job was to clean up the Metro cars when they came into the yard every night, and in the morning, when he went home, all the cars would be clean.

He liked it better here, at the downtown yards outside Union Station. He'd built up enough seniority now so his wishes counted for something, and his first big wish was to get transferred from Shady Grove, which was way out in Maryland. There, if he finished doing all his work early, wasn't anything to do but sit around and twiddle his thumbs. There wasn't much to do here, either, but Norman liked to walk around and look at the city lights when he had the time. Another thing was, he lived nearby. If an emergency came up, he could run home. From Shady Grove, he'd be lucky if he could send a telegram.

Norman finished the platform, pulled back his broom like a matador with a sword, and turned around.

And there was someone in the car.

"Damn," Norman said. "Second one this week."

Some weeks, it happened more than that. Weren't any conductors on the Metro, see, so when the line shut down each midnight, anybody who slept through the loudspeaker announcement wound up here with Norman.

Norman walked down to him, keeping his broom handy. He didn't *look* bad, a small old white man with gray hair. He was a white man, even though his skin was darker than Norman's—he just had one of those tropical tans. Maybe he was a Congressman back from one of those junkets or something.

He didn't look like one of the dope fiends who sometimes nodded out on the Metro, and sometimes died there. The suburbanites who came into the city and tied one on a little too big usually were a lot younger than this guy. And you never got winos and derelicts on the Metro. The phrase for them now was "the homeless," but Norman Jones, who had worked very, very hard for the last thirty-nine of his forty-nine years to keep a roof over his head and the rest of the heads he was responsible for, still thought "bum" was the word that said it best. Anyway, whatever you called them, you didn't get them on the Metro. Not in the cars, anyway. Sometimes in those big barns of stations, but not in the cars. It cost too much. This wasn't like New York, where one dollar let you ride as long as you wanted. There were fancy computer tickets here, and the longer you rode, the more it cost.

Anyway, this guy didn't look like any of those, but Norman didn't take any chances. He walked up the aisle to a distance of about eight feet from the sleeper.

"Yo. Mister, wake up. Hey, wake up."

No answer. He didn't even stir.

"Come on, I'll show you where to get a cab. You're lucky. You could have wound up way the hell out in Shady Grove."

Still no answer. Norman prodded him gently with the broom handle.

"Dammit, Mister, I've got work to do. If I have to get the guard, you'll be in no end of trouble, wait till you see the fare they're gonna hit you with—"

Norman stopped because the prodding had caused the old white man to move at last. He moved right out of the seat and slumped to the floor. That was when Norman saw the ice-pick handle sticking up from the man's back.

Chapter Eight

Stamford, Connecticut

The door to apartment 6B looked different from the others on this floor; it was cold when Trotter touched it. Metal. His old friend must be having a hard time adjusting to freedom.

Trotter rang the doorbell and waited. A peephole in the door opened, then clicked shut. Then followed a series of gliding, grating, and clicking noises as various locks and bolts were undone. Finally the door swung open.

The man in the doorway had aged since Trotter had seen him last. Age, which it had seemed would never touch him, had begun to caress him gently. There were lines around the eyes, now, and a touch of gray in his hair. He was still the handsomest man Trotter had ever seen.

"Come in, my friend. This *is* a surprise." The man was smiling broadly. He seemed almost too happy over some unexpected company on a Wednesday afternoon. Then Trotter realized that a lot of the smile must be from relief. When a man is constantly expecting unknown dangers, a known one can be almost a comfort.

Trotter looked around while his host locked the door back up. A nice place, modern and roomy. There wasn't a lot of personality to it, but Bulanin hadn't been here very long yet. The only personal touches Trotter could see were the metal shutters on the insides of the windows, and the big gray desk with a word processor on it and papers scattered all over.

"Sit down, sit down," he said. "Are you still Trotter?"

Trotter smiled in spite of himself. Bulanin had built a career on that charm. What the hell, he thought. "Call me Allan, Grigory Illyich."

"Can I get you something to drink, Allan?"

"No, thanks. You seem to be settled in."

"The work helps." Bulanin had built himself some kind of clear drink in a very large glass. He sat down, pulled at it as if it were lemonade, and looked at Trotter as if daring him to make something of it.

This was new. Bulanin was an atypical Russian in many ways, and one of them was (or had been) that he had never been much of a drinker. He had had ambitions of someday ruling the Soviet Union. Maybe, Trotter thought, he no longer had any reason to keep his head clear.

Trotter had encountered Bulanin a few years ago in London. The Russian was the top KGB man there at the time, and in an attempt to score a coup that would boost his career, had backed a terrorist's plan to kidnap the Congressman's British counterpart. That had ended badly for Bulanin—if he hadn't defected, his own people would have killed him. Painfully, as an example to others.

So Bulanin had come to the United States. He had been an invaluable source of information, so valuable that the Congressman had taken no chances on Bulanin's former comrades' finding him and taking him back home as a show monkey, or simply killing him. Bulanin had been interned in a compound in the Maryland mountains not far from Camp David. He'd all the comforts he could ask for, but he'd also had a cadre of grim Israelis for guards and a deadly electrified fence between him and any place the old man didn't want him to go.

Bulanin had taken it calmly for a while, but then he started going stir-crazy. He began agitating for his release.

The way Trotter looked at it, they had already received full value from the man. Furthermore, during his confinement, he had learned nothing that could really hurt the Agency. And he did not dare go back to the Russians no matter how much he *might* have learned, because sooner or later, they would kill him. So when Trotter took over the Agency, the first thing he'd done was tell Bulanin he was free, as long as he let the Agency know where he was.

He'd sent Joe Albright to him with the news. As Joe reported it, there had been ten seconds of unbridled elation, followed by a growing concern. Bulanin hadn't gone so far as to change his mind about being set loose, but he asked a few questions about how he was going to keep the KGB from liquidating him.

Trotter had passed word along that Bulanin was to make up a security plan for himself, and if it cost less than maintaining him for one year at the Maryland compound (which cost a fortune), the Agency would spring for it.

Bulanin had done that, and here he was. He had a new name, his first. That was an oddity in Trotter's world, where names were like placemats— only good as long as they have nothing dripped on them. He had chosen to live in a small city in the shadow of a huge city. He had taken an apartment and turned it into a fortress.

He had even found a job for himself. He was a translator, Russian and

French. The reports Trotter had checked before coming here said he was doing very well at it, almost doubling the subsidy the Agency paid him.

And he had started to drink heavily. Well, Trotter thought, he's still wound up a lot better than most people in this business do.

Bulanin took another pull on his drink and smiled the charming smile again. "To what do I owe the pleasure of this visit?" he asked.

Trotter took a piece of paper from his pocket, unfolded it, and handed it to Bulanin. "Do you recognize any of these names?"

Bulanin looked it over quickly, then again more slowly. "Yes," he said. "I do. Three of them."

"All right," Trotter said. "Don't make me beg for it. Who? And in what connection."

"Samuel Currus, Arnold Gillick, and Jacob Feder."

"Gillick and Feder," Trotter said.

"And Currus. They are all buggers."

"I assume," Trotter said, "that you are not using British slang."

Bulanin laughed. "My friend, I sometimes think that if you had been Russian, or I American, we might have ruled the world together."

"If that's your idea of a good time," Trotter said.

"It might be nice to try for a month or so," Bulanin said. "But to answer your question, no, I was not using British slang. Though for all I know, any or all of these gentlemen might be buggers in that sense as well. No, what I was talking about was electronic surveillance and all that implies. When I was in the Washington KGB office, Currus, who lived in San Francisco, and Gillick, who lived in New York, I believe, were on a list of people who would do good work for the proper money, without asking from whom the money came. I myself never used them, but some of our people did."

Trotter nodded. It made sense to use nationals of the target country for things like bugging, if you could find them, and save your own people for the absolutely most delicate cases. You never knew when one of your experts had been made by the opposition until you ran a lengthy and strenuous security check. And your own people were in for a tougher time if they were caught. They could do you more damage in that case, too.

"What about Feder?" Trotter wanted to know.

"He was—what is the phrase?—a must to avoid. He works for you people. Doesn't he? At least for the U.S. government in some regard."

"Do tell," Trotter said dryly. His father was going to love hearing about this. You spend years congratulating yourself on how well a cover works, then you find out the opposition has been laying off your boy because they know he's yours and they don't want to make complications.

"Oh, yes," Bulanin said. "The word was that he was the best in the business, too. He even had an open reputation in the private sector, and an enormous private income from it. That was another reason to leave him be, of course. If he was doing the espionage work for something other than money, he had to be a true patriot."

"Patriot enough to be killed?"

"I don't know what you mean."

"Feder's dead. All the men on that list are dead."

"Under suspicious circumstances, I presume. Or—"

"Or I wouldn't be here, right. I had the research department up all night on this. Somebody is murdering electronic-surveillance experts. Does that make any sense to you?"

Bulanin frowned. "Not really. It would seem to me that the tape, or whatever else technology has come up with recently, could be expected to outlive the person who made it."

"It seemed that way to me, too," Trotter admitted. "But I thought I'd ask if your old firm had any plans along these lines."

"No. It doesn't make any sense."

"I was about to say that I respect your brain and ask you if you could make any sense out of it."

Bulanin scowled. He looked at the glass of vodka in his hand as if he didn't know how it got there. He raised it to his mouth and took a long pull, then scowled again.

"The only thing . . ." he said. "But that doesn't make any sense, either."

"Let's hear it."

"Well, if *one* of the names on that list had learned something he shouldn't, or had betrayed the KGB in some way, they might well correct his manners. That was Borzov's, you know. Borzov would never say 'kill.' Yes. They might correct his manners, and it occurred to me that it might occur to the KGB as a good idea to leave a few other bodies around as a smoke screen, but doing it this way would only draw an investigator's attention to the skill that led to his association with my old firm in the first place."

"It would be a much better smoke screen to slip a bomb on the guy's bus and surround him with stiffs of a bunch of civilians."

"Precisely," Bulanin said.

Trotter rose. "Yeah," he said. "Well, think about it, will you? You know how to get a message to me."

"What are you going to do?"

"What would you do, Grigory Illyich?"

"I would find a few such specialists as were still alive, question them closely, and provide protection, if I felt it necessary."

Trotter looked at him and smiled. "Maybe we could have ruled the world, at that. I'll let myself out. Take care of yourself."

The Russian rose and shook his hand. "You too, my friend," he said. "You, too."

Chapter Nine

Moscow, USSR

General Borzov reached for a fresh handkerchief from the stack on the upper right-hand corner of his desk. He brought it to his mouth and coughed into it. Then he opened it and looked at it. Disgusting. Truly. But he was under orders.

Borzov was not used to taking orders. This desk, this simple scarred piece of wood, had been the site of origin for some of the most important directives in the history of the Motherland. Borzov would never say such a thing himself, of course, but the trait that more than any other had made him who he was was his ability to accept facts. And the fact was, he was one of the most important men in the history of the Soviet Union, and therefore, of the world.

The fact that few people at home or abroad would ever know of his importance bothered him not at all. Borzov lived to serve his country as long as his country needed him.

And the time of the Motherland's need of him had not yet passed. He had that from the Chairman's own lips. Glasnost and Perestroika were all very good (in Borzov's opinions, better than very good—*superb* as propaganda; tolerable as actual policies) but there would still be the need for the Menagerie Men.

Borzov smiled. It was his old ally-turned-adversary, the Congressman, who had coined that term, one cold night in 1943 in German-occupied Yugoslavia. Menagerie Men were war horses with the cunning of a fox, the courage of a lion, and the sting of a serpent. Borzov possessed all of those in full measure; until recently, he had also had the constitution of a bull. Now he was old. No—he had been old for a long time. Now he was old and infirm of body. *That* was the problem. That was what took getting used to.

And that was why he had submitted himself to the orders of someone other than the leader of the nation. To a mere colonel, a woman. Because Borzov had, of all things, a virus. It had kept him in bed for several days, until Comrade Colonel Doctor, who resembled an upright piano with a straight blond wig on top, had decided he would be more tranquil and recuperate better if she let him go back to work.

Tranquil. Borzov snorted just thinking of the word. He had a delicate mission under way, one that he had been preparing for the better part of two decades. It was vitally important. On the rare occasions Borzov allowed himself to daydream, it did not seem unreasonable to think of it as decisive. And it would all be decided in the fall, when the Americans chose their next President.

Once this operation could be successfully concluded, Borzov would be perfectly content to die. He would have left the Motherland in such a secure situation, that whatever young fool they chose to succeed him, said fool would be hard-pressed to ruin things.

So he did what the doctor told him, in order that he might live the required time. He made sure Madame Piano had the necessary information.

Such as the color of his phlegm.

General Borzov estimated that in person or through his subordinates, he had been responsible for the gathering of more information than any human being who had ever walked the earth. This information had been gathered through stealth and seduction and theft and extortion and assassination and torture, but none of that had *ever* been as distasteful to General Borzov as the constant monitoring of the color of his phlegm.

And now he had to cough again. Borzov took another handkerchief, coughed, looked. Grayish, he supposed. Yellowish-gray. Curse that doctor, anyway. What he ought to do was to parcel up the used handkerchiefs and send them to the doctor at the end of the day. Let *her* contemplate the color of his phlegm. He had more intriguing things to worry about.

Like the problem of who was killing the electronics experts. Indiscriminately. Some he had used, at least one the Congressman had used. Most of the dead men had never knowingly or unknowingly been involved in the operations of any government at all.

The Americans weren't doing it. It didn't feel like them at all, and Borzov's great age was a testimonial to the wisdom of trusting his feelings. The GRU denied it was one of their operations. Borzov supposed he believed them. Though "Army Intelligence" was a contradiction in terms as far as Borzov was concerned, this indiscriminate killing seemed too much even for them.

Borzov sighed. It was ridiculous to let the GRU have such latitude. All it did was duplicate the KGB's efforts, and frequently get in Borzov's way. *That* was something to live for after the Atropos operation was done. He would (somehow) get around the Army's objections and subsume the GRU into the KGB.

He laughed. It would only take another hundred years or so. The laugh turned into a cough. Borzov looked. Same color. He wondered how much phlegm he could produce for the doctor, should he live another hundred years. Enough to drown her in, he hoped.

In the meantime, he would try to puzzle out these killings. They didn't have the earmarks of a professional operation. Neither did they seem to be the work of one of those quaint lunatic killers the capitalist system had a knack for turning out.

Someone was doing this for a reason, but what could the reason be? It couldn't be to stop the men from taking or completing a given job. At least, that couldn't be the reason for all of them, since some of the victims, including Gillick, one of the ones Borzov used to use, had been retired for some time.

Gillick, Borzov thought. He was, he supposed, just as glad to have Gillick dead, especially now, with Borzov's masterpiece so near completion. Borzov might even have neutralized Gillick as a possible source of embarrassment himself, if it had occurred to him. So to one way of thinking, this killer had done Borzov a favor.

Borzov did not like to be grateful to unknowns for unasked favors. It bothered him. A spy master should know his allies as well as his enemies.

Borzov felt another cough coming on. He told himself he would suppress it for ten seconds. He began counting. At the count of seven, he cursed and reached madly for a handkerchief, bringing it to his mouth just in time.

CHAPTER TEN

Kirkester, New York

Sean Murphy was glad he'd picked Regina Hudson's office as the place to offer his suggestion. If he'd done it anywhere else, she would have walked out on him.

"Sean," she said. "That's disgusting. I thought you were supposed to be looking out for me."

Sean pushed his wire-frame glasses up his nose. "Your mother," he said, "asked me to *help* you. I assumed what she wanted me to help you do is become a first-rate journalist. I'm a reporter, not a baby-sitter. If you need looking out for, you should look somewhere else."

"But Sean, I *slept* with the guy." The tone of her voice and her body language made her seem too young to sleep with a teddy bear, let alone guys, but Murphy knew that could be deceptive.

"I know," he said, and waited.

Regina opened her mouth to speak, then realized the turn the conversation had been taking and closed it again. She turned a firm pink, but she pressed on. "You know what I mean!"

"I know that you are supposed to be running the Hudson Group," Murphy said. "And that the masthead of *Worldwatch* says you are the publisher of it. I also know that you are in a unique position to get information that the other newsmagazines can't get. That *was* you I was sitting next to at the meeting the other day, wasn't it? You did hear that everybody said this was the one interesting story of an otherwise boring campaign? So why are you being so fastidious?"

"It might not even work."

"If it doesn't work, we haven't lost anything."

"The last time I saw him, I told him to drop dead."

"He probably loved you for it. Those people don't get told to drop dead too often."

"I don't even *like* him anymore."

"I'm not telling you to like him, I'm telling you to call him on the phone and ask him a couple of questions."

Regina made patterns with her finger on her desk blotter. Murphy had known her since she was a little girl. All she'd ever wanted to be was a good reporter, and whatever that Trotter character had done to her, he hadn't been able to wipe that out completely. Right now, she had to be thinking how nice it would be to get the beat on this, how proud of her her mother would be.

"Sean," she said. "This doesn't feel right to me. I mean, it doesn't strike me as completely ethical, getting a story from someone you used to have a relationship with."

"Don't be ridiculous," Murphy said. "There's no connection at all. You were finished with this guy when? Four years ago?"

Regina looked at the ceiling for a second, waved a few fingers. "Almost five," she said.

"Okay, then. So it's ethical to ask. I mean, it's impossible that you slept with him just to get the story, right?"

"No," Regina said. "Definitely not."

• • •

Regina had slept with Mark Van Horn because she had been confused and lonely and horny and sad. It was late in her junior year of college. She had spent most of the year in love (she thought) with a classic poor-but-honest case who was at Whitten on a scholarship. He was witty and considerate, and an enthusiastic and tender lover, Regina's first.

He was also, it turned out, a snob. Since Patty Hearst had disappeared, the children of the rich had been drilled in not broadcasting exactly who they were. Hudson was a common-enough name, so Regina didn't need to use an alias the way some people she knew did.

When PBH found out she was of the Hudson Group Hudsons, he became a completely different person. He started *apologizing* all the time. For his clothes. For the fact that he didn't have a car. Whenever he didn't have enough money to pay for a movie or something. Before he'd found out who Regina was, he'd never given it a thought.

Regina tried to kid him out of it. She tried logic. She wound up throwing things and screaming. Nothing worked. PBH was never going to learn the basic concept of American democracy—the only way having money showed you were better than anybody else was that it showed you were better in getting or holding on to money.

After two months of this, Regina had called it off. PBH had taken it with a sigh. His bearing and attitude said, "I've been expecting this, rich girl like you, poor boy like me, just slumming, I should have known," and Regina wanted to kill him.

Then Mark Van Horn, who had transferred to Whitten College at the beginning of the second term, asked her out.

"It will be fairly gruesome," he'd said. "Some people up here have invited me to tea."

"Party people?" Regina asked. She meant, of course, the Van Horns' political party.

To Mark, to any Van Horn, there was no other sort of party. "Old friends of the family, though I've never met them. They said I could bring someone along, and I want to, in case one of them has a daughter with thin blood and buckteeth."

Regina laughed. "So you asked me."

Mark nodded. "You're one of the few people I know here, and I know you can go to a tea without laughing at the idea. Also, you're very pretty, and I like you. I didn't know whether it was less insulting to ask you to do this as a favor or as a date, so I'm trying to make it a little of both. What do you say? I'd like your company, and I need the favor."

Regina went. It had been absolutely as terrible as Mark had said it would be, and they'd laughed about it over dinner later. Three more dates, and they were lovers.

The relationship had a lot to be said for it, most of which was said by others. Regina's roommate thought she and Mark looked dreamy together, and that it was fate that sent Mark there. Regina suspected that her roommate had a serious case of damp panties for Mark herself, but nothing was ever said out loud. Mark treated the roommate the way he treated practically everyone else—with the smooth manner and easy smile his father gave to the constituents.

The three parents involved thought it was simply marvelous. The Senator, no doubt, had visions of adding the weight of one of the nation's largest communications companies to his already legendary clout. Besides, a lot of the Van Horn money came from pulp forests. The marriage could be an economic and political masterstroke. Mark's mother, Ella, now divorced and drinking on the French Riviera on a more-or-less permanent basis, was hoping that Regina would marry her son to save him from some, quote, gold-digging tramp, unquote. The fact that she had married Senator Van Horn not too long out of her family's bakery in Fort Wayne, Indiana, seemed to have been rinsed from her mind completely.

Petra Hudson had been all for it, too. She'd done everything but start publishing a magazine for brides and force Regina to proofread the whole thing. Regina had found her mother's behavior very puzzling, considering her lifelong dedication to keeping the Hudson Group free of political entanglements. It was only recently that Regina had figured it out. Petra Hudson, renegade Soviet spy, had wanted her daughter married to the son of one of the most powerful politicians in America, in case her secret came out. She wanted a hold on the Senator, leverage on him.

That might have been enough to make Regina hate her mother, but she had already ordered her heart to issue the woman a blanket pardon by the time the explanation for the whole business occurred to her. There was also the fact that Mother, while she had been sad when Regina broke up with Mark, had not nagged her or pushed her in any way to take up with him again.

Regina was not so crazy about the relationship as all that. Mark could be fun, and he certainly understood as much as Regina did about money and power. But he was selfish and demanding (and I thought *I* was spoiled, Regina thought), and he could be very nasty when he didn't get his way.

The only thing that kept them together for three months was the fact that Mark didn't have all that many things he wanted his way about. He was totally indifferent to what he ate or drank, or to what he or Regina wore. He wouldn't even bother to ask her opinion—he'd just wait for her to express a preference. Sometimes, Regina thought that if she waited long enough before saying anything, Mark would starve to death out of pure indifference.

But Mark had to pick the movies they saw, the records they listened to, the people they went out with. He simply refused to have anything to do with something he didn't like. Or thought he might not like. "Wait till I'm not around," he would say. "You'll have a better time."

Sex with Mark was scary. He had a beautiful body and knew what to do with it, but he was so cold and businesslike, Regina sometimes wondered if she wouldn't be better off with a vibrator. Mark knew, it seemed, a million positions to do it in, and was determined to work his way through them one by one, as if he were accumulating points for a merit badge.

The only time there'd been any real passion in their relationship came during the Great Anal Sex Argument. Mark wanted to; Regina absolutely refused. The very idea disgusted her, and still did. She felt now that Acquired Immune Deficiency Syndrome, whatever else it was, was a mammoth vindication of her instincts.

Mark had been furious. He'd called her silly. He'd called her a coward. He said she was repressed and provincial and bourgeois.

Regina had said, "I don't care," and Mark had really gotten upset.

That had been the beginning of the end. Once Mark knew that there was at least one thing in which he was never going to get his way, he stopped treating her with any kind of respect at all, sniping at her in public and private with snotty remarks, showing up late or not at all, and all the rest of the things a person can do to get on someone else's nerves.

Finally, he'd done one too many, and Regina had told him to drop dead and walked out. He transferred again at the end of the term (Mark didn't seem to last long anywhere) and Regina hadn't seen him since.

• • •

Now, she was supposed to call him up and ask him for a favor.

She took a deep breath. She was going to do it. She had promised Sean, and she kept her promises. She didn't *want* to do it, but she would.

She wasted a little time analyzing why she didn't want to do it. She decided that it was because she found it embarrassing to have gone to bed with someone basically because she knew her mother would approve of him. She wanted to forget all about Mark Van Horn, but here she was, dragging herself back to his attention. Asking, she knew, to be told to drop dead. Or worse, to have some of the famous Van Horn charm (Mark could show the full measure of that when he wanted to) poured over her.

All right, she told herself, all right. Get it over with. The first thing to do was find him. She had her secretary ring Senator Van Horn's office. Regina picked up when the connection was made.

"Hello," she said smoothly. This was her Corporate Voice. She often thought that if anything happened to the Hudson Group, she could use the Corporate Voice to get work as an announcer on a classical-music radio station. "This is Regina Hudson, of the Hudson Group. I'd like to get in touch with Mr. Mark Van Horn, the Senator's son—" Regina winced. *They* knew he was the Senator's son. The Corporate Voice, however, never missed a beat. "—and I was wondering if you might tell me how."

"Just . . ." The person on the other end hesitated for a second, as if listening to someone else. "Just a moment, Miss Hudson. Please hold."

She wasn't on hold long, just long enough to wonder what kind of luck would let Mark be in his father's office at that particular second. Regina had been looking forward to another round of dithering once she found out where Mark was.

"Miss Hudson!" said a happy voice after the hold clicked off. Not Mark's voice. "This is Ainley Masters."

Ainley Masters, Regina thought. He was another one who'd thought Hudson–Van Horn nuptials would have been a marvelous idea. Maybe the worst of them. Rumor had it that he had been drawing up a pre-nuptial agreement the size of the Federal Budget when Regina pulled the plug.

"Good afternoon, Mr. Masters," Regina said politely.

"I understand you want to talk to Mark."

"Yes, I do."

"Perhaps I can help you."

"No, it's personal." Kind of, Regina added silently. If there were no personal element, this phone call wouldn't be happening, that was for sure.

"Well, then," Masters said. "You're in luck. I don't know where Mark is at the moment, but he's due in town within the next couple of days. I'm sure he'll want to call you immediately."

"That would be nice," Regina lied.

"If you'll just give me a number where you can be reached . . ."

Regina gave him a couple.

Masters repeated the last few numbers, then complimented her on the smooth transition at *Worldwatch*. He said he hoped he'd be seeing her again soon, and hung up. He even seemed to hang up cheerfully.

Well, Regina thought, I made his day. If Allan were around, she would have been delighted to give him the opportunity to make hers, so to speak.

Where the hell *was* he, anyway?

CHAPTER ELEVEN

Minneapolis, Minnesota

If striding along on a pavement so cold it makes your feet ache, with your hands stuffed into inadequate pockets and your head pulled turtlelike into your jacket can be called strolling, Allan Trotter was strolling down the Nicholette Mall that Sunday afternoon.

For all the company he had, he might as well have been on the moon. They apparently had some strict blue laws in Minnesota. Here it was, 1:30 P.M. Central Standard Time, and the bars weren't even open yet.

It had seemed like such a good idea when he'd thought of it yesterday. The computer had regurgitated Carl Gottfried, of CG Electronics, Minneapolis, Minnesota, as the most likely duck to be lined up in the bugger-hater's shooting gallery.

After eleven murders, of course, you'd think the computer could give you copies of the killer's grade-school report cards. As they said, garbage in, garbage out. What the Agency had been able to glean from police reports from around the nation and its own files hadn't exactly been garbage, but it hadn't been a feast either.

The victim profile it turned out was useless. The dead men were different in age, religion, marital status and financial well-being. What they had in common, nobody needed a computer to find: They were all white males, they were all electronics experts respected in their field, and they all had a reputation, earned or otherwise, for having done secret stuff. There was no consensus on that, either. Some people had supposedly worked for the Russians, some for what Trotter laughingly thought of as Our Side, and some had big industrial-espionage reputations. And, of course, they had all been killed.

And there was one other thing. While several of the men on the list had retired by the time they were hit, all of them had been active through the years 1973–1977. Trotter wondered how much that was worth. It would be like someone running around killing everyone who'd worked for McDonald's in the summer of 1982. It would give you an interesting cross-section of victims, but what could you possibly have *against* all of them?

Anyway, Rines had had the idea of feeding the computer all the information they had on electronic-surveillance people (which was quite a bit—there are certain people your government likes to keep track of) and having the computer cross-check it with the profile. "Maybe we can ask the next guy why somebody wants to kill him," Rines said.

The computer gave them Carl Gottfried of CG Electronics, Minneapolis, Minnesota.

The Congressman had looked at the huge sheet of printout with the one lonely name on it and said, "My Lord, he's cleared the table, hasn't he?"

"One name," Trotter said.

"And even he don't exactly fit," the old man said. "He didn't even start up in the business till spring of 1974."

"I'd like to talk to this Gottfried," Trotter said.

"That's what I just said," Rines told him.

"I don't mean question him, I mean talk to him now, this very minute. Did it give us his phone number on that thing?"

It did. Two of them, in fact. Trotter got no answer at the office number, but found Gottfried at home. He told him he had some business for him, urgent business, and he'd like to see him as soon as possible.

Gottfried was amenable. "Well, you're more than five hundred miles away from Minneapolis; how soon can you get here?"

"How did you know that?"

The computer had come up with a picture of Gottfried along with the data. He was thin, balding, wore glasses. He looked like a high school nerd who had found a long-term and very satisfying revenge on the rest of the world.

"I'm an electronics expert, Mr. Trotter."

Trotter could almost see the picture smirk. He could definitely hear it in Gottfried's voice.

"I'll fly in tomorrow morning," he said.

"Okay. Your plane will probably be late. The weather is a mess. Call me at home when you get to the airport, and I'll come into the office to meet you. You have my office address?"

Trotter repeated it.

"Third floor," Gottfried reminded him. "On second thought . . ."

"Yes?"

"No, nothing. Tell you what. Call me here, like I said, and if there's no answer, call me at the office, all right?"

"Fine with me," Trotter had said. "Take care of yourself."

Gottfried said, "Huh?" but Trotter was already hanging up.

"Get me on a plane to Minneapolis," he said.

"Send a man," his father replied. "I don't want you flying into any blizzard."

"No time to brief him. Look, our friend, whoever he is, moves fast. In less than a year, he's killed almost a dozen men. And they weren't innocent bystanders, either. These were people who'd made it to the top in the suspicion business. The killer knew who these men were, and had the resources to find them, get close to them, and kill them."

Rines scratched his chin. "Yeah. And he did it in so many different ways that we only caught on to him a couple of weeks ago."

"All right," the old man said. "You've convinced me. Not that you had to. You're running the Agency, remember?"

Trotter smiled. "I don't want to throw my weight around unnecessarily. I just wish I didn't have to wait till tomorrow to get there. How come you never taught me to fly a jet?"

"It was on the agenda, son. You ran out on me before I could get around to it."

"Don't expect me to apologize." The meeting broke up.

Trotter called Regina that evening and told her it would be another day or two before he got home. He was pleased to find himself thinking of it as home.

Regina was disappointed—that also felt good—and told him about the call she'd made to Mark Van Horn. Trotter had heard the story of Mark Van Horn a long time ago. He wasn't worried. He told Regina to go ahead and ask him her questions. "Interview him in person, if you have to. If you want to. It's your magazine, and it's your decision."

"You don't mind?"

"Do you love me?"

"Isn't it obvious?"

"Do you love him?"

"I never did."

"Then what do I have to worry about? Or you either. I'll see you soon, Bash. We've got a lot to talk about."

• • •

Trotter called Gottfried from the airport. No answer at his home. Busy signal at the office. He tried a few more times. Same results. Finally, he said to hell with it, and went for a taxi. The line was busy; the odds were that someone was in the office.

He told the driver to drop him off at a hotel about five blocks from Gottfried's office. Not only was this a standard precaution, it was also good for his cover as somebody with a problem he needed a security consultant's help with. It was all probably a waste of time, since it was all but certain no one was following him, but as his father had often said, if you make your precautions habits, you don't have to waste time deciding whether you need them.

That was true wisdom, and had stood him in good stead over the years, but Trotter wished that this time it had occurred to him to precaution himself about three blocks closer to his destination.

He could feel the blood congealing in his legs by the time he reached the right door. He was glad he had gloves on when he grabbed the handle. He wondered what kind of brain would put brass handles on an outside door in the middle of the frost belt. What did the unfortunate bare-handed person do? Stand there until spring?

Trotter went inside and stood there for a few seconds, warming up. Slowly, he let his head inch free from his coat.

Then he realized he was stalling.

It made him angry, because he didn't know why. He took a few seconds to figure it out. When he did, he was angrier still.

He was stalling because he was afraid of what that busy signal might mean.

Bad. Very bad. Fear was all right. Fear was good. It put an edge on you. But not if you refused to face it. Trotter took a deep breath, then exhaled, fogging up his glasses again. He waited until they cleared.

Too long out of the field, he thought. Then headed for the stairs. Gottfried's office was on the third floor.

He was out of breath by the time he got there. All that damned working out, and he *still* wasn't in shape. He caught his breath and made his way down the hall.

The doors here were wood, top to bottom, with gold letters announcing who occupied what office. There was no glass to let Trotter have a look inside before he committed himself.

There it was. CG Electronics. Trotter didn't knock. He grabbed the knob firmly and twisted it slowly. It made no noise. The door was open. When he could feel the latch had cleared, he threw the door open and jumped aside.

Nothing happened. Trotter shrugged. That would also be good for his cover, if his cover was posing as a paranoid nut.

He went inside. The office had been trashed. A man lay on the floor to his right, out of immediate sight of the doorway. A telephone receiver dangled just above his hand. The man's face was turned obligingly toward Trotter. Obligingly, because it enabled Trotter to see instantly that the dead man was Gottfried, and because it is considerably less unpleasant to see a small black hole in someone's forehead than it is to see a big red mess where the back of someone's head used to be.

The gun was on the floor about fifteen feet from the body, a regulation police thirty-eight. Trotter was happy to see that the killer had saved everyone a lot of irritation by not trying to set this up like a suicide or an accident or something. The position of the wound, the lack of powder burns, would have told the truth no matter what the killer had tried to set up.

Trotter went over and picked up the gun. "*Always* pick up the gun," his father had taught him. "You come upon a dead body, and the gun is lying there, *you pick it up*. A dead body and a gun means a *killer's* been around, boy, and for all you know he's still there or just came back. Don't worry about your fingerprints, you worry about your life first."

Trotter still had his gloves on, so he didn't have to worry about leaving fingerprints, just smudging the killer's. In the unlikely event the killer had left any. He worried instead about what he was going to do for leads now. The combined genius of the Congressman, Rines, himself, and some very high-priced computers had come up with the name of this now rapidly cooling corpse. He could only hope the killer hadn't retired.

Trotter laughed at himself. Aren't *you* the sweet one.

But he didn't take it back. Trotter was not equipped to go back over old cases and patiently follow clues. He had been trained to take charge, to grab hold of a situation and not to let go until he had twisted it into a shape he liked.

Now, there might not *be* a situation. The situation might be (probably was) over. Might as well try to grab a handful of steam. The whole situation would bother him less if he had some inkling of what the hell was at stake.

He decided to forget about it. He arrived at that sort of decision a lot more frequently than he was able to carry it out, but he always felt better just for telling himself he was allowed to put it aside. He'd go back to Kirkester, to Bash. Make wedding plans, if she still wanted to. If something was going to happen that would make some sense of this mess, Trotter would find out about it.

The only thing to decide now was whether to let poor Mr. Gottfried wait till tomorrow for someone to find him, or to make an anonymous call to the police before he left town.

Then he didn't even have to decide that much, because the police were there, pointing guns at him, and yelling at him to drop his.

Trotter did what they said. He put his hands on top of his head, though they hadn't asked him to do that. And he worked hard at not smiling. He didn't think they'd understand.

Chapter Twelve

Washington, D.C.

He lay naked on the bed, relaxed, happy. It had been a very hectic six months. Twelve of the bastards killed. Life would have been a lot simpler if he'd just been able to find out who the right one was, of course. Doing something unfamiliar once was a lot easier than doing it twelve times. He was glad it was over. He was beginning to get the feeling that someone suspected something was going on. That guy they busted in Minneapolis—they'd let him out of jail altogether too soon. That's what his sources said anyway, and he had no reason to doubt his sources. That guy might have been released because he was cozy with the police. So what—whatever he was, he'd shown up just an hour after Gottfried's death. That was cutting it a little too close.

He rubbed his chest and told himself again how glad he was that it was over. He had to smile. They'd all been so *surprised* when he'd pulled his gun or grabbed their throats or whatever he'd decided to do to that particular one. It was an amazing feeling of power, watching them realize that though Nature or God or whatever they wanted to say had put them in this world, *he* had decided to take them out of it.

It wouldn't be the same, of course, if he'd had to kill somebody with a shred of decency. But these men were scum. They earned their bread by nosing into people's dirty secrets. They deserved to get it. There must be a lot of people who deserved to get it.

He had the heat in the apartment way down. He could feel cool air currents against his body. He liked it. He liked to go naked. He was more alive that way, more in touch, as though the world loved him.

One more, he thought. One more to be rid of, but that could wait. That *had* to wait. In the meantime, he had nothing to do but live his life.

There was a phone call he was supposed to make. To a woman. He felt something stronger than the wind down in his groin. He raised his head. His dick was twitching. He looked at it as though he'd never seen it before.

"What is this?" he asked it. "Nostalgia?"

He started to laugh. He rolled over and grabbed the phone and dialed. He was still smiling when the call went through.

"Regina?" he said. "Hi. This is Mark Van Horn. I understand you've been trying to get in touch with me."

PART TWO
LACHESIS

She who measures the thread of life . . .

Chapter One

The Year Before

Mark was doing a favor for his mother. That was the rationale. The real reason was that he had always wanted to poke around inside his father's safe. Mark Van Horn had been forbidden very little in life, but he had been forbidden to look into that safe.

What was even more amazing was that this order came not from the housekeeper, or from Ainley Masters, but directly from the Senator himself. Mark was forbidden to mess with the safe and, more amazing still, further forbidden from telling anyone his father had mentioned it.

It was silly, in a way. At the time the safe had been put off limits, Mark had been a twelve-year-old kid with a fixation on caper movies and a toy stethoscope, with which he used to listen to all the locks in the house, and through which it was impossible even to hear his own heartbeat. If he wanted to cat-burgle any place (as he frequently did), he had to steal a key or sneak in through the window. He had about as much chance of getting into a combination lock as he had of growing up to be a member of the Other Party. All the Senator had succeeded in doing was filling his son's mind with curiosity about that safe, and making him carry on his burglar fixation long past the time it would have died a natural death. Mark had very nearly (but not quite) been thrown out of two private schools for testing his continually developing skills on safes in headmasters' offices.

The Van Horn name and Van Horn money smoothed over those situations, and by the time he started college, Mark had more or less lost his mania for getting into places. Or rather, the nature of the places he wanted to get into had changed. Regina Hudson had been one of the nicer places he had gotten into.

The only lock he still wanted to open was on his father's safe. One day, on a visit to Switzerland to see his mother, he decided to break the second part of the law.

"Ella?" he said. His mother liked him to call her Ella. She said being called "Mother" made her feel too old. "Ella, what does the Senator keep in the wall safe in the bedroom?"

"What bedroom, dear?"

"The master bedroom in the Georgetown house."

"There is no wall safe there."

"Yes, there is."

Ella sniffed. She had a fine, thin nose. Delicate nostrils. Very good for sniffing. "If there is, he put it in after I left him."

"I suppose so." Mark's parents had split up when he was twelve, and he was thirteen before he found out the safe existed, so it was possible. He had just assumed it had always been there, since he hadn't been aware of its installation. On the other hand, he was away at school so much, they could have installed lead lining and turned the place into a fallout shelter without Mark's necessarily having been aware of it.

"In any case," Ella went on, "it can't be anything very important. Ainley Masters takes all the important things and puts them in a vault somewhere underground. I tried to tell your father that someday, Ainley will sell that stuff back to the Van Horn family for a billion dollars, but he wouldn't listen to me." She sniffed again. "He never listened to me. I think Ainley poisoned his mind. Would you care for a drink, dear? I'm going to ring down for one."

Mark had checked his watch. Eleven thirty-five A.M. One of Ella's better days.

"I don't know how important it is," Mark said, "but he told me never to go near it or he'd whip me."

Ella's blue eyes widened. "Your father said that?"

"He did. He also told me never to mention it to anyone. Including Ainley."

Ella's eyes lit up. She half-sat, half-collapsed into a chair. She spread the fingers of a bone-china hand across her chest and sat there blinking.

"Ella? Mother? Are you all right?"

"Oh," Ella said. "I wonder if it . . ."

"What do you wonder?"

"If the *letter* could be in there?"

"Letter?"

"Oh. Oh, Mark dear. I don't know if I should tell you."

There was a knock on the door. A pitcher of dry martinis for his mother. Mark took it, poured, and handed his mother the glass. She sipped at the top layer as if she'd never tasted gin before and wasn't sure how she liked it. Mark knew the pitcher would be gone before the sun went down. That was one of the reasons his visits to his mother were so infrequent.

"After the size of your reaction, I'd say you have to tell me, now."

She sampled the liquor again, rolling it around in her mouth and looking heavenward, still trying to decide if she liked it. This would go on for five minutes. Then she'd decide she loved it.

Ella sighed. She had a good nose for sighing, too. "I suppose you ought to know. You're not my little baby anymore, you're a strong man now. I should trust you to take care of me."

Mark smiled sadly. The habit of loving his mother had not been broken, but he knew that habit was all it was. His mother was weak and venal and ineffectual, everything he despised.

"Tell me about the letter, Ella," he said.

She told him. It was after one of the Senator's multitudinous extramarital flings, but "before he burned up that Italian girl, of course." Instead of facing the situation with her usual resignation, Ella had gotten angry and, worse, had threatened to make a fuss. She knew how the Van Horns felt about fusses.

The Senator had been contrite. He wrote her a letter, begging forgiveness.

"It was quite sweet, in a way," Ella said. "He said it was a weakness that grew from the strength of his Dutch sea-captain forebears, and other romantic lies. The truth, of course, is that your father's brains are in his testicles. In any case, he begged me to forgive him, and while he couldn't promise to conquer the weakness once and for all, he did say I was the only one he had ever loved, and if he ever did anything to drive me away, he would quit politics and sign over completely his entire share of the family businesses."

"He didn't," Mark said.

"Oh, he did, dear, and signed it. The whole thing, in fact, was in his handwriting."

"He must have been crazy. You could destroy him at any moment. You still can."

Ella looked horrified. "I never would!" she said. "If I let your father throw it all away, he can't leave it to you, can he, dear? I know you've been preparing yourself to be everything it means to be a Van Horn. *I'm* certainly not going to ruin it for you."

She sniffed, then took a long pull at her drink. This martini stuff was pretty good, after all. "Besides," she went on, "I couldn't if I wanted to. He got the letter back somehow. I used to keep it in my overnight case, you know, the one I kept packed for when your father would be just *too* outrageous with some woman. Then came that Italian girl. I waited a decent interval after he managed to get himself cleared—protecting the family to the last, you see—then walked out for good. When I got to my hotel, I looked for the letter. I was going to mail it back to your father, you know, a noble gesture. But it was gone."

"He had ample opportunity to take it back," Mark said.

"I know, I know. It's just that you wondered about the safe. That was all I could think of that he'd want to keep secret from Ainley Masters."

Ella smiled at her son. "But, of course, that's foolish. Lord knows your father isn't Einstein, but even he wouldn't be stupid enough not to burn that letter once he got hold of it again." She looked up from her drink. "Would he?"

Mark smiled back. "You'd like to find out, wouldn't you?"

"If it still exists, I'd like to get it back again and send it to your father. I owe myself the grand gesture, don't you think?"

Mark continued to smile. "Next time I visit him," he said, "I'll do what I can to find out. If the letter's there, I'll mail it back to him in your name."

Ella pouted. "But Mark, dear, it's supposed to be *my* grand gesture."

"You might forget."

"Listen to you talk. A person would think you didn't trust me."

"What kind of son wouldn't trust his own mother?"

"A smart kind," Ella said flatly, and suddenly, it was impossible to tell she'd had anything to drink at all. "You just keep it up, dear. And remember to take care of your mother when you're running the country."

• • •

There had been nothing to it. All he had to do was arrange his end-of-term visit to D.C. so that he *just missed* his father, who'd be back in the home state keeping them happy in the outposts of the empire, or off on a fact-finding trip to some balmy place with a comely member of his staff to take notes or whatever else the Senator was dishing out. No suspicion was aroused. That sort of thing happened often enough by accident. Mark would do what he always did—let Mrs. Rodriguez spoil him for a few days, then take off himself. The only thing he had to worry about was being caught in the master bedroom with a stethoscope.

The first night, he went to his father's empty room just to look the thing over. It had been years since he'd seen it, and he'd known nothing about safes at the time. Comparing his memory of it with what he'd learned since, he didn't think it would be much trouble, but if he was going to need anything special, better to know now.

There was a mirror in front of the safe, rather than a picture. Mark was sure that had never aroused any suspicion, either. The Senator's major asset as a Senator was his Senatorial good looks, and he was quite well known for never missing an opportunity to admire them. People would have been more surprised if Hank Van Horn *hadn't* had an extra mirror hanging on the wall of the bedroom.

The mirror swung away from the wall on hidden hinges. The knob read "MasterSecure 500." Nothing great, but not total garbage, either. Not much harder than what a headmaster might keep in his office, at any rate. Mark wasn't going to do this with just his fingertips, though. If he was really serious about getting into this thing, he might have to drill it. Nitro, of course, was out of the question. Mark smiled and shook his head at himself for even thinking of it. He must have wanted into that thing even more than he'd been willing to admit to himself. Well, he'd have to go back to his room and decide just how badly he did want to get in there, because he wasn't about to do it tonight.

Unless . . .

How stupid *was* his father? Or, how mentally sloppy had a life of effortless power, of having all his messes cleaned up after him, made him? Maybe they were both the same question. Either way, Mark's answer was "Quite a bit." So he stood there for a while and twiddled knobs.

This kind of safe would carry a four- or five-digit combination. The Senator certainly wouldn't carry a slip of paper around with the combination written on it. He'd want something that would be easy for him to remember. That was the kind of thinking that had let burglars into a thousand safes. The Senator usually got better advice than that. Ainley Masters, for instance, wouldn't have let him get away with it for a second.

But this was the Senator's own secret. Ainley Masters was to know nothing about it. No one was to know anything about it. Mark had found out only because he had been a nosy little kid, poking into everything. The Senator had figured him harmless.

Even now, Mark wasn't sure that he intended his father any harm. His mother's story had given him the impetus to do this after years of merely wanting to, but Mark wanted to get into this safe as much to find something to admire about his father as about anything else. What was it, he wondered, after a lifetime of letting his life be run by his grandfather, his older brother, Ainley Masters, that had led Hank Van Horn to his first act of defiance? Since, Mark was sure, it would fall to him to run his father's life, it was his duty to the family to find out.

He tried combinations. He tried his father's birthday. He tried his mother's birthday, which might have been suitable if all this really turned out to be that stupid letter. On the same theory, he tried the day his parents had been married, and the day they split up. No luck. Mark tried his own birthday, then 7-4-7-6 in the hope that the Senator had set the combination in a fit of patriotism.

Nothing. Mark frowned and started to turn away. He'd be back with a drill. Or not. It all depended on how this escapade looked in the light of the morning.

Then he had a hunch. He didn't know, and would *never* know, where it came from. It was just *there,* and it refused to be ignored.

Mark spun the dial to 8-8-7-4. August 8, 1974. The day before the resignation of Richard Milhous Nixon as President of the United States. The date Miss Giuseppina Girolamo had been reduced to a few greasy ashes. He could almost feel the tumblers meshing.

Mark felt something crawling on his forehead. Sweat. He grabbed the handle, hoping that it wouldn't move when he pulled it.

It practically jumped in his hand. The door swung open before Mark had even told his muscles to pull.

Inside was a small, rectangular parcel wrapped in stiff white paper that was yellowing at the bent places. Mark could see bumps and lines embossed in the side of the paper toward him. Typewriting. Not just a piece of paper. A letter.

Not, however, the letter his father had written to his mother. That, according to Ella, had been handwritten.

Mark reached inside the safe and removed the parcel, then swept his hand around to see if there was anything else inside. Nothing, not even dust.

The paper had been neatly folded around whatever was inside, but it hadn't been sealed. It was stiff, but not brittle enough to break or tear when Mark removed it. He was grateful for that. All he needed to do was to leave little flakes of paper on the floor in front of the safe. It would be nice to be able to refold the thing and put it back the way it was, if that's what he decided to do.

The rectangle was a tape cassette. A cheap one. The label said "Exceptional Tape Company," which made Mark think it was probably from Hong Kong, or someplace else that hadn't found out that in the United States, "exceptional" was now a euphemism for "retarded." Gray plastic, gray-and-white label. Nothing had been written on it. The tape was rewound and ready to go. Mark knew then that the parcel was not making its way back to the safe. Not tonight.

He looked at the note. It read, "Senator—This is one copy. A thousand or more could be made. You will be contacted." No signature.

Mark closed the safe and spun the dial. He was so eager to get the hell out of there he almost forgot to put the mirror back.

He forced himself to walk calmly back to his room. It was just past 1:00 A.M.; a servant might still be awake. It wouldn't do for Mark to be seen sprinting through the house.

He had to dig through a lot of stuff in his closet before he found his old Sony Walkman, one of the first ones. He'd grown tired of his before most people knew they existed. There was several thousand dollars' worth of stereo equipment in this room, but as it happened, the only earphones were attached to the Walkman. Whatever was on this tape was not going to be let loose to blend with the atmosphere.

Mark cannibalized a couple of batteries from a flash gun, put the headphones on, and got ready to play the tape.

He fumbled the tape into the machine. His hands weren't exactly shaking. They felt as if they had too much blood in them, as if they were swollen and hard to bend.

He took a deep breath and forced himself to concentrate. He got the tape settled, got the machine closed.

As he listened to the hiss of the leader going through the recording head, he thought, *blackmail*. Blackmail, for God's sake. It was ridiculous. Van Horns didn't pay blackmail. It was ridiculous. There was no need. Van Horns brazened it out. That was the advantage of being bold about your vices. Van Horns drank. Van Horns womanized. Van Horns used every bit of financial and political power to help their friends and screw their enemies.

Besides, the Van Horn family had paid with blood and spectacle for long-term kid-gloves treatment from the press.

What could the Senator have possibly done to be blackmailed over? What in the world could there be that Mark's father was afraid to tell *Ainley Masters,* a man for whom the death of Pina Girolamo had been a public-relations exercise?

Voices came to Mark's ears.

"Do you want to eat first?" a woman asked.

"After," the Senator said.

The woman laughed low in her throat.

There was more small talk, then creaking bedsprings and moans and the sticky-valve sound of sex.

Then there was more talking. "I thought you were taking care of that," the Senator said.

"Hank, darling, nothing works all the time. I'm sorry."

Talk about an abortion. Talk about blackmail. Then Mark's father saying, "Bitch," followed by more creaking bedsprings, this time accompanied by choking noises and gurgles rather than moans.

More talk about abortion.

The asshole doesn't know he's killed her, Mark thought.

"Come on," the Senator said. "Don't sulk." There was silence for a long time. No more talk after that, just movement in the room, followed by a crackling that got louder and louder until it ended in a squeal.

That was the microphone melting, Mark thought.

Mark hit the rewind button and listened to the tape hum its way back to the beginning. He was amazed at how calm he was.

He listened to it again, then rewound and listened a third time. It didn't change.

Mark pulled the earphones off and shook his head. He took the cassette from the Walkman and stuffed it down behind the bottom drawer of his dresser. The note he folded up and put in his wallet, reminding himself as he did that he must be very careful not to have his pocket picked or to be hit by a car.

Mark, who had been twelve years old when it happened, but already a true Van Horn, had put the odds at about forty percent that his father had killed that girl. A few years later, he had decided that if he had, he had done it because she'd gotten herself pregnant and was being difficult about it.

But this—this was beyond belief. To choke her by accident in a *bugged room*. He didn't even want to know who had been bugging the room. Yet.

Mark had always known it was coming. He always knew that someday he'd have to take control of the family. He'd just always figured it would happen after he'd served a few terms in Congress, then made the move up to his father's Senate seat, as Hank Van Horn was trundled off to one of the more prestigious ambassadorships.

But that wasn't the way it was working out. If Mark expected there to be anything of the Van Horn name and power left to inherit, he had to take charge *right now*.

He'd also have to have a long and not especially pleasant talk with his father, but not now. Not for a while. There were things to do, first. Some facts had to be learned, and some people had to die.

CHAPTER TWO

The Present—February—Concord, New Hampshire

One of the two major candidates for the Party's Presidential nomination lay back on a lumpy bed in a quaint New England inn. It was late afternoon now, and he'd been on the go since before 6:00 A.M. A campaign breakfast. Pancakes, great slabs of bacon, butter, maple syrup. The candidate usually had nothing but black coffee until he ate a small salad around 2:00 P.M., and the meal had been enough to make him gag.

He did not, in fact, gag. He smiled and cleaned his plate. And asked for more when the cameras turned toward him. He'd made four speeches since. Or rather, he'd made The Speech four times, and each time it had taken a greater and greater effort to repress vicious, heartburn-inspired belches. What fun Dan Rather would have had with that.

Finally, he had fought his way through mobs of reporters back to the inn. A lot of reporters, a few New Hampshirites. New Hampshirians. To hell with it. He'd just keep saying "The People of New Hampshire." The People of New Hampshire had a good thing going, as far as the candidate could tell. They had turned the primary into a major industry, getting suckers to come in and spend millions. In February, for crying out loud, when it was cold enough to freeze your feet to your shoes and your underwear to your groin. Amazing what people would go through to get to be President.

The candidate was running a little behind schedule. Candidates *always* ran behind schedule. This was due to having schedules that made them so exhausted they could no longer move.

Now, for instance, the candidate was supposed to be donning a tuxedo in order to attend a dinner being thrown by the state party chairman. The other candidate would be there, but the understanding was no debating, no overt campaigning. He just hoped the other guy would be as late as he was.

The candidate groaned. Dressing for dinner. He had managed to get as far as shedding his jacket and tie before collapsing on the bed. A little work with his feet, and his shoes were off, too. That was progress. He had better not be there too late. He had lost in Iowa; not a big deal, perhaps, but when you lose in Iowa, you'd damn well better win in New Hampshire.

The thing was, he wasn't even sure he wanted to be President. He thought he was doing a good job where he was. The people who had put him where he was had no reason to complain.

And they *weren't* complaining. They were just ambitious. This was the culmination of a glorious plan, and of the candidate's glorious career. He supposed it wasn't *that* bad an idea. It was hard to remember when you were tired and cold and faced with a procession of endless days finishing only in November (and then only if you *lost*) that the reason you had gotten involved in the business in the first place was that you had ideals and goals and a vision for the human race.

The money wasn't bad, either.

With a mighty effort, the candidate sat up on the bed. He sighed. The problem was, they had already practically guaranteed him the nomination and the Presidency. It had all been arranged. He would have had a lot more interest in this if they'd told him it all depended on him.

The candidate was about to collapse back to the bed when someone knocked on the door.

"What is it?" he asked, trying not to sound grumpy.

"Mr. Augustus Pickett is here, sir. He'd like to talk to you, if it's convenient."

Gus Pickett. That was good. That was better than good. Gus Pickett was the richest man in the Party. He was into gold and bauxite and gypsum, practically anything that could be found in the ground. He lived in Colorado. If he had come to New Hampshire it had to have something to do with the primary.

The candidate sprang from the bed. He was about to tell his aide to have Pickett wait until he was dressed. Then he thought, no. Here was a chance to be Presidential and human at the same time.

"He can come in right now," the candidate said. "If he doesn't mind watching me dress."

There was a gravelly laugh from outside the room. Pickett liked it. Good. He'd have to see that the press found out about this.

The candidate went over and opened the door and welcomed his visitor. Gus Pickett was a small man, but tough. He had a mop of thick white hair and pale, cold, blue eyes. Everything else about him was brown. The grooved skin, stretched tight over a face that was all planes and angles; the suit, tie, shoes, overcoat.

"You should have let one of the kids take your coat," the candidate said.

"It's all right, I won't be here long. I just wanted to say hello, ask how you're doing."

Change jingled as the candidate let his pants fall to the carpet. He started to unbutton his shirt.

"I'm fine," he said brightly. "Not too much time to rest, but that's campaigning."

"Sure," Gus Pickett said. "Politics ain't shelling peas."

The candidate looked at him. Gus Pickett? He stood gaping for a moment, then said, "I thought the expression was 'Politics ain't beanbag.'"

Pickett smiled. "Peas, beans, what's the difference?"

There was no doubt about it, now. Sign, countersign, confirmation. Gus Pickett, it seemed, was not just the richest man in the Party, he was the richest man in the *party*. The room had already been checked for bugs and was clear. Now that the signs had been given, whatever Pickett said next, the candidate was to take as coming directly from Control. From Moscow.

The candidate stood there in his socks and underwear, listening to Gus Pickett tell him how Control was going to place the candidate in the White House.

The plan was brilliant. He couldn't see how it could fail.

Gus Pickett seemed pretty sanguine about it, too. The grooves of his face rearranged themselves into a bright smile. "See you at the dinner, Mr. President," he said.

Mr. President. I might as well get used to hearing that, the candidate thought. He was going to be President! He would remove America as a threat to World Peace. He could lead his country the rest of the way into true Socialist justice. He would be one of the great heroes of history.

Then he saw himself in the mirror. The Great Hero of history looked at himself in his underwear, smiled sheepishly, then hastened to get dressed.

CHAPTER THREE

Kirkester, New York

Trotter had come back to Kirkester depressed. His little expedition had been a total washout. Worse—he had to have strings pulled to get the police to let him leave Minnesota. It is never good to leave people wondering what's so important about you.

And though New England was freezing (according to *USA Today*'s weather map), Central New York had just undergone the annual Midwinter Thaw. This meant that the snow that had fallen since late November had melted all at once, which meant in turn that everything that was not paved was mud, and much of what *was* paved was covered with mud.

The only good thing about his return was seeing Regina again.

When the welcome-back kisses were finished, she said, "I'm not pregnant."

"Ah." Trotter was strangely sad. He knew he was being stupid but he went on feeling that way. There'd be a lot more chances, and trying to make her pregnant was fun.

Then he realized how she probably knew she wasn't pregnant. "Does that mean we can't . . . ?"

Regina frowned. "Not for a couple of days, anyway."

"Doesn't matter. We'll have a quiet dinner and snuggle."

Regina smiled and shook her head. "I have a hard time figuring you out," she said. "I know what you've been trained to do, and I've seen you in action. You're the tough, deadly spy."

"The spy who loved you," Trotter said.

"Yeah, exactly. Then when it comes to you and me, not only are you sweet and gentle, you're almost sappy, like a high school kid."

"Sappy?"

"I *like* sappy. It's just a strange picture, you know?"

"I guess. Maybe it's because I never had a chance to do any sappy stuff when I was the right age for it. I'm a late bloomer. Maybe I'll grow out of it. Probably by the time we're eighty or ninety, I won't be sappy at all."

They had their quiet dinner and snuggled, then went to bed. Trotter spent a large part of the night staring at the ceiling wondering about what he'd had in mind when he talked about being eighty or ninety years old. Had he meant it? He hoped not. There had been a time when Trotter had been convinced he wouldn't live to see thirty. That birthday was safely past, but the one thing someone in his business, even in the administration end, could not allow himself, was the future. The only way you could go on living was to be ready to die at any second. The man who called himself Allan Trotter was beginning to doubt he was.

The next day he decided to go into the office, more because he wanted to be in the same building with Bash than anything else. He went to the basement, where the Kirkester *Chronicle*'s offices were, and made his way to the desk he barely used.

As he sat down, he heard hands clapping from across the room. Trotter looked up to see Sean Murphy grinning sardonically at him.

Murphy walked across the room to him. "Regina said you'd be here. I could hardly believe it. Glad you could find your desk."

"Secret homing device inside. What can I do for you?"

"How about a drink?"

"First you make remarks about my showing up, now you want to haul me out of here."

"I have to talk to you."

"So talk."

"Not here. Come on."

"Isn't it a little early for a drink?"

"Bars open at eleven. It'll be eleven by the time we get to one. That's the one trouble with having your paper on a big estate like this. No bar next door. All the great journalistic enterprises have bars next door."

"All right," Trotter said. "Don't want to overdo it, anyway." His smile was a challenge. Murphy rolled his eyes a little but he didn't say anything. He *did* have something on his mind.

"We'll take my car," Trotter said.

"Mine's right outside," Murphy protested.

"I am not letting a man who's got to find a saloon at eleven o'clock in the morning drive anywhere. You might kill me, or you might kill you. And you're too valuable to the Hudson Group."

"Your concern for the Hudson Group is touching."

"Thank you. Got any particular bar in mind?"

Murphy picked a place called John's in downtown Kirkester. They knew him there. Murphy waved to the bartender, who was still taking chairs off tables, and told him they'd be sitting in a booth in the back when he was ready.

They only had to wait about half a minute. Murphy ordered a double Irish; Trotter had a club soda. The bartender gave him a suspicious look. "You want lime?" he said.

"No, thanks," Trotter said. The bartender walked away, apparently mollified. He turned to Murphy. "What does he want from me at eleven o'clock in the morning?"

Murphy sipped his whiskey. "This is a serious drinking bar. I used to be here a lot."

"Yeah. I didn't want to say anything, but your behavior this morning doesn't make you seem like someone who's cut way down."

"This is different. This is therapeutic."

"For what?"

"Stomach trouble. Lack of guts."

Trotter considered digging for the meaning in that, if any, but decided against it. "Okay," he said. "We're here, you've got a drink, can you finally tell me what your problem is?"

Murphy took another sip. "Not yet. I have to work up to it. We can talk about other stuff, though."

"Fine. How long do you think it will take for the mud to freeze up again?"

"Usually takes three days to a week. Here, let me start a topic with a little more body to it. Regina has decided that *Worldwatch* is going to urge the new President to press forward with Star Wars."

"I know."

"You wouldn't have anything to do with that decision, would you?"

"Not a thing. I'm proud of her, though."

"I'll just bet you are." He tossed off the rest of his drink and called for another one. "I advised her against it, you know."

"I know," Trotter said. "I wondered why."

"It's an unpopular issue. Discredited."

"With the kind of bullshit press it's gotten, I'm not surprised."

"A little hard on your colleagues there, aren't you, Trotter?"

"I wear glasses. Does that mean I have to approve everything a nearsighted person does? Besides, it's immoral to oppose SDI."

"Im*moral*? How do you get that?"

"I get it from the fact that SDI is designed to blow up Russian missiles. Everything else we've ever built—anything we *will* ever build with a policy of Mutually Assured Destruction—is designed to blow up Russian children."

"It will cost trillions."

"What's civilization worth to you, Murphy?"

"That would be swell if it worked."

"Uh-huh. I told Orville, and I told Wilbur, and now I'm telling you, that thing will never get off the ground."

"So you think it *will* work?" The second drink had lasted a much shorter time than the first. Murphy got started on the third.

"I know it will work."

"Oh, come off it. A bunch of technology that doesn't even exist is going to keep us one hundred percent safe from atomic missiles. Right."

Trotter smiled. "Let me ask you a question. If SDI is such a pipe dream, why are the Russians practically shitting their pants in an attempt to make us give it up? They're not stupid, you know. Besides, they're building one, too."

"How the hell can you be so sure about *that*?"

Trotter smiled. He could be so sure because he'd seen the satellite photographs of the construction of Russian SDI command stations. It probably wasn't a good idea to say so.

"All right," he said. "Let's leave it I am strongly of the opinion that they are. I'm not a hundred percent sure.

"And speaking of one hundred percent, it was the press who started this crap about 'one hundred percent safe' from Russian missiles. What bullshit. You might as well say that a welfare program is a failure if anyone in the United States feels hungry for ten minutes."

"So you're saying a nuclear missile here and there is okay."

"I'm saying that all SDI has to do to be worthwhile is make it impossible for the Russians ever to think they can knock us out of action with a first strike. Period. If we can protect half our missile silos from a first strike, they'll never attack. They're *not stupid*. They want to control a planet, not a cinder."

Murphy was looking skeptically at him. Trotter shook his head. "I know. I know. God forbid you should actually *think* about something for thirty seconds. Might unsettle your prejudices. Look, I'll make it simple. There are four possible reasons to oppose SDI: It costs too much, which means making your society safer from Armageddon is not something you care about. You think it won't work, in which case you think the Russians are a bunch of assholes, because they would practically give Minsk to get us to stop. You're against it *because* the Russians want us to stop, though why an American gives a shit about what the Russians want is beyond me. Or you simply prefer the idea of wasting schoolkids, grown-ups, cats, Russian wolfhounds, millions of lives, to the idea of blowing up hardware."

Trotter leaned back. "Now. You pick one of those and tell me how it's a moral choice."

Murphy poured the rest of his drink through a thin smile and said, "You're good. It's not your arguments, your arguments are simplistic bullshit—"

"That's not going to refute them."

"—it's your face and your eyes. And of course, you're brave. You took that fall off the catwalk saving Regina from *something*, though us poor working stiffs were never allowed to know exactly what. I can see why Regina is so taken with you."

"Yeah," Trotter said. "Her mother likes me, too."

"I didn't say I like you. As a matter of fact, I'm kind of afraid of you."

"Afraid of me?"

"Do you think I had to jump off the wagon and get myself sloshed to get up the guts to talk to you about *Star Wars*, for God's sake?"

"You mean we're finally getting to the point?"

"Yeah. I'm drunk enough now not to give a shit."

"Finally."

"Yeah. Who the hell are you, Trotter?"

"You just used my name."

"I mean, who are you *really*? You're not who you say you are, I'll tell you that. I mean, your name might be Allan Trotter, but you're no reporter."

"Did you get hold of my résumé and check me out?"

"You know I did, you slippery bastard. And it checks out, all the way down the line. That's the scary part. For instance, it says you worked for the Baltimore *Sun*. I've got dozens of friends on the Baltimore *Sun*. You never worked for the goddam Baltimore *Sun*."

"Maybe your friends have poor memories."

"Yeah, good, make me laugh. I'll like you better. And another thing. Nobody here has ever *seen* you write a fucking thing. Christ, listen to my fucking mouth. I must be drunk."

"You are. I think you wanted to tie one on, so you made up some kind of paranoid fantasy about me for an excuse."

"Don't try to hand me that shit. I'm drunk now, but tomorrow morning I'll be sober, and I still won't trust you any farther than I could throw a rhino by the dick."

"You don't have to trust me. Your boss trusts me."

"Yeah, that's the bitch of it, isn't it? Too bad she doesn't remember Tony Prolone."

Trotter kept his face straight. "Who's he?"

"Feature writer. I used to work with him in Phoenix. Won the Pulitzer way back."

"What about him?"

"You write—or the stuff that gets printed with your name on it, at least—that stuff is identical in style with his stuff. Absolutely fucking identical. Like you had his brain in a jar or something."

"Maybe you ought to check with this Tony Prolone and see if he's ghosting my stuff."

"I would, but he's dead."

"Oh, too bad."

"Yeah. He drank and gambled himself into a hole and wound up giving a gas pipe a blow job. Six years ago. I was at the funeral."

Trotter knew all about it. He'd been at odds with the Agency then, but his father had filled him in. Tony Prolone had gotten in too deep and he screamed for help. That cry, like the cry of anyone at the end of his rope who could be of use to the Agency, reached the Congressman. He provided Prolone with a fake death, a new identity, and a decent living, in exchange for the journalist's furnishing the Agency with whatever readable writing it needed. Trotter made a mental note to tell Rines to make sure that Prolone had remained discreet about his new identity.

"You're not making a lot of sense, Murphy," Trotter said.

"I'm making perfect sense. *You're* the one who doesn't add up. You, my friend, are running a goddam scam. I don't know how or why, but you are."

"I still don't know what the point is."

Murphy leaned forward and thumped the table with his fist. "*This* is the point, you son of a bitch. Regina Hudson is a sweet kid, and I'm sick of you messing her around."

"We're getting married," Trotter said. He hadn't planned to say it, but now that he saw the effect, he was glad he had. If he'd smacked Murphy, the man couldn't have been more stunned. "I wanted you to be the first to know. We haven't even told her mother yet."

"You bastard," Murphy breathed. "You *bastard*. That's your scam. You're not after a slice of the money, you want the whole Hudson Group."

"Murphy," Trotter said, "you're kind of a jerk, but I like you. Let me tell you one thing. No man has ever been more wrong than you are right now."

"I'm not done with you," Murphy said. "You cocksucker. I'll get the goods on you yet. It's bad enough you've got Regina climbing all over you as it is, but to marry her—" Murphy ran out of words. He tightened his lips and sawed his head viciously side to side.

Trotter said quietly, "You're in love with her yourself, aren't you?"

"*Of course I'm in love with her, you fucking asshole!* Since she was a little girl, I've loved her. I waited, I—oh, fuck you, Trotter. I know I'm just a pathetic old fart with a pipe dream. But you're *no good for her*! The only way you can keep me from breaking it up, I swear to God, is to kill me right now. Are you going to?"

Trotter sighed. "Murphy—"

"Then get the fuck out of here! I'm going to drink until I pass out."

"I don't think so," Trotter said. "You get going good, you may never crawl out of the bottle, and the Hudson Group needs you. I want it in perfect shape when I take it over."

"You bastard," Murphy said. His eyes were hot.

Trotter grabbed him under the arm and yanked. Murphy had thought he wasn't going to budge, but to his own surprise, he rose.

"Come on," Trotter said. "The sooner we get you sobered up, the sooner you can start shafting me."

"You'll see, you bastard. Just wait."

Trotter paid the check, left a good tip, and led him from the bar.

Chapter Four

Moscow, USSR

Borzov didn't really feel like it, but he went to Troylev's liquidation anyway. Borzov's presence at events like this had been a matter of ritual since before the Hitler war. If he were to start skipping them now, the young wolves would scent weakness. They would say Borzov was old, and losing his stomach for duty.

The worst part of that was that it was true. Borzov *was* old, and he was losing not only his stomach, but every organ in his body. There remained only his will, and his love of the Motherland. He knew this was no time to allow even the possibility of dissention in his department. The Chairman was in the midst of bold and hazardous plans for the future of the Soviet Union. The plans held the potential to lull the West into a sense of security. They also held the potential for destroying the Soviet State.

There was a time when Borzov would have been content to wait and see, then act when action seemed advisable. Now, he feared he would not live to see whether glasnost and perestroika led to the ultimate victory of the workers, or to chaos. He might not even live long enough to notice the first indications of one or the other.

So Borzov, as his last gift to his beloved country, would do what he could to ensure its survival no matter what might happen. He would deliver America to Russia. Or more precisely, he would deliver the White House to the Kremlin. The plan had been building for years. It had begun building even before it existed, ever since a certain young man of obvious qualifications and sincere devotion to the Soviet cause had been recruited and told to keep his sympathies absolutely secret. The young man had been guided into politics, carefully advised and financed, and led from success to success until now he had a good chance to become President of the United States.

The plan—with his love of mythology, Borzov called it Project Atropos—was designed to make that chance a certainty.

Senator Henry Van Horn was essential to the plan. When Borzov had heard the tape of that corrupt weakling murdering his concubine, Project Atropos had sprung to his mind. Not in detail, of course, but in general outline. It was Destiny. Borzov had only ordered the bugging of the places the Senator frequented because he'd wanted to know what this influential man was going to do in committee about a pending trade bill.

Now the influential man belonged body and soul to Borzov, though he himself wouldn't admit it. Van Horn was allowed to maintain the fiction that he had "agreed" to consultations with the General's representatives in the interests of "World Peace."

It didn't matter. The man was a coward and a hypocrite and a fool. But he knew who the boss was. He'd jump for the Devil himself if that was who had the goods on him.

No less essential to the plan, though, was Troylev. Because for the trap to be properly sprung, there were certain things the Americans had to believe. Troylev would die to convince them of the truth.

The Americans had thought for the past ten years that Vladimir Petrovich Troylev was working for them. What they didn't know was that Borzov had planted him on them, on the theory that if Borzov *gave* the CIA a mole in the particular branch of the foreign office in which Troylev worked, they would not try to recruit one of their own.

Through Troylev, Borzov had fed the Americans a steady diet of valuable, if unspectacular, information, all to build up the man's credibility to them, so that they would believe when Borzov had him feed them a lie.

It was ironic, Borzov reflected, that that time had never come. To the end, Troylev had told them the truth. Borzov had decided to capture the White House for the Motherland with a truth. The truth was this: One of the two contenders for the Presidential nomination from Senator Van Horn's party was an agent of the Soviet Union.

At Borzov's orders, Troylev had fed it to them. He would die to make sure they swallowed it.

This room, down the hall from Borzov's office in the cellar of Lubyanka, the old KGB headquarters in Dzerzhinsky Square, had seen hundreds of liquidations. It was windowless, square and gray in the light of the bare bulbs that dotted the ceiling. It smelled of old fear.

Radowsky was waiting for him. Colonel Radowsky was one of the wolves, an ambitious man, a child of the War, who, as he closed in on his fiftieth birthday, was beginning to see General Borzov not as a leader, but as a cork who was keeping men like Radowsky from bubbling to the top of the Komitet.

"The traitor Troylev is prepared for execution, Comrade General," Radowsky said.

He *looks* like a wolf, Borzov thought. A blond, blue-eyed wolf. Borzov had always wondered if the Aryan-looking colonel had been fathered by one of Hitler's soldiers.

Borzov put it from his mind. What did it matter? He was only speculating about Radowsky to avoid the necessity of looking at Troylev.

The false American agent wore white shirt and black pants. He was gagged, and tied with stout rope to a plain wooden chair. The chair was placed in the middle of a galvanized tub some two meters in diameter. Troylev's eyes were wild. When Borzov appeared, he began straining against the ropes and the gag. The chair made clanging sounds as Troylev's desperate wigglings caused it to move slightly against the metal floor of the tub.

Borzov met Rodowsky's eyes. He didn't know if he could meet Troylev's. "Proceed," he said.

Radowsky drew his gun and stepped into the tub. "Vladimir Petrovich Troylev. You have been found to be a traitor; I am now about to execute sentence as ordered by my superiors."

He raised the gun to the bound man's temple. Troylev's eyes screamed.

Radowsky looked blandly at Borzov. "Unless *you'd* rather do the honors, Comrade General? It is within regulations."

Borzov had to do it. He must show no weakness, none. As he took the gun, he made a vow that before he died, he would see Colonel Radowsky sitting in the galvanized tub. It was the only way to keep himself from shooting the wolf right now.

Borzov put the gun to the innocent Troylev's head. The man was whimpering behind the gag now. Tears squeezed from tight-shut eyes.

Borzov pulled the trigger. The shot echoed sharply in the room. He handed the gun back to Radowsky and without a word walked to the door.

Behind him, Radowsky barked orders to his men. The men would untie Troylev and lay him in the tub. With knives and bone saws, they would dismember him. The tub would catch the blood and viscera, as it had caught the spray that followed the bullet from the far side of the man's skull. The pieces would then be burned, along with the chair. The tub would be washed and put away for its next use. (Radowsky, Borzov hoped.) It would be as if Troylev had never been.

But the Americans would know he was gone. They might even find out what had happened to him. Borzov was not naive enough to believe that the only sources of information the Americans had were ones he had planted on them.

It didn't matter. The Americans would know that Troylev had ceased to be after he'd told them that last bit of information. They'd believe it. They'd go frantic trying to discover who.

Before they could make any significant progress toward finding out, however, Borzov would tell them.

And America would be his.

CHAPTER FIVE

Kirkester, New York

Rines felt it necessary to come to Kirkester to confer with Trotter.

"The CIA is having kittens," Rines said. "He gave them the news and disappeared. Some of their sources say Borzov shot him, in person."

"You said all this on the scrambler."

"I didn't say which one. Neither did Troylev."

"What if it's neither?"

"They shot him to death."

"Uh-huh. Or maybe they gave him plastic surgery and a new job in a new town. Maybe he was dying of cancer or something, and was glad to be shot to put one over on the old USA."

Before he had met Trotter, Rines had thought himself cynical. "And maybe not," he said. He was beginning to get exasperated.

"Maybe not," Trotter conceded. "Maybe they just took this guy and executed him in cold blood. But do you think the mind that conceived of having women bear children expressly so they could be sacrificed in the Cold War is going to hesitate to waste one innocent man in order to put an operation across?"

Rines made a face. He always looked like a small-town banker. Now he looked like a small-town banker with an ulcer. "We can't shrug this off, Trotter."

"Of course we can't."

"Well, heck, it's nice to hear you say so."

"But we can't panic, either."

"Trotter, I think the idea of a Russian agent in the White House is cause enough for panic."

"We need more than an idea before we do anything drastic."

Rines looked at him. "I wish I could figure you out."

"It's simple," Trotter told him. "Easy to lose sight of in the craziness we live in."

"The craziness you dragged me into," Rines corrected.

Trotter smiled. "You were begging for it. But listen. We lie, spy, cheat, kill, manipulate and do whatever we can think of to protect this country."

"I know that well enough."

"We've sold our souls."

"Feels like it, sometimes."

"Yeah. Well, if we're going to get anything out of the deal, there are certain things we don't dare mess with without being sure we're doing the right thing. And elections are one of them. If we start arranging who gets voted into office, what's the difference between us and Borzov?"

"If a Russian puppet winds up in the White House, what's the difference between us and Bulgaria?" Rines could hear himself starting to shout.

Trotter stepped in while he was catching his breath. "All right, all right. Maybe we're arguing about nothing. What do you want to do about this?"

"I've got everyone available digging like mad to try to find out which one."

"Keep at it."

"Of course we'll keep at it. We've only got until the convention." Rines scratched his head. "What I want to know is, what are we going to do if we *don't* find out before then."

"We'll think of something."

"What? Short of having them both assassinated, what can you do?"

Trotter showed him an innocent face. "We'll think of something," he said again.

Rines looked at him. Finally, he said, "Jesus Christ," and stormed from the room.

CHAPTER SIX

April—Washington, D.C.

Ainley Masters left the office early in order to get home in time to change for the party. The Senator was throwing a party. That was remarkable. A Van Horn did not have to throw parties. Washington parties were given by rich women who enjoyed meeting and feeding the powerful, or by lobbyists interested in influencing them. They were practically never given by the powerful themselves. It had been known to happen, of course—President Johnson's famous barbecues were an example—but only when the powerful had some jawboning to do, some heavy-duty convincing in order to get backing for a pet program.

But Hank Van Horn didn't work that way. He got by on looks and his family's previous martyrdoms. Hank's father, "a hero in war and peace." Hank's brother Roger, the astronaut, who died "pushing back the barriers of human knowledge." That was how the Senator's publicity releases usually put it. Roger, of course, was also attempting to make himself unbeatable for his own projected political career while he was at it. Still, Roger's death had been tragic. God knew he would have run the family (and a Senatorial career) much better than Hank did.

So Hank was not throwing this party to convince anybody of anything. A Hudson Group reporter named Sean Murphy once said after a session with Hank that he felt like a Philistine—he'd spent two hours being smitten with the jawbone of an ass.

Even more remarkable, the Senator was throwing his party *without Ainley's help.* Not, of course, that it was especially difficult to throw a party in Washington, where politicians and bureaucrats and journalists streamed to free food and liquor like lemmings to the sea, especially if your name was social magic in and of itself. It was just that for so many years the Senator had shown signs of being unable to undo his own zipper without dampening his pants that the sudden change was disconcerting.

Ainley had at least been allowed to see the guest list. That had been a surprise, too. It was perfect. The right mix of friendly and unfriendly diplomats, politicians from both parties, both major Presidential candidates from his own party, visiting dignitaries, opera singers, artists, and journalists.

Apparently, Mark had been consulted as well, because his little friend Regina Hudson was coming. For a while, Ainley had thought that the possibility of the Great Dynastic Marriage he had envisioned so fondly when the children were in college was alive again. Regina had come to Washington for a few days, and spent most of the time with Mark. They'd gone to the Kennedy Center together, and a couple of parties. They had started tongues moving, and had set typewriters warming up. Then Regina had flown off back to that godforsaken town she kept her printing presses in, and announced her engagement to one of her reporters. *He* was coming, too, it seemed. Ainley couldn't wait to get a look at the young man without a name who could beat Mark Van Horn's time with an heiress.

Still, if Mark were to become involved with a woman, it would upset things, and Ainley was quite happy with the arrangement as it was. Mark had settled in with him as a long-term house guest, his return to law school on an indefinite hold. It didn't matter. What Mark was learning now would be vastly more important than anything a law degree could give him.

Ainley put his briefcase down on the welcome mat and reached in his pocket for his keys. Before he had them, though, the lock clicked, and the door to his apartment opened a crack.

One of Mark's blue eyes and a lock of damp hair appeared in the crack. "I heard you jingling," Mark said. "This may be a high-security building, but the soundproofing is terrible."

"Maybe you just have sharp ears."

"Yeah," Mark said. "That must be it." He swung the door wide and let Ainley in. "I figured you'd probably want to take a shower, so I took mine just now."

"I would have guessed," Ainley said.

Mark looked down at himself and grinned. He had a chicken leg in one hand and a pale-green towel in the other. In between, he was naked. Drops of water gleamed in the blond hair of his body.

"I suppose so," he said.

Ainley did not smile. "Suppose we close the door, all right?"

"What? Oh, sure." He promptly closed the door.

"I wish," Ainley said, "you wouldn't do that. Parade around with no clothes on the way you do."

"I just stepped out of the shower when the munchies hit, so I dashed to the refrigerator." He bit into the chicken leg. "That's where I was when I heard you outside and thought I'd save you the trouble of digging out your keys."

"I understand, Mark, and I appreciate your consideration. But instead of carrying the towel around, you might have at least wrapped yourself in it."

Mark gave him an embarrassed grin. He held the drumstick in his teeth and quickly wrapped the towel around his waist.

"I've been living alone too much," he said. "Sorry. I had a roommate at one of my colleges who used to be bothered by it, too. I'll try to remember."

"It doesn't *bother* me in the slightest," Ainley said, suddenly feeling enormously bothered. "I just don't think it's necessary for anyone to get any ideas."

"Most people in Washington never had an idea in their lives," Mark said. Ainley couldn't help joining him in a smile. The boy had charm; he would carry the Van Horn empire to new heights.

"True," Ainley said. "But the thoughts they *do* have are all too frequently put there by journalists. That's a process we want to keep under control."

"Right, Ainley. As usual. Well, it's way too early to put on my tux. I'll tell you what—my mother gave me this hideous silk robe for Christmas last year. I'll go get it and give it its maiden voyage."

"Thanks, Mark. When you come back, we can talk about what your father ought to do when the farm bill comes out of committee."

"Good. I can bowl him over at the party with my mature wisdom."

If he can recognize it, Ainley thought.

Mark came back in a robe so red it could be found in the dark. They had a laugh over it, then sat and talked about the farm bill. When they were done, Ainley looked at his watch and said, "Well, I think I'll take that shower you mentioned."

"Good," Mark said. "I'll start getting dressed." He started walking toward the room Ainley had given him.

"Oh, Mark," Ainley said.

Mark looked back over his shoulder. "Yes?"

"You don't have to answer this if you don't want to, it's just curiosity on my part."

Mark was amiable. "Okay," he said.

"Why did you have your father invite Regina Hudson and her fiancé?"

"Trotter," Mark said. "His name is Allan Trotter. Boy, did I get an earful of him. But I didn't."

"You didn't?"

"Didn't get Dad to invite them. It was strictly his own idea. Maybe he's a member of the same club as you and my mother."

"Club?"

Mark grinned. "The 'It's a Shame You Two Broke Up Club.'" He shrugged. "It wouldn't have worked out, in any case. Regina could never have loved me as much as she loves this Trotter. In a way, I'm kind of eager to get a look at him."

"I had the same idea."

"Besides, Regina is a terrific girl, but the older I get, the more I see she's not my type."

Ainley rubbed his beard. "What is your type?"

Mark's grin turned sly. "We don't have enough time to go into that. Maybe Dad just wants to make things interesting for the Russians. Especially this new guy, Dudakov. He seems to be important enough to have been one of the first to know that Regina's mother was tired of spying for the KGB."

Ainley thought about it for a second. Now it was his turn to grin. "That should indeed be entertaining. But isn't it a little subtle for the Senator?"

Mark laughed. "You should have more respect for your employer," he said.

"I have always had the greatest respect for the Van Horn family," Ainley replied.

"And that, my friend, is unresponsive—and you know it."

"You've learned *something* in law school, I see."

"We could always *ask* my father, I suppose."

"Yes," Ainley said. "Perhaps we should."

Mark went to get dressed.

Chapter Seven

Special Agent Joe Albright was nervous as he waited for the elevator that would bring him to the offices of Rines Investigations. He wondered what the maniacs who ran the Agency had in store for him *this* time. He'd never been summoned like this, in the middle of the day, to come get orders from Rines, at least not since Rines had supposedly gone out on his own. Usually they met at the Lincoln Memorial, like tourists, or on line at a bank, or something like that.

It had been different, of course, before Rines had left the Bureau. Then he just had Albright report to his office. Now things were a lot more complicated. As Rines (and Trotter, on those rare occasions Joe spoke to him) never got tired of saying, Joe was now the Agency's main man in the FBI. They were depending on him.

And thank you so very goddam much, Joe thought bitterly. *I* never wanted to get involved in this sort of crap in the first place.

He had Rines to thank for this. Joe had been getting along very nicely, working for the Bureau out of the Portland, Oregon, office. One day, he'd had orders passed along to him—orders, he later found out, that originated with Rines—that he was to find a man named Allan Trotter and bring him to Washington, D.C. He should have known something was wrong when they gave him fifteen different descriptions for this Trotter character, and told him not to threaten the man in any way.

All Albright had done was follow orders. But before he was done with that one simple assignment, he knew who Trotter was, and he knew a certain small office building in Silver Spring, Maryland, just past the District line, was more than it appeared to be. The way these people thought, that meant they either had to recruit him, or kill him.

Of course, they'd never planned to kill him. Rines had sniffed him out for the mysterious whoever who actually *ran* the Agency. Joe sometimes wondered what kind of being this Trotter was willing to take orders from, but never out loud.

Joe pushed the elevator button again, which was dumb but made him feel better. About ten seconds later the doors slid open, and he got on with a bunch of other silent, impatient people. You'd think they were *all* spies.

It was too crowded for Joe to get to the buttons. He said, "Eleven please," to the woman nearest the control panel. He was glad that his voice didn't crack.

Now that he was safely on the elevator, at least one of his fears was receding. He'd been more nervous than he'd wanted to admit about running into someone from the Bureau. It wasn't just that he'd been looking around for something to worry about, either. It could happen. Rines hadn't moved far away from his old haunts at Justice, and there were a lot of insurance companies and things like that here. None on the eleventh floor, though. A smart agent—and they were practically all smart—would wonder why Special Agent Albright would be consulting a private eye, even a private eye who'd once been pretty big in the Bureau.

Of course, they had a cover story worked up to use if they needed one—Joe was coming in to get Rines's take on a bank robber Rines had arrested during his days with the Bureau—but it sounded pretty lame to Joe.

Number 11 lit up above the door of the elevator, and the door slid open. Joe muttered excuse mes as he elbowed his way out. He walked a few steps, opened a door and gave his name to Rines's receptionist, who showed him to the man's office and announced him.

Rines got up and actually walked around his desk in order to shake hands with Joe. The man was constantly showing him these little unforced rituals of courtesy and respect. That was one reason that, no matter what Rines had done to him, Joe had a tough time disliking him.

"Sit down, Joe," Rines said.

Joe sat.

"We've got a big job for you tonight."

"I've been expecting this. I don't know if I can do it."

There was sincere confusion on Rines's face. "What are you talking about?"

"Don't be coy, all right?"

"I'm not being coy."

"You have a big job for me? After making me practically sneak away from the Bureau and come here in person? You want me to bag somebody, don't you?"

"Don't be ridiculous. For God's sake, Joe."

"Now you're going to tell me the Agency would never stoop to such a thing."

"Now I'm going to tell you that in the *rare event* we are forced to stoop to such a thing, we call upon a professional wetworker to do it. Is that clear?"

The Agency was a whole different culture. Here the man had more or less just confessed to having the occasional murder committed, but Joe was the one who felt sheepish.

Joe cleared his throat. "Why the big buildup, then?"

"You're about to get an assignment that means meeting your boss."

Joe supposed it didn't make any difference—he was in this outfit for life, anyway. At least he could satisfy his curiosity about whoever it was who could make Trotter jump through hoops.

"What's the assignment?"

"The Congressman will tell you himself."

"Congressman?"

"You'll recognize him," Rines assured him. "Can you think of a better cover for the Agency?"

Joe rubbed his lip. "No," he said, "I guess not."

"Neither could he." Rines stood up. "Come on," he said. "Be quiet, though. He's probably on the phone."

Rines eased the door open and allowed Joe to precede him into the room. Rines had been right. Joe *did* recognize him. It was that Southern one, the one who'd had a stroke a while ago. The one, Joe remembered now, who was chairman of the House Intelligence Oversight Committee. The cover got better and better.

The Congressman was in fact on the phone. Joe could hear both sides of the conversation, because the old man was leaning back in a chair with his eyes closed and his hands folded across his lap, talking into a speaker phone.

"No, Senator, I understand how busy a man in your position can be. I've put plenty of people on hold, myself." He chuckled.

Joe was amazed to hear that rich, Dixie voice coming from the wasted body of the man in the chair. It was almost as if the Congressman were lip-syncing to a recording of a healthy man's voice.

"To tell you the truth," the Congressman went on, "I never expected to talk to you personally at all."

"Nonsense," a voice boomed from the speaker. That was Senator Van Horn. "Always time to talk to one of my colleagues. How are you coming along? You sound quite well."

"Well," the Congressman said, "I wouldn't go so far as to say I'm *quite* well, but I'm feeling well enough to try to wangle an invitation to your party tonight."

"What? Oh—oh, of course! I'll arrange it with my secretary. Needless to say, if I'd known you were feeling up to going out again, you would have gotten one of the first invitations."

"That's awfully kind of you, Senator; I know this is really the most atrocious bad manners—"

"Not at all."

"*Very* kind, but I understand both the Party's major candidates will be there, and I haven't had a chance to talk to them yet, being laid up and all. And since I don't really think I'm going to be up to going to the convention, I thought—"

"Please, Congressman, no explanation is necessary. It will be an honor to have you."

"Well, I'm afraid I haven't come to the end of my bad manners yet, Senator. I'll have to ask if my nurse can come, too."

"Well, give her name to my secretary, and she'll take care of everything."

"Actually," the old man said, "it's a male nurse, a young man named Joseph Albright. He's terrific. You'll never know he's there."

"That'll be fine. I'll put my secretary on now. Nice talking to you, Congressman."

"Thanks again, Senator, see you tonight."

There was a click, and a female voice came on the line. The Congressman gave her details, said good-bye. He sat up and strained a feeble arm toward the button that would break the connection. Joe was going to do it for him, but thought better of it. It took the old man a good fifteen seconds to reach the button, and when he did he scrabbled around the top of the box before he could push it.

He collapsed back in his chair, puffing as if he'd just run a mile. Joe was beginning to think that if the Congressman really wanted to go out tonight, he'd be better off getting a real nurse.

"So you're Albright," the Congressman said. He smiled. The smile was lopsided, but it did involve both sides of his face. Either the stroke he'd had had been fairly mild, or this old man was curing himself through sheer willpower. "I've heard a lot of good things about you."

"I'm glad to hear that, sir."

"That boy Trotter thinks you're the ant's ankles."

"I'm honored."

"What do you think about him?"

Oh, boy, Joe thought. "I . . . I think he's a remarkable human being, sir."

The old man laughed. "Remarkable. I like that. That's the word, all right. Remarkable. You're a very tactful boy, Albright."

Joe felt a twinge of anger at the word "boy," but he decided to be tactful and stifle it. Besides, he'd just called Trotter a boy; it probably wasn't a racial thing. Even if it were, the only thing he could do about it was pull his weapon and shoot Rines and the old man. He sure as hell couldn't pound the desk and resign in a huff.

"Tactful," the Congressman went on. "You've got to be surprised to find me the boss of this outfit, but you don't say anything about it."

"I try to take things as they come, sir."

"I saw your hand twitch when I tried to hang up the damned phone. Why didn't you help a poor old man?"

"I figured you're used to giving orders. If you wanted someone to push the button, you would have said so."

"All right, then. All right. You're going to be my male nurse tonight. Basically, you just have to help me upstairs, carry my medicine, like that. *And* keep your eyes and ears open, but you already know how to do that."

"I assume nobody at this party is going to make me as an FBI man."

"That'll be taken care of," Rines said. "Don't even worry about it."

"Just bring your piece," the old man said.

Joe raised an eyebrow.

"I may need to borrow it." The Congressman was grim. "I may need it to shoot a Russian son of a bitch or two."

Chapter Eight

Trotter had been planning to take a cab from the hotel to Senator Van Horn's party, but that was before the Congressman's phone call. Now they drove up in a stretch Cadillac limousine, a very special one. Inside those shiny black panels was armor that would stop anything short of an 88-millimeter shell. All the windows were bulletproof. The driver was an employee of the Agency, though he probably didn't know it. Trotter looked at the back of the driver's head through another sheet of bulletproof glass, saw the well-trimmed salt-and-pepper hair and the old scars on his neck, and decided the man probably thought he was working for Army Intelligence. It wouldn't do to ask.

This limousine symbolized two facets of the Congressman's genius in setting up the Agency. One, hardly anybody who worked for it was aware of it. If anybody were to get the notion that it would be interesting to learn what this driver could be forced to say, the man would hold out as long as he could. When he spilled, he could spill nothing but misinformation, because that's all he would know.

The other neat trick was that the Congressman never let the Agency's assets lie idle. This car belonged to the Agency, but to the world it belonged to TranSecure, an outfit with branches in major cities that specialized in renting bulletproof vehicles to people who thought they were in danger. And who could afford high rental fees.

The Agency was glad to have the money. Its official budget had to be hidden among appropriations for a dozen innocent government departments. Obviously, the smaller this official budget was, the easier it was to hide.

And TranSecure, with a little judicious bugging, could gather the odd bit of information from the VIPs who needed to ride in bulletproof comfort. All in all, a tidy little arrangement.

Trotter wished he didn't need to use it.

He looked across at Regina, who was gorgeous in a black gown with diamonds at her ears and throat. Her hair was drawn back, and there was a pretty display of collarbone and cleavage.

Tonight, she didn't look like a kid. Tonight, she actually *looked* like the head of one of America's biggest media conglomerates. Tonight, she might really be in danger.

The Congressman's call had come while Bash was in the shower. They had just made love. She had been even more responsive and passionate than usual. Trotter realized this was excitement at the prospect of facing an old lover on the arm of a new one, one who had fucked her brains out just a few short hours before.

It wasn't, Trotter was sure, that she had anything against this Mark Van Horn, who seemed to be as nice as any heir to that much power could be expected to be. It was that centuries of male dominance had led women to develop these little ways of scoring points. They had become ingrained; Regina probably didn't even realize it herself. It would take more than a few decades of being liberated before new behavior patterns could develop.

His father had told him who was supposed to be at this party, and what that meant.

"Great," Trotter had said. "I've always wanted to lay eyes on him." It wasn't until the words were out of his mouth that Trotter realized how much he meant them.

"Yeah, well, I think he'd kind of like to get a look at you, too, son. I'm beginning to think that's the whole reason for this party. Or at least for your being invited to it."

"How could they swing that?"

"I don't know. Maybe they told the Senator they're crazy about the Hudson Group newspapers."

Trotter laughed.

"Maybe they're working it through the son. Don't have any information. Maybe we'll spot some at the party."

"We?"

"You heard me."

"Sure you're up to it?"

"Joe Albright's coming as my nurse. I'd go if I had to crawl, son. I want to use my eyes some, too. Make sure it's who I think it is before I get all excited. But there's one other thing."

"What's that?"

"This fellow's got a pair of eyes, too. He'll use them on you."

"He already knows who I am, if he's not an idiot."

"He's no idiot, boy. Don't you be, either. The thing is, he's going to see you with that gal. He already knows you're fixing to marry her. If he gets the idea that this is anything but a move to put the Agency in charge of the Hudson Group, any time he wants to get you, he'll get you through her."

The Congressman paused. When he spoke again, he was almost apologetic. "I *told* you this was gonna happen, son."

"Right, as usual. Okay, it's my problem, I'll deal with it."

"If she wasn't so damned famous, we could send her away, hide her somewhere—"

"All *right*," Trotter said. "I said I'd deal with it. Anything else?"

"I've told Albright to arm himself. It might be a good idea for you, too."

"Yeah," Trotter said. He hated guns.

"No tellin' what these people might be up to. He hasn't used that name, or left home, since 1946."

"I'll consider it. See you later."

Then he hung up the phone and tried to decide just how he was going to deal with it. What he *wanted* to do was to tell Regina to stay away; that he'd go to the party without her and have some muscle from the Agency watch over her.

He realized as soon as he thought of it that it was a bad idea. He might as well install a neon sign over Regina's head that blinked V*A*L*U*A*B*L*E H*O*S*T*A*G*E in green and red.

To skip the party himself was not an option. Trotter had never been elected by anyone (except Fate), but he felt his responsibility to two hundred million Americans every bit as thoroughly as the President did. Going to this party was definitely part of the job, and it was his job to do.

All right. He couldn't keep her from going, he couldn't refrain from going himself. Didn't he at least owe it to Regina to tell her what he might be letting her in for?

The answer was yes. The only decent and honorable thing to do would be to warn her that they might be walking into danger tonight.

Trotter had not been raised to be decent and honorable. He had been trained from birth to do whatever would work the best toward attaining his objective. Regina had been trained for the executive suite of the newspaper business. She wasn't an agent; she wasn't an actress. If Trotter had told her she was going to be in danger, she would show it. And that might give people ideas. People in Trotter's profession were often like cattle—they could smell fear, and they could catch it. Trotter would just have to handle the deceit for both of them.

A touch brought him out of his brooding. Bash had put her hand in his and squeezed. He looked at her and returned her smile.

The car stopped. "We're here, Mr. Trotter."

"Thanks. I'll call the office when we want to be picked up."

The driver said that would be very good, then came around and opened doors. Trotter joined Regina on the sidewalk and took her arm. The .32 revolver he had holstered in the small of his back dug into him like an accusing finger.

"Now let's go meet that old boyfriend," he said.

Chapter Nine

So these, Joe Albright thought, are the movers and shakers. Well, at least they had a well-padded environment to do their moving and shaking in. If they moved too close to a wall, there'd be a big antique chair or a leather sofa to collapse in. If they shook so hard they fell over, they'd simply land on a carpet so deep that, standing in it, Joe could hardly feel his feet.

Senator Van Horn had quite a place, all right. The party was being held in what the man in livery who'd taken his coat and the Congressman's had said was the "Georgian Room." This turned out to be a place that lacked only books to be a dead ringer of the old Carnegie library in Joe's home town. There was a high, vaulted ceiling, held up, it seemed, by fluted columns set halfway into the walls. Grapes and grape leaves and things like that were carved (or molded in plaster—Joe didn't really know much about this sort of stuff) at the tops of the columns. Everything was bone-white, except for a band of blue outlined by two strips of gold about two-thirds of the way to the ceiling.

"How do you get to be able to afford this?" Joe muttered.

The Congressman's chuckle told him he'd been all too articulate. "Hank Van Horn did it the hard way—he inherited it."

"That strikes me as the easy way," Joe said.

"All depends on how you look at it, Joe. You can do things to try to arrange *your* getting money. How do you arrange for your father or grandfather to have done it already?"

"What?" Joe said. "Oh, yeah. Right. Good point." What a weird old guy. No wonder Trotter was so nuts. Joe would probably be just like them in three years.

People with big smiles on their faces were coming over to talk to the Congressman, telling him how happy they were to have him back. The Congressman introduced Joe to every single one of them. And there was the same look in the eyes of every single one of them, like the red gleam of an LED when you turn on your calculator. You could almost hear the facts clicking into place. *Young. Black. Have not met previously. Introduced by Congressman. Protégé? Reporter? Not reporter—Congressman would have told me. What can I gain from this man? What should I fear? Examine further. Placate in the meantime.*

Every one of them, Republican or Democrat, male or female, black or white, in office or trying to be, pumped Joe's hand vigorously and told him how happy they were to meet him. They did not go so far as to tell him how much they liked Motown music, but in a different era they would have.

Joe was interested to find out if Abweg and Babington, the big boys at this particular do, would be the same. Maybe the rarefied air in the high places near the Presidency removed this when-in-doubt-kiss-ass instinct. Joe hoped so.

But he didn't get to find out, at least not just then. The Congressman disengaged himself from a guy who was trying very hard to conceal the fact that he would kill his mother if that would get him a high-level job in the State Department, and turned to Joe. "I need to sit down. Bullshit is always exhausting, and my tolerance has dropped through lack of exposure to it. Think you can get me over to that sofa there?"

"Sure. Just hold my arm. Should have brought your walker."

"Joe, my boy, when a vulture sees a man is weak, it will fly down and peck his eyes out to hasten death."

"I've heard that," Joe conceded.

"A vulture," the Congressman said, "is a philanthropist compared to a politician. Never forget that."

Joe got the old man seated under a portrait of some nineteenth-century Van Horn who scowled at the room from between a really impressive set of side whiskers.

The Congressman matched the scowl. "Where the hell is he?" Joe assumed the old man was talking about the Russian son of a bitch he might have to shoot. "I get off my deathbed to see him, and he's not here."

"Maybe he's in the bathroom," Joe suggested. "Maybe he didn't show up yet. Maybe he's in the kitchen."

"The kitchen?"

"Every time *I* throw a party, everybody winds up in the kitchen."

The Congressman changed the scowl to a smile. It was remarkable how quickly he could do that. "That's wholesome, Joe. America is proud of you. Most people your age, it seems all their parties wind up in the bedrooms."

"That kind of party is a lot smaller, when I throw one."

"All right, all right, spare me the details. Listen, I'll be all right here. You go mingle and try to find out where the Russian is."

"I don't want to leave you."

"I didn't bring you here to fuss over me. I'll be fine. Go. Talk to people. Eat hors d'oeuvres. Bring me back a bourbon and soda."

"Bourbon?" Joe's voice was very severe.

"All right, all right, just soda. You're worse than the damn doctor."

"That's better." Joe nodded. He realized even as he did so that the old man had engineered the whole little bit of business to lend credence to the idea that Joe was indeed a male nurse. If anyone was watching. Of *course* someone was watching. What was it Trotter had told him? "In any public place, always assume someone is watching you and act accordingly. You can live a lot longer that way."

Fine, Joe thought. Someone is watching me. Now what do I want them to see?

"Don't just stand there," the Congressman growled. "Go mingle."

"Yes, sir. Do I go on letting people think I'm somebody?"

"Joe, don't let Jesse Jackson hear you say that. You—are—*somebody*! Right?"

"Oh, absolutely." Joe smiled and shook his head. This man, old and feeble and crippled as he was, could carry you along with his personality so easily it was frightening. Joe felt a little sorry for Trotter and Rines, who had apparently had to deal with him at full strength, before he'd had his stroke.

"You just let people think what they want to think. If they ask you any questions, just tell the truth."

"Right," Joe said. What the Congressman meant, of course, was the truth as defined by the Agency—i.e., the current cover story.

Joe went to mingle. He took a glass of champagne from a passing tray, and a shrimp the size of a badminton shuttlecock from another. The shrimp was delicious. The champagne was cold and dry, served in fine crystal. The trays had been gold. The people carrying them, one man and one woman, were black.

Joe considered the political ramifications. On the one hand, it was pretty stereotypical. Joe's father had been a waiter at a country club, and had put Joe through the University of Missouri on tips, so Joe was making no judgments. On the other hand, this was Washington, D.C. Eighty percent black, high unemployment. To find white waiters and bartenders, you'd *really* have to discriminate. On balance, then, Joe figured it was the right move.

Across the room, Joe saw Trotter and Regina Hudson talking to a six-foot-tall blond woman. Trotter caught his eye, then looked away. Joe got the message. It was better not to know each other. He wondered if the Hudson girl was in on all of this. He wondered how well she'd pull it off if they had brought her in on it.

Not his problem. His problem was finding Russians and obtaining a glass of club soda for the Congressman.

As he zeroed in on the bar, someone tugged Joe's sleeve. He turned around and found himself in a group with two African diplomats and Senator Van Horn himself. One of the Africans wore robes and a fez; the other had on a London-tailored silk suit. The Senator had on his professional smile.

"Excuse me," said the man in the robes. "I know I am rude."

"Not at all."

"I just wished to ask something of a black American."

"I'm one," Joe said. The diplomats laughed; the Senator continued to smile. "Joe Albright, pleased to meet you."

The Senator stepped in and performed introductions, giving the names and countries of the diplomats, and acting as if he had known Joe all his life, when Joe knew for a fact the man had never heard of him before today and almost certainly didn't remember him.

The man in the suit spoke. It almost shocked him that the man's voice was thin and reedy. Movies and television had left him with the impression that African diplomats are all supposed to sound like William Marshall or James Earl Jones, and the first man had lived up to the image.

"We have been telling the Senator that we know more of some of his countrymen than he does. Do you not, as a black American, feel a *personal* outrage at the existence of the terrorist state of South Africa? Do you not feel, in a sense, threatened that your nation, in which you are a minority, could countenance such a government?"

The Congressman had told him to tell the truth if anyone asked him any questions. He also said, let them think what they want. So Joe answered simply, "Yes. I feel outraged at apartheid. And oppressive governments threaten everybody."

The diplomat in the robes turned to the Senator with a contented smile on his face. "You see, Senator, it is as we have told you—"

"I'll tell you something else that outrages me just as badly," Joe said. They turned to him. "The fact that every day, hundreds and thousands of people flee from black African countries *into* South Africa. Including yours."

The two diplomats, and the Senator, too, looked at Joe as if they had suddenly forgotten how to speak English.

"I mean, how screwed up *are* you people, that thousands of your citizens would up and leave and *choose* to live where the very law practically defines them as subhuman? What goes on in your countries that your people see an obscenity like South Africa as an *improvement*? Talk about frightening."

Joe thought, oops, got a little carried away there. What happens now, fisticuffs? I get invited to leave the party? War?

What happened was nothing. Less than nothing. The two diplomats and Senator Van Horn turned away from him as if he had ceased to exist.

"Ah," the Senator said. "General Dudakov." The backs of three heads receded.

Joe got a glimpse of a short and stocky figure, an iron-gray crew cut and the gleam of medals before a crowd gathered around and cut him off from view. It was amazing how assiduously these Washington party types went after a man they'd probably never heard of until he'd gotten here three days ago.

The Congressman would never be able to fight his way through that mob. Joe supposed the old man could wait awhile. He went and got the Congressman his drink.

• • •

The girl's name was Helen Fraser. Her father was something in the Interior Department. She was here as Mark Van Horn's date.

So, Regina thought, he's jealous of me, after all. Why else would he dig up a blond bombshell to come to the party with? One who asked you what sign you were five minutes after you met her. One who wanted to tell you about her channeler, the one who could let you talk *personally* with the spirit of Alexander the Great.

"It's really opened my mind," Helen said. She nodded solemnly.

Allan nodded back. "As soon as we started talking, I said there is someone who has made a lot of space in her mind."

Helen said, "Exactly!" Regina suppressed a giggle.

"Of course, growing up so close to the Interior Department . . ." Allan went on.

"I have a natural affinity for open spaces! My channeler says that, too!"

"Ah . . . How much does this guy charge you?"

"Do you want to see him, too? He's very select about his clientele, you know, but I bet he would see you." She looked at him. She was so tall that when she looked Allan in the eye (as she frequently did; she'd been coming on to him, with Regina standing right there, since she'd first laid eyes on him) all Regina could see of her was the bottom of her chin.

Helen waited breathlessly (she did everything breathlessly) for Allan's answer. Regina was pretty interested to hear what he would say, too, but she would never know because just then, Mark Van Horn and Ainley Masters joined them.

"I see you've already met Helen," Mark said. Introductions were made all around. Ainley said it was so nice to see her again.

Mark pumped Allan's hand vigorously. "Trotter. I've heard so much about you."

"Well, of course that always raises a question, doesn't it?"

"Oh, good things, all good. Our little Regina is quite devoted to you. You're a lucky man."

Our little Regina, Regina thought. I can't believe it. This is a spite party, at least as far as I'm concerned. Does he really think showing up here with someone tall and blond and thin, while I am short and dark and not thin, is going to bother me? And calling me our little Regina? When I have

Allan? The poor dope. All she felt was sorry for him. And a little disappointed. She guessed Van Horns weren't used to not getting things, even if it was something they manifestly had never wanted.

"When's the big day?" Mark asked.

"We haven't set the date yet," Regina said.

Mark smiled at Allan. "Don't let her get away."

No chance of that, Regina thought.

• • •

There was noise from the room with the bar in it. "That must be either the candidates or the Russians," Trotter said.

Mark Van Horn smiled at him. He was smiling so hard it looked as if he might sprain his cheeks, but his eyes were dead, just blue holes in his head for pouring information into his brain. He stared at Allan over the top of that painful smile like a kid watching a magic act. Trotter wondered what Mark expected him to do.

"I think it's the Russians," Mark said. He was working the smile so hard his voice was starting to strain.

Helen noticed it. "Mark, honey," she said, "relax." She put her hand on his arm. "I can feel beta waves all through you."

Mark shook her off. "I'm fine," he snapped. Then he turned to her and said more gently, "I'm fine, really." He turned to Regina. "Come and meet the General. He's told my father he wants to meet as many representatives of the press as possible."

"He doesn't want to meet me," Regina said.

"Let's go, Bash," Trotter said. Using his pet name for her in public was an informal code they'd worked up—when he called her Bash she wasn't to ask questions, just go along.

She went. She didn't take it with a lot of grace, but that didn't matter. Mark took Regina by the hand and took off through the crowd. He never looked around for Helen, but he made sure he knew where Trotter was every moment.

As they drew nearer the center of the knot of people, Trotter could feel some beta waves or whatever the hell they were rising in himself. He told himself to calm down, but his subconscious didn't listen. He knew why.

This was the man behind the Cronus project. This was the sick mind that sent a hundred women to America, each assigned to become the perfect woman for a soon-to-be influential American, to win him, and to bear him children in case he ever needed hostages. This was Trotter's other father, and Regina's. This was the man responsible for Trotter's own twisted life. And now he was going to see him face to face.

And he was just an old man.

You could see him on park benches anywhere in America, at family picnics, in the solaria of nursing homes. A man who had been powerful in youth; who had been rounded and melted by age. A potential mugging victim.

The Congressman twisted my life, made me a Cold-War monster, to fight *him?* Trotter brought himself up short. Appearances meant nothing. Trotter's father was the only man in the world Trotter was afraid of; General Dmitri Borzov, whatever he wanted to call himself, was the only man the Congressman feared. He had to be treated with respect. Age had ravaged the bodies of both men (even now, the General was stifling a cough) but the minds remained deadly.

"General Dudakov," Mark Van Horn said. "I'd like you to meet Regina Hudson, a very good friend of mine. Miss Hudson is publisher of the Hudson Communications Group."

The General smiled. "I am delighted. You are young to hold such an important position."

"I have a lot of help," Regina said.

Dudakov/Borzov offered a chuckle. "Still, responsibility rests with the leader, does it not? It is not a burden everyone can carry. Your appearance indicates that for you, carrying this heavy load has served you merely as healthful exercise. If I may say so, you seem to be thriving."

And how *charming* of you, you old bastard, Trotter thought. Regina was practically blushing.

"Why, thank you, Gen——"

"I knew your mother," Borzov said.

Trotter had been trained since childhood to show no emotions except on purpose. Surprise now gave that training its toughest test ever. What the hell was going on here? What happened to the General's strict incognito as a Kremlin functionary? Had age turned the KGB's best brain? This was dangerous stuff. Everyone in America who could read knew that Regina's mother had been sent by the Russians to infiltrate the American press. A lot of people knew Borzov had done the sending. A small number, including Trotter, knew or suspected that Borzov was here right now.

Maybe, Trotter told himself, he's going to defect. He suppressed a smile. Maybe he was going to announce that a Russian-backed coup d'état had just taken control of the United States. That was about as likely as the defection would be.

"How?" Regina said. "How did you know my mother?"

"Oh, we worked in the same department for a time. Before the intelligence people got hold of her. She was very young. But even then, I could see her strength. Her beauty was apparent to anyone."

Borzov started to smile, then went off into a coughing fit. Trotter could see he was serious about it. The skin of the Russian's face reddened, and it looked as though he'd have trouble staying on his feet. An aide rushed forward to hold him up, but Borzov waved him away. Borzov got a handkerchief from his pocket and brought it to his mouth. Somehow, muffling that jagged, choking cough only made it sound worse.

Trotter noticed that the crowd had formed a circle around Borzov, one that got wider with every cough. They wanted to give him room to collapse.

Just when it seemed the old man's breath was gone for good, the coughing stopped. Borzov pulled in a great breath, then closed his eyes and breathed deeply for a few seconds. He took the handkerchief away from his mouth, looked inside, and made a face.

The aide stepped forward again. Borzov handed him the handkerchief, which he took without a moment's hesitation, as though being handed a flower from the Queen, instead of maybe a quarter of a cup of mucus. He'll go far, Trotter thought.

It seemed safe to talk now. A chorus of "Are you all right?" rose from the crowd. Trotter thought he could make out Senator Van Horn's voice. Borzov held up a hand and said, "Just a moment, please, it is nothing."

The aide had gotten rid of the handkerchief. *Stuck it in his pocket?* Trotter thought. Yuck. In any case, he replaced it with a gelatin capsule and a glass of water. Borzov popped the capsule in his mouth, washed it down with the water, then smiled and turned to Regina as if he'd never missed a beat.

"And as it was with your mother, my dear," he said, "so it is with you. The Soviet Union's loss is America's gain."

"I'm quite happy with the way things turned out, General," Regina said. Trotter almost kissed her on the spot. "Are you sure you're all right?"

Borzov spread his hands. "For a man as old as I, merely to be alive is to be 'all right.'"

He turned to Trotter. "And you, young man. Have I understood correctly? Your are to have the good fortune of marrying this young woman?"

"I'm the one," Trotter said. He looked in the General's eyes. It was strange, almost frightening. There was little resemblance between the Russian and the Congressman, aside from the wrinkles of age and the gray hair, but their eyes were the eyes of twins. Worse than that; the light that glinted in the eyes of both men, the intelligence that lived behind them, was identical.

"Take good care of her, Mr. Trotter."

"Oh, I will," Trotter said.

"That's very good," the General said. "Very good. Now, perhaps, Mr. Trotter, you can be of assistance to me. There is a man whom I especially wanted to meet during my time in America. I was told he would be here this evening. A comrade of mine in the war against Hitler. I knew then that he would achieve great things. Indeed, now he serves in your Congress."

"Oh?" Trotter said. "What's his name?"

Borzov told him.

Trotter covered confusion with a smile. What *was* this man up to?

"I haven't seen him," Trotter said truthfully. "But why do you ask me where he is?"

"Oh, in some ways you remind me of him. And you seem to be a man of intelligence." Borzov was smiling; behind his eyes, he was shouting with laughter.

"Here I am, you old pirate," the Congressman's voice said. "If the damned crowd will just let an old man through—thanks. Excuse me. No, he's with me. Come on, Joe."

The Congressman appeared, walking with just a cane. Joe Albright stood behind him with his hands open, ready to catch the Congressman if he fell. Trotter could have told him not to worry. The Congressman wasn't about to fall. Not now. Not here.

Borzov's face lit up with what looked like genuine delight. "Comrade!" he said, and threw his arms open.

The Congressman said "Dmitri" and did the same.

Trotter stood there watching his father embracing his oldest and toughest enemy, and decided that at last, he'd seen everything.

Chapter Ten

Mark looked around at Helen Fraser's apartment. You'd think a person who'd had so many past lives as Helen claimed to would have accumulated more personality. While the exterior of the building was gingerbready Victorian brownstone, not too different from the Van Horn place, Helen's second-floor apartment might have been carved from the inside of a scoop of vanilla ice cream. White walls and ceilings. White carpet. Glass and chrome and white leather. In the bedroom, there were a white pine bureau and a white pine vanity with a lighted mirror. Big, round, white lights. Mark currently reclined on a white pine platform bed on top of a white tufted spread. The only color in the whole apartment, Mark knew, was in the bathroom. Helen used pink soap. And pink toilet paper.

She was in there now, putting in her diaphragm—a pink one, Mark supposed. Sometimes he wondered why she bothered. True, they always wound up having intercourse, but that didn't seem to be the main point of things for Helen. When he thought of straitlaced little Regina Hudson refusing to take delivery in the rear, and compared her with Helen, he wanted to laugh.

What he didn't want to do was to play any of Helen's games right now. He had too much on his mind. He had to think through what he'd seen tonight. Maybe Helen would understand.

Who am I kidding? he thought. Helen could never understand the necessity of anybody's thinking, because she never did any herself.

She was going to insist on her goddam "challenge"; if he refused, she'd cry or fight, and he'd never get any thinking done unless he left, and he didn't want to leave. If he left, he'd have nowhere to go but to the Senator or Ainley Masters, and he didn't want to be around either of them tonight.

The idea was to think of a challenge that would keep her busy without involving him too much. He didn't want to be buckling leather or clinking handcuffs tonight. Come on, he told himself. The woman's a bubblehead. You ought to be able to think of something.

Helen came out of the bathroom wearing a satin robe, white, naturally. "Mark," she said irritably, "you're still *dressed*."

"So I am," he said. He had exchanged his tux for ratty old sneakers, jeans and a blue work shirt before he left his father's place, but he'd been so preoccupied, he had forgotten to shed them for Helen.

Inspiration struck. "Of course I am," he said. "It's part of your challenge."

Helen said, "Oh," and looked very serious, like a second grader whose teacher has said she's about to say something *very important*. "I thought you forgot."

"I didn't forget," Mark lied. "Take off your robe."

Helen slipped it from her shoulders. She really was beautiful. Given her proclivities and her looks, Mark reflected, it was a shame Helen had been born the daughter of a prominent civil servant in this, the era of AIDS, because her true calling was to be a porno star. Maybe she'd been one in a previous life.

One thing she knew was how to give her looks the best advantage. She stood with her hands on her hips, thrusting her red-tipped breasts forward. She angled her body so the lamp struck gold sparks in her pubic hair. She let him look, apparently expecting him to melt. He never did. That's what she liked about him.

"I'm ready, Mark," she said.

"Now undress me," he told her.

The lovely, patrician face scowled. Parts of her bounced in anger. "What the hell kind of challenge is *that*?" she demanded.

"Shut up," he said.

Helen shut up.

"Undress me," Mark said. "But don't use your hands. If one of your hands touches me, I'm out of here."

"How—"

"I don't care. You wanted a challenge. This is it."

Helen's breath was heavy. She was going to love this. Because Helen couldn't get off without being humiliated first. She had to be spanked or tied up or insulted. She found more release in tears than in orgasm. Maybe it had something to do with being born with money and beauty, the daughter of a powerful man. She'd been insulated from fear and humiliation her whole life, and she didn't really have the brains to imagine them. They were exotic to her, and therefore exciting. Maybe the sex games, the "challenges" she needed were the poor dim child's only way of feeling anything.

Or maybe not. Mark was no psychiatrist, and he really didn't give a damn.

Helen said, "I don't know how . . . I don't know . . ."

"Start with the shoes and work your way up," Mark said. "It'll be easier."

Helen brightened. "Oh, right. Like getting your pants off." She climbed up on the bed, knelt, bent, and began working on his shoelaces with her teeth.

Mark left her to it and got back to his thinking.

When he'd first found that tape, and realized someone had had his father by the balls for years, he suspected that someone to be Ainley Masters. It made sense. Hank came as close to being a loose cannon as any Van Horn, trained from the cradle in smart politics, could ever be. It would be natural for Ainley to want to know what the Senator was up to in greater detail than the Senator would be willing to tell him. Ainley would find out almost without trying whom Hank was screwing; it struck Mark that Ainley was the type to want to know what the pillow talk had been.

"There!" Helen said. She had grabbed the rubber heal of Mark's right sneaker in her teeth and pulled it free. She brought a long leg around and kicked it to the floor. She knelt again and bit the toe of his sock.

It wasn't as if the Van Horns or the people who worked for them were too noble to stoop to bugging, either. Mark had gotten his list of electronics experts from an old file in Ainley's office during a flying visit to town. One of the reasons he'd wanted to stay with Ainley when he'd come to Washington this time was to see if Ainley betrayed any concern, or even any knowledge, of the deaths of these men. He hadn't, at least as far as Mark could tell.

Besides, Ainley did not seem to be a man with a secret stranglehold over the Senator. He seemed to be a man *losing* control of the Senator, and he seemed to have no idea why it was happening. Granted, Ainley hadn't won and held his position without being an expert at deception; Mark thought he could trust appearances in this case. Mark believed that because he was convinced Ainley had the hots for him in an ancient-Greek, elder-mentor-loving-idealized-youth sort of way.

Shoes and socks were gone now. Helen's chin was digging into his belly as she worked on the heavy leather of his belt. Then the belt was open, and she went to work on the brass button of his fly, pushing at it with her tongue. It wasn't working and it wasn't working, and tears of frustration were close now.

"Tastes awful, doesn't it?" Mark asked.

Helen screamed into the denim, and the button came apart. She grabbed one side of his fly in her teeth and pulled down the zipper. She started to struggle to get the pants down, nudging him first onto one side, then the other to get them past his butt.

His father's party tonight. As soon as he learned about it, learned who it was for, Mark knew that it was the Russians who had been holding his father's leash all these years. And worse, they hadn't been pulling it. He couldn't think of a single vote of his father's since Pina had gone up in smoke that was inconsistent with what the Senator would have done if nobody knew anything about him. So they were saving him. And you don't save a big gun (even if he is a loose cannon) like Senator Henry Van Horn unless you intend to fire him at a very large target indeed when you get around to it.

And this was a Presidential election year.

The jeans had joined the shoes and socks on the floor. Helen surprised him. She went to his chest and, instead of unbuttoning his shirt, *bit* the buttons clean off, giving a muffled cry of rage each time she got one free. Mark laughed, and she spit a button in his face. Tears were pouring down her cheeks now. "You *bastard!*" she said.

She turned him over with her head and pulled his shirt off by grabbing the collar at the back of the neck and pulling straight down. Then she nudged him back over. She was a strong girl.

But what was it with Dudakov and Trotter? Dudakov's presence, and Hank's sucking up to him, meant the payoff was soon. Hank might have to rush the last phase of his plan.

But what the hell did *Trotter* have to do with it? If Trotter were a Russian spy, sent to take the Hudson Group back over for the KGB, he and Dudakov (who *had* to be a KGB man) wouldn't get within miles of each other. It was bizarre. What they acted like was a pair of old enemies, and that was impossible. Mark just couldn't understand it, and he didn't like what he didn't understand. He'd have to find out more about this Trotter. If he could figure out a way to do it.

Helen had Mark's briefs down to his hips now, her wet mouth rubbing against him, her heavy blond hair tickling his belly. He was reacting in spite of himself. Helen gave a final tug, and his dick sprang free. Helen pulled the shorts down past his feet, then crawled back up him and took him in her mouth. Just as Mark closed his eyes, she bit him, hard.

"Fuck me now, you bastard," she said. "I earned it. Fuck me this fucking minute!"

Mark grabbed her and flipped her hard on her back. She was still cursing when he entered her; she came before he was all the way in.

CHAPTER ELEVEN

Trotter threw himself down on the Congressman's black leather sofa. He let out a breath that matched the whooshing of air from the cushion. The Congressman and Rines were sitting on chairs, facing him. Nobody seemed to want to speak first.

They were in the Congressman's apartment in the Watergate. Two rooms, kitchen, bath. It had cost the old man a fortune. He lived here, the old man said, because it was only inside the goddam ugly place that you were safe from looking at it.

Trotter had never been here before; all his meetings with the Congressman had been in open air, or in carefully selected safe houses, of which Fenton Rines Investigations was just the latest.

The idea had been to avoid anyone's seeing them together, thereby protecting both their covers. Now, with Borzov running around Washington, shaking Trotter's hand and making in-jokes in front of Washington society, including two Presidential contenders, that particular sort of caution seemed a little superfluous.

This was to be a council of war. The idea was to plan strategy and tactics so brilliant that they would confound Borzov and gain a decided advantage for the United States in the never-ending Cold War. These were to be discussions too hot even for Joe Albright to hear. Albright was (discreetly) bodyguarding Regina back at the hotel.

It occurred to Trotter that these discussions could never achieve the brilliance that was their destiny unless somebody said something.

So he said something. "For starters," he yawned, "I resign."

"Don't shit around, Trotter," said Rines, who never swore.

"I have never," Trotter said, "been more serious in my life." He turned to his father. "Congressman, if you are well enough to walk across a crowded room to embrace your greatest enemy, you are well enough to run your Agency again. I quit."

The Congressman stared at him. "You quit," he said.

"That's right."

"Then get the hell out of here!"

Trotter sat back. "What?"

"Get the hell out of here! I'm good and sick of you. All your worthless life I've had to chase you around and drag you back to do what you can do better than anybody in the world, what you were born to do. I'm sick of it. I'm sick of you. You'd run out on me now? On your goddam country? Hell, I wouldn't piss on you if you were on fire. Get out. Be a rich girl's pet."

"Hey, wait a minute—"

"I'm not waiting any more minutes for you, boy. Something big is on, something B-I-G. Borzov wouldn't be here, otherwise. And it don't take a *whole* lot of brains to see it has *something* to do with the election. There's gonna be blood and fire over this, boy, I can smell it. You could, too, if you'd just be true to yourself. But maybe your nostrils have gotten delicate. It don't matter. Rines and me will handle it. At least we *care* what happens to our country. We don't need anybody who doesn't. You just get."

Trotter looked at him in silence for a full thirty seconds. At last he said, "Are you done?"

"You still here, boy?"

"I'm still here. I'm not going anywhere."

"After people resign," Rines said mildly, "they usually leave."

"Agency fever," Trotter said. "You finally caught it, Rines."

"And what did you catch, that makes you run out in the middle of a crisis?"

"Jesus Christ," Trotter said, "for a couple of intelligence agents, you two are being pretty stupid. I'm not walking *out* on you. I'm resigning as head or acting head, or tri-head or whatever the hell you want to call it, of the Agency. I'm not leaving the Agency itself."

"You're not?" The Congressman sounded like a kid who had just found out he wasn't going to be spanked after all.

"No. I'm not. At least not now."

"Ha!" the old man said.

"Not until this business with Borzov is squared away. As you said, our country might be at stake."

"Don't say that like you're joking, boy. I mean it."

"I know you do. You've got me scarred to death."

"That's the proper attitude," his father told him. "Why are you stepping down? Even assuming I'm up to taking on the whole thing again, which is more than *I* can be sure of right now, I'll tell you that—even assuming that, how long do you think I can keep this up? You ought to be running the show, son."

"No, I shouldn't. I'm terrible at it. You trained me for fieldwork, not for administration."

"You've been doing fine."

"And no serious emergencies have come up yet, either."

"As opposed to comical emergencies?" the Congressman said.

"Droll," Trotter said. "You know what I mean."

"I'm not sure I do, son. What is it exactly you want?"

"I want Borzov. I want to handle the situation."

"Handle it? You mean, *handle* it?"

"I want to run it in the field."

"You mean the kind of thing you used to run away from? The kind of thing I used to have to kidnap you, or threaten to kill some innocent person, to get you to do?"

"Exactly. I'll bet that makes you happy."

"Gives me the warm fuzzies all over. What have you got in mind, son?"

"You never used to ask me that before."

"Maybe I just can't believe my good luck."

"I want to ask you some questions. You too, Rines."

Rines had a sour look on his face. Probably facing the fact that again there was nobody between him and the top of the Agency if anything happened to the old man. "Sure," he said. "Ask away."

"Why do you think Borzov is being so *blatant*? I mean, we all agree why he's here—he's got something so big coming to a head he doesn't trust it to anyone else. But why go to *parties,* for God's sake? Why use the cover name he used with you during the War? Why was he so obvious with me? Okay, fine, he had to know my name from the Azrael business, but why so up-front about it? He's a pro—"

"Son, he practically invented the game," the Congressman said.

"My point, exactly. Yet here he is, almost like he's *toying* with you and me. Like he's sleeping with our wives or something. If we had wives."

"Well, you seem to be planning to have one, son," the Congressman said.

"If his plan is to get next to Regina, we've got nothing to worry about."

"I think," Rines said. He cleared his throat. "I think he's dying."

"We're all dying, Rines," the Congressman said. "Besides, he's an old man. Older than me."

"I mean I think he's dying soon, and ugly. I think he's got lung cancer too bad to do anything about. The coughing, the phlegm you mentioned on the way over here—I remember my grandfather going through the same thing. The operation may be as big as you say, I think it probably is, but I bet the real reason Borzov is over here is to make sure you realize, when whatever it is happens, that he's the one who did it to you."

Trotter and the Congressman exchanged skeptical looks. "I'd think," Trotter said, "that the moving genius of the KGB would be past that kind of thing."

"You two don't realize the effect you have on people. What do they call it? Charisma? Star quality?"

The Congressman rapped his cane on the floor. "Don't be an ass, Rines. We both would have been dead long since."

"Oh, you can be inconspicuous when you want to. At least, Trotter here, can. I've never seen you inconspicuous, Congressman, with all respect. But when Trotter's doing it, it takes an effort on his part. When he lets up, he gets . . . *noticed*. Like you, Congressman. Or, from what I hear, like Borzov himself. You've all got enormous egos—" Rines held up a hand. "I know, we couldn't do this sort of work without it. I've got an ego myself. And I can tell you that if I were supposed to be a genius, and I could outsmart everybody in the world but one or two men, and I wanted to beat them if it turned out to be the last thing I ever did, and I was convinced that I was *about* to beat them, and it *would* be the last thing I ever did, I don't think I'd be able to resist the opportunity to show up in person to rub it in. If it could be managed, of course, without jeopardizing the operation. I don't know about the jeopardizing; it does seem to have been managed."

Trotter scratched his head. "That's something else I've wondered about. Visitors like 'General Dudakov' have to be approved by the State Department. Even if the State Department doesn't know the Agency exists, the CIA must have let them know that Dudakov is Borzov. That cover is practically transparent to anyone in the business."

"I arranged it so that he would be let in," the Congressman said.

Trotter had taken off his tie; now he was removing the cuff links from his shirt. He smiled across at Rines. "You see, Rines, this is the sort of thing that makes me decide I'm not cut out to head the Agency. Not only would it never occur to me to let Borzov into the country, any more than it would occur to me to let a weasel into a henhouse, but the Congressman here didn't even feel it necessary to tell me Borzov was going to be in the country at all. Until this afternoon, when he kindly called and told me I was going to meet the man face to face. Come to think of it, neither did you, Rines. Maybe I *ought* to walk out of here."

"I . . . ah . . . I arranged for you not to be told. Don't blame Rines."

Trotter's voice was calm, but he could feel himself seething. "Why?" he said.

"Why did I have them let Borzov in, or why did I not tell you?"

"Either," Trotter said. "Both."

"Well, I didn't tell you because I was afraid you might talk me out of it. Or worse yet, forbid it altogether. After all, you are—were head of the Agency."

"Not so's you'd notice. Go on. You didn't tell me because you were champing at the bit to be back in charge, and were starting to undercut me already."

The Congressman scowled. "I suppose I deserve that."

"Worse," Rines assured him. Trotter didn't know Rines had it in him.

"Okay. Now tell me why you cleared the way for Borzov to come here." The Congressman mumbled.

"What?"

"I said, I'm getting old, too! I wanted that bastard where I could get my hands on him, all right? He's murdered millions, son. No exaggeration. *Millions*. Whatever you think of me, I've never done that. As screwed up as this country gets sometimes, we've never done that.

"But as long as he stayed in Moscow, what could I do about him? Just wait for him to have another bright idea like the Cronus project, and try to fight off the effects.

"But then he wanted to come to America! *My* territory. And it was for damned sure that bastard wasn't coming to look at the Statue of Liberty. So he had something on, something dirty and nasty, and I thought, if I could only *catch* him at it, I could die happy.

"Of course, I knew no matter how tightly I had him sewn up, I could never put him on trial. Even if he didn't have diplomatic immunity (which he does), the government and the press have poured so many *glasses* of *nost* down the public's throat that the whole goddam country is Russia-drunk. They'd hush this up for the greater good, and I hate to say it, but it would probably be the right thing to do. They'd ship him back to Russia, and maybe pull a few tonnes of wheat off the Russians' table.

"But Borzov would be through. Maybe they'd do a wet job on him right near his office. Maybe they'd just put him out to pasture. Wouldn't matter. He'd be through and America would be a lot safer."

The Congressman looked at his son. "That's why," he said.

"Sounds good to me," Trotter said. "Let's do it."

"Oh, terrific," Rines said. "How? We don't know what he's doing, who he's doing it with, or when it's supposed to happen. All we have to do is catch him at it."

"I've got a couple of ideas about that," Trotter said.

Rines shut up, and the skeptical expression left his face. He leaned forward in his chair.

"It's a pretty good guess," Trotter said, "that this has something to do with the election, right?"

Rines nodded. The Congressman said he'd be willing to bet on it.

"Fine. Let's take the candidates to the cleaners. I'm talking wiretaps, surveillance, background checks up the kazoo, everything illegal and effective we can think of."

"We have a man we can trust in the Secret Service," said Fenton Rines, who had once been the "man we could trust" in the FBI.

"Still, put the best people on it. They'll have the best chance to turn something up without stepping on anyone's toes."

"First thing in the morning," Rines said.

"Good."

"What are you going to do, son?" the Congressman asked. There was a gleam of pride in his eye. It made Trotter furious at himself to be so happy to see it there.

"I'm going to try to induce General Borzov to let us know what he's up to, or at least who he's working with."

"How are you going to do that?"

"Well, the first thing I'm going to do is try to kill him."

Chapter Twelve

Stamford, Connecticut

By the time Grigory Illyich Bulanin got around to making the bomb, he had stopped complaining, even to himself, about the unfairness of it all. He was property; he had to work for the good of the State. It had always been that way—just because he had defected, he had no right to expect his fate to change. So the Americans—well, some of them; fewer and fewer all the time, as far as Bulanin could see—*some* Americans professed to believe that the individual should *not* be compelled to labor for the good of the State. What of it? Bulanin had spent his entire adult life in Intelligence. He knew as well as anyone that what a government did had precious little to do with what it professed to believe. Every Soviet citizen, for example, was promised in the Soviet Constitution a job and freedom of religion.

One of Bulanin's first jobs for Borzov had been harassing Jews in their workplaces, making the job intolerable for them. As soon as they ceased to tolerate it, they were through. If they attempted to end Bulanin's taunts and tortures through force, they were known as "hooligans," and sent to jail—after a good beating by Bulanin, of course. If they simply stayed away, they became parasites or refuseniks, and were sent to mental hospitals, until their appreciation of socialism returned to full flower.

Some, of course, were eventually allowed to leave the Soviet Union, but not before they were made to realize that they were the property of the Motherland until such time as it was the pleasure of the Motherland to let them go.

The only way around that, of course, was to defect, which Bulanin had done. Unfortunately, he was not a musician or a ballet dancer, free to use his talent to grab huge handfuls of the unimaginable wealth that was

America. He was (or had been) a spy, and his talents were useful only to a select few.

The Congressman, for instance. Trotter. He belonged to them; he would do what they said, or die. They didn't even have to kill him. They could just abandon him. Without the shield of false identity and false background that the Congressman's Agency provided for him and kept in repair, the KGB would find him soon enough. They weren't about to give up; Bulanin had been an important man. The unfortunate thing about defecting was that it was a move that could only be made once. There was nowhere else to go.

Bulanin spread newspapers carefully on his kitchen table, then carefully split open one of the shotgun shells he had bought yesterday. He had driven up Route 8, to the northern part of Connecticut, to buy them. It was a different world up there. He had driven above Waterbury, then picked an exit at random. He drove along a country road for about fifteen minutes, then, just as Trotter had told him he would, he had come to a place where he could buy what he needed. He had smiled at the sign above the door—GUNS/Sandwiches/Coffee/AMMO. Bulanin had purchased three out of four. The coffee and the sandwich were standard American fare—they did what they were designed to do without being especially notable.

The same was true of the shotgun shells. Twelve-gauge, from a national manufacturer, one of many headquartered right here in Connecticut.

Bulanin peeled back the stiff paper covering and the plastic collar, removed the wadding, and spilled the black powder and shiny pellets onto the newspaper. He repeated the process with every shell in the box.

It was messy, smelly work. Plastique was so much more pleasant, and, since it didn't move with a stray breath, you could smoke while you worked with it, if you felt adventurous. Bulanin had smoked for years. He had not cared for the habit, but had embraced it as a way to gain time while he thought things over. He found the action of smoking, though not the tobacco itself, calming. He had quit the habit soon after his defection, but he'd begun to feel the urge once again.

He opened another box of shells, slit and emptied them. Then, with a piece of cardboard, he swept the powder and pellets into a small plastic bag. He rolled it up until it was as round and tight as a sausage, sealed it with cellophane tape, and put it aside.

He repeated the process until he had enough small sausages to fill a child's lunchbox. The lunchbox he had bought at a CVS pharmacy in Bridgeport on his way back from buying the shells. It had a bad painting of a movie actor on the side of it, with the word RAMBO appearing in the middle of an explosion. Appropriate, Bulanin supposed.

The bomb was to be set off by a simple sparking mechanism that would be activated when the paper wrapping was taken off the cardboard carton

Bulanin planned to send it in. Not that it ever would be unwrapped, Bulanin thought.

He sighed as he finished the job. Using his left hand, he addressed the parcel in sloppy, American-style block letters. Tomorrow morning, he would take it to a busy post office in another town and mail it, carrying his part of the charade through to the end.

CHAPTER THIRTEEN

Kirkester, New York

It was exactly the kind of headache, Sean Murphy knew, that a couple of quick shots of bourbon would fix right up. Well, maybe not *fix*. Maybe "delay" was a better word. The bourbon would push the headache into a corner of his head too remote to be felt, where it would stay until the bourbon wore off.

Then a few more shots would banish it again. This was a process that could go on for days, even weeks—Murphy knew that from experience. Drinking for him was like a ride in a fast car on a mountain road. There was always a crash somewhere ahead, but the trip leading up to it could be exhilarating.

He caught himself licking his lips. You goddam idiot, he thought, and bit his tongue, hard. Tears came to his eyes; he tasted blood. It was his own home-grown brand of aversion therapy, and so far it had been working. He hadn't had a drink since he'd braced Trotter about his past.

Not that this wouldn't be a good time for a drink. Celebrating a triumph and all that. Because he had him. He had Trotter dead to rights. Right here on the screen in front of him. Murphy could almost take pride in this particular headache. It had nothing to do with alcohol; it had to do with staring into the bright lights of a microfilm projector every spare minute since he'd started the project. Why couldn't microfilm stay in focus? More than once, Murphy had walked out of the Hudson Group's microfilm morgue seeing double and too tired to drive home. He'd been sleeping on the couch in his office. His clothes were rumpled, he needed a shave, he smelled bad—Christ, he thought, I might as well *be* drunk.

But it was worth it. Here was the picture, in a late-summer issue of *Worldwatch* magazine from a few years ago. Elizabeth Fane, the daughter of a defense contractor, had been kidnapped by terrorists. There was a picture of the officials in charge of trying to get her back.

One of them was Trotter. He was heavier in the picture, his hair was lighter, he wore different glasses. The caption identified him as "State Department Official Clifford Driscoll." But it was Trotter. Anybody could see it.

Now Murphy knew why Trotter had bothered him from the start. Murphy had been National Affairs editor at *Worldwatch* at the time of the Liz Fane case. He had undoubtedly selected this very photograph. Subconsciously, he must have recognized the man when he'd turned up as Regina's lover. (That hurt. Even thinking the phrase "Regina's lover" hurt).

Murphy had thought it was simply logic on his part to look for Trotter (or Driscoll or whatever) in accounts of tragedies involving rich young women. He was afraid for Regina; he wanted evidence that would scare Regina away from Trotter—it seemed like the best way to go. Now he realized that his subconscious had been steering his logic.

It didn't matter. The question was, what was he going to do now?

Should he take it to Regina? She was back in town; she and Trotter had returned from Washington a couple of days ago.

No. She was in love with Trotter, and by now Trotter had undoubtedly told her the way Murphy felt about her. What an idiot he was to have admitted he loved her. He didn't dare say anything against Trotter. She wouldn't believe it. Worse, she would lose whatever affection she felt for him.

He'd have to take it to Trotter.

No! Trotter was not a normal man. Trotter, Murphy was sure, was not a man you could threaten. He was a blade with a brain. Murphy ran the tape back and reread the story of the Liz Fane case. People died when Trotter was around. People died nasty.

What else could he do with it?

Causing it to be printed in *Worldwatch* or any other organ of the Hudson Group would be worse than bringing it to Regina. Not only would he have attacked Trotter, but he would have gone behind her back and expropriated her own property to do so.

The police? The FBI? Some other part of the government? They'd laugh in his face. Or lock him up or have him committed. The theory was that Trotter was already working for the government, remember?

So he'd have to take it to Trotter. God help him.

But not naked. Not without *something* to back him up.

Murphy had the microfilm librarian pull him some copies of the photograph. He didn't like the first batch—not clear enough. He ignored the technician's mutterings as he tried again. Much better, this time.

Murphy clutched the photos to his chest as he returned to his office. He ignored the terminal on his desk and pulled an old Smith-Corona Silent Super portable out of the bottom drawer. What he was about to type would go into nobody's memory banks. He sandwiched paper to make an original and two carbons. He rolled the paper in and hit the keys.

An hour later, he was finished. He put a picture and one copy of the document in each of three manila envelopes. He addressed two of the envelopes, left the third blank. He told his secretary he'd be gone for the day. He took the elevator to the parking-lot entrance. He got to his car and delivered the two addressed envelopes in person. He kept the blank one on the seat beside him. As he drove, he touched it lightly from time to time, as though he expected it to scorch him. Maybe it would.

He tried to think of what he would say to Trotter.

God, he wanted a drink.

No. No. He would not have a drink. The last time he faced Trotter with a bellyful of Dutch courage. This time, he'd just have to home-grow some of that, too.

Chapter Fourteen

"Murphy," Trotter said as he opened the door. He sounded almost glad to see him.

"I've got to talk to you," Murphy said.

"I got your message last time," Trotter said. One friend to another. You couldn't find a threat in Trotter's tone if you played a tape of it over and over for a year. Murphy shivered.

Trotter must have seen it. "Come inside," he said. "It's cold out there—I don't want to tighten up." Trotter turned his back on Murphy and went back inside. Murphy followed.

"Come down to the basement," Trotter said. "I've got a couple more miles on the exercise bike and I'll be through for the day. We can talk while I do that. Or grab a drink and wait."

"I'll come down."

Trotter was wearing sneakers and socks, shorts and a sweatshirt. His face looked drawn. Scars like white zippers marred both legs. There was stiffness in the younger man's walk as he went down the stairs, as if he were forcing himself not to limp.

Murphy felt faintly encouraged. It was closer to human than he'd ever let himself imagine Trotter to be. On the other hand, Murphy had about convinced himself that Trotter's reported heroics on the catwalk had been a fabrication. Here was evidence the man really had thrown himself and a gunman thirty feet through space to a concrete floor. He'd had a bad smashup with something, that was for sure. A man who'd get himself hurt like that *on purpose,* Murphy knew, was dangerous. He swallowed.

Trotter climbed on a sleek object in textured white plastic with matte-black accessories. The only thing that marked it as an exercise bicycle were the pedals. Trotter pushed a few buttons, then began to pedal. Aside from beeping once in a while, like a microwave oven, the thing made no rattle, no whiz, no noise at all. Murphy decided he didn't care for exercise equipment that wasn't even human enough to clatter every once in a while.

Trotter's voice was breathy, but calm. "What can I do for you?"

Murphy took the photo out of the envelope. Trotter took one hand off a dull black rectangle that was supposed to pass for handlebars and took it from him.

Trotter looked at the picture with no expression whatever. Then he looked up, pointed to a stack of towels on a nearby table, and asked Murphy to get him one. Murphy complied. Trotter handed the picture back when he took the towel. He removed his glasses and wiped them carefully with the towel, then wiped his face. He put the glasses back on and asked for the picture again.

He's stalling, Murphy thought. I've stung the bastard. He doesn't know what to say.

Murphy thought he'd help him along a little. "Recognize it?"

Trotter was still looking at the picture. "Mmm?" he said, without looking up.

"I asked you if you recognized it."

Now Trotter met his eyes. His face was bland. "There's a caption right here."

Murphy kept hold of his Irish temper. "That's not," he said quietly, "what I meant."

"I know," Trotter said. He smiled. The son of a bitch was smiling at him. Like he was kidding around with an old friend or something. "Of course I recognize it," Trotter went on.

"You do?" It couldn't be this easy.

"Sure. It's Cliff Driscoll. He used to work at the State Department. People used to say we looked alike."

Murphy had his eyes closed. "What people?"

"People who knew us both. When I worked for the *Sun*. Baltimore's not all that—" There was a long beeping noise. Trotter let out a sigh and let his legs stop pumping. He took the towel from where he'd draped it on the pseudo handlebars, took off his glasses and wiped his face again.

If I had a knife, Murphy thought, I could stab him in the belly when he's doing that, when he's wiping his eyes. I could kill him. I could kill him and not even go to confession after.

Trotter put his glasses back on, smiled, and picked up his train of thought. "Baltimore's not all that far from Washington, you know."

"I'd like to interview this guy. This Driscoll. Maybe you could help me get in touch with him."

"Can't be done, Sean."

Murphy could feel his fingers tightening into fists. "Why's that, Allan?" Even to himself, his voice sounded like the voice of a man being strangled.

"Because Driscoll's dead."

"Driscoll's dead," Murphy echoed.

"Right after Liz Fane was returned. He had a car crash on his way back to town to take part in debriefing. Girl's mother was killed, too."

Murphy was kicking himself for not having followed up on the career of "Mr. Driscoll" after he'd found the photograph. There was undoubtedly something fishy about this Driscoll's "death." Murphy might have been able to spot what it was.

Too late now. Better to brazen it out than to let himself be tossed any curveballs.

"Bullshit!" he said. "Driscoll isn't dead. *You* are Driscoll, and I'm giving you just five seconds to admit it!"

Trotter wiped his face again, muttering something into the towel.

"I can't hear you," Murphy said.

"I said, 'Five seconds to admit it, or else *what?*' What have you got besides a wish to make me play along with your fantasies?"

"It's no fantasy, damn you. And if you don't do what I tell you, this picture and the rest of the evidence I've collected gets a blanket release to the media, not just the Hudson Group."

"Uh-huh." Trotter threw one scarred leg over the exercise machine and stood up wincing. "Ouch. That's it, screw the sit-ups today. What do you want me to do?"

Murphy could feel himself losing it. He was an experienced reporter; he'd played cat and mouse with too many people too often not to know that if he were in control of this situation, it wouldn't seem so easy.

Nothing to do but play it out. "I want you," he said, "to disappear. Fake your death. If Driscoll could do it, so can you. Just take off. Get out of Regina's life before you get her killed. Before you hurt her worse than she's already been hurt."

"Uh-huh," Trotter said again. "I suppose you've got a lot of those envelopes squirreled away with people you think you can trust."

"Enough. And if anything happens to me, they all go out."

"You're afraid something is going to happen to you?" Trotter sounded incredulous. "Come on."

The fact was Murphy had *not* been afraid that anything might happen to him. Until right now. He suppressed another shudder. He was glad he'd taken precautions.

"I suppose," Trotter went on, "that the very first packet of evidence, whatever it is, goes to Regina herself."

Murphy stared at him.

"Doesn't it?" Trotter asked. "It's not that hard to figure. What you want to do is get me away from Regina. Or her away from me, I guess, from your point of view. The best way for you would be if I take this conversation to heart and just split. The next best would be for you to discredit me just in

Regina's eyes. If she doesn't trust me, I can't achieve whatever nefarious things you think I'm up to."

"Go to hell."

"The media blitz is the last resort. It would, the way you see it, neutralize me, but it would also make a new scandal for the Hudson Group, which has barely gotten over the last one. And anything that hurts the Hudson Group hurts Regina. Hey!"

Murphy jumped.

"I'm being a terrible host," Trotter said. "You've been sitting on that stool all this time. Let's go back upstairs; the chairs are more comfortable and I've got to drink some Gatorade before I cramp up."

"Lead the way," Murphy said.

Trotter grinned. "Okay, but I'm pretty slow going upstairs these days."

"I'm in no hurry."

"And you're not letting me get behind you, either. Okay, okay. Here goes." Trotter walked over to the stairs and started lifting himself up. "I'm so damned stiff," he said. He looked back over his shoulder at Murphy, who was keeping a cautious, four-stair distance between himself and his host. "Oh. How am I doing, by the way?"

"You're getting there. Don't put on a show for my benefit."

"I wish it were a show. But I'm not talking about the stairs. How am I doing at figuring out your strategy?"

"Nobody ever said you weren't smart."

Trotter brought him to the living room. "Take a chair. I'll be right back."

"Where are you going?"

"To the kitchen. That's where the Gatorade is. Want to come along, see I don't come back with an Uzi or something?"

"No, thanks. Anything happens to me, those documents go out."

"Right, right, the documents."

Trotter walked stiffly from the room. Murphy could feel himself growing more paranoid by the second. What if Trotter was calling for help? What if he had agents tracking down and killing everyone Murphy could trust, so those documents couldn't go out? Murphy tiptoed across the rug to the doorway and listened hard. He heard a refrigerator open and close. He heard ice clink in a glass. He heard liquid being poured. He heard footsteps returning.

He just got back to his chair before Trotter returned. The younger man had a tall glass with ice and a pale-green liquid in his right hand, a squat bottle of the same green liquid in his left.

"You want anything?" Trotter asked, plunking himself down in the middle of the leather couch.

"Nothing."

"Right," Trotter said. "Might slip you a hypnotic drug and make you get the documents back by yourself."

"I don't find anything about this funny, Trotter."

"Sean, I like you. I really do."

"Don't like me," Murphy heard himself saying. "Don't you *dare* like me."

"I can't help it. But forget that for a minute. Can I ask you a question?"

"You haven't answered any of mine yet."

"We've got plenty of time. I might surprise you."

"Ask. I don't promise to answer."

"Why do you hate the idea of my being with Regina so much? What is it you think I *am*?"

"I know damn well what you are. You're a spy, almost certainly for the American government. You work for a group so secret I couldn't get a *sniff* of you through ordinary channels. You were there in the Liz Fane case, and a lot of people, probably innocent people, died. I get the feeling you didn't care, as long as you got your job done. Now you're working on Regina, you've got her to the point where she thinks she's in love with you; for God's sake, she thinks she's going to *marry* you. You're setting her up for something, and I won't have it."

Trotter pursed his lips. "Well," he began.

"You sound like Reagan."

Trotter laughed. "Are you accusing me of being Reagan, now?" He waved it away. "It doesn't matter. I deny it. I deny everything, of course."

"I don't care what the hell you admit or deny. Just get out of town. Out of Regina's life."

"You wanted to talk. We'll talk first." Trotter's face told Murphy it was not a request.

Trotter drank Gatorade. "Let's assume, though, just for the sake of argument, that you're right. That I *am* a spy, in deep cover, working on some top-secret operation. You say yourself that if I were, it's the United States I would be working for. Doesn't that make a difference?"

"Don't make me laugh."

"Hey, it's *your* government I'm working for, according to you. I could be engaged in a project that could save millions of lives, bring world peace, if only I got a chance to finish the job. Wouldn't that give you second thoughts about blowing the whistle? Could I appeal to your patriotism at all?"

"I'm a reporter, Trotter. I have a job to do. I'm bending my ethics enough just offering to let you skip town. I should have phoned you for a comment, then plastered your face across the front page of this afternoon's papers."

"Even if it would have ruined months, maybe years, of delicate maneuvering and secret negotiations? Even if lives would be lost and a chance to increase your country's security is ruined?"

"I do my job, Trotter. Don't try to snow me."

"Okay, let me see if I've got you straight. A reporter has a job to do; he has to print what he thinks he's found out, no matter what."

"Don't you know that? Aren't you supposed to be a reporter?"

"We're pretending I'm a spy, remember? So he prints what he knows, no matter what. Unless, of course, he has some personal ax to grind, the way you do, then he uses the information for blackmail. Right?"

Murphy wanted to shout indignant denials, but honesty compelled him to admit to himself that that was exactly what he was doing. He could argue he was doing it for the good of someone he loved, but that wouldn't carry a lot of weight, since he'd already scoffed at the idea of Trotter's doing what he did for his country.

"Go on," Murphy said.

Trotter nodded. "Our ideal reporter, then, just does his job. He does what he's been trained to do, what he's promised his employers he'll do."

"That's right."

"He doesn't give a shit who gets hurt."

"No, he doesn't."

"Then what's the difference between you and me, friend? Why the hell should *I* give a shit about Regina, or you, or anybody else?"

Trotter was leaning off the couch now. His eyes shot flames. Murphy could smell Trotter's sweat, a feral smell. *The last thing the rabbit knows,* Murphy thought, *is the breath of the wolf.*

Trotter closed his eyes and let out his own breath in a whoosh. He leaned back, took a sip of his drink, and opened his eyes again.

"Let's take it from another angle. If I didn't like you, I'd just let you publish the stuff and be done with it. *You'd* have to leave town."

"Don't be an ass." Murphy had been afraid his voice would crack; he was proud of himself that it hadn't.

"You'd be a laughingstock. Look, you checked me out, Allan Trotter. Everything you were able to find supported the idea that I'm who I say I am. Now you say that Clifford Driscoll isn't dead, that I'm Clifford Driscoll. Okay, you dig him up, you compare dental records, fingerprints, whatever. How much would you like to bet everything you check supports my version of things? And makes you look like an idiot?"

Murphy clutched his envelope tight. He'd put it together believing his salvation was inside it. He couldn't let go of it now, no matter what Trotter said.

Trotter was far from through. "You say I'm a spy, but you'll never find a nickel paid to me on any government payroll ever. An agency you can't even get a sniff of? Who's going to buy it?"

"Oh, you're right about one thing. Nothing would ever happen to you. If you were to have an accident, conspiracy nuts might begin to take you seriously. On the other hand, if you go ahead with this, everybody will take it as the pathetic spleen of a lovesick drunk."

Murphy stared at him. The envelope slipped from his fingers. He had come here this afternoon fighting the fear that Trotter would kill him. Now he almost wished he would.

"No," Trotter said. "Wait a minute. Sean. I know that look in your eye.

Don't go planning any of your own accidents to lend yourself credibility, okay?"

"It never crossed my mind," Murphy lied. "But why not?"

"Because there's something else you didn't think of. Or wouldn't let yourself believe if you did."

"What's that?"

"That whoever or whatever I am, I truly do love Regina Hudson. That whatever there is to know about me, she's known since before I went off the catwalk."

"But . . . but . . ."

"You're shocked that she hasn't printed it." Trotter shrugged. "From the publisher's chair, maybe journalism is a little more complicated. Or maybe Regina can just see around the edges of it a little bit better."

"You're lying to me."

"Well," Trotter said, then smiled. "Reagan again. We're just supposing here, remember. For now. Unless you're wired. I'll tell you what. You talk to Regina. I'll tell her to limit what she tells you only by her trust for you. From what she says about you, that's a pretty loose limit."

Murphy didn't believe it. He didn't dare believe it. But he was damned if he could figure out what the trick was.

"When is this supposed to happen?"

"Today. Now. I'll call Regina right away." Trotter reached for the phone. He paused with his hand on the receiver. "Oh," he said. "Just one thing."

"I knew there was a catch."

"If *you* in your nosy amateur way do anything to put Regina in danger, I'll kill you."

"Pretty aggressive talk for a reporter."

"If you put the woman I love in danger, I'd kill you if I were a soda jerk. Still want me to make that call?"

"Make it."

But he never did. Just then, the phone rang. Trotter brought it to his ear and said hello. "No, as a matter of fact, I had my hand on the phone." He said yes a few times, then he said "Jesus." He said he wasn't alone and couldn't go into details. He said he'd be down there by tonight. He hung up the phone.

To Murphy, he said, "You've got to leave now."

"What about the call to Regina?"

"When I get the chance. Tonight, probably."

Trotter was on his feet, somehow propelling Murphy toward the door.

"I know a stall when I hear one, Trotter."

Trotter rolled his eyes in exasperation. "To hell with you then. I've got no time to go easy on you. Publish whatever you goddam want."

The door slammed behind him. Murphy was out on the front walk. He didn't have his envelope. He thought of knocking on the door and asking for it, but he'd used up all the courage he could muster for one afternoon.

He wondered if he'd accomplished anything this afternoon. He wondered what he was going to do now.

And, as he had from the moment he'd met the man, he wondered what the hell Trotter was up to.

Chapter Fifteen

Washington, D.C.

"Senator, have you heard from the kidnappers?"

"Senator, do you have any indication that your son is still unharmed?"

"Was your son involved with Miss Fraser, Senator?"

"Senator, how about speculation that—"

"Senator, is it true that—"

"Senator, would you say—"

"Senator—"

"Senator—"

They were going to get their shot at him sooner or later; Hank had agreed with Ainley that it would be wisest to get it over with right away. Hank knew from experience that if a thing like this happened, the smart move was to get the press on your side as soon as possible. Of course, sometimes, as in the Pina thing, you couldn't actually get them over to your side, the best you could do was to keep them from being mad at you for not cooperating with them. Something else Hank had learned over the years—the one thing the press can't ever forgive is your trying to ignore them. They didn't like that. They needed the constant reassurance that they were as important as they thought they were.

This would be simple compared to the Pina thing, since Hank was absolutely innocent. He didn't know a damn thing more than these vulture reporters did.

Yesterday morning, the maid had shown up at Helen Fraser's apartment to find the Fraser kid lying on the floor with a hole from a 9-millimeter automatic between her eyes, wearing her overcoat, and surrounded by the contents of a bag of groceries she'd been carrying when she entered. She hadn't been raped.

Mark's fingerprints were all over the place. People pretended to be surprised, but Hank knew that for the hypocrisy it was. For one thing, everyone in Washington who counted had seen them together, and for another, if Mark had been spending time in the company of a girl that good-looking without collecting her scalp, the boy wouldn't be much of a Van Horn. And everybody who counted knew that, too.

Mark's car had been found parked nearby, which helped scotch the nasty rumors that Mark had done for the girl himself, and arranged for his own disappearance. People had such nasty minds. Hank had found that out for himself. Here the poor kid's girlfriend had been killed for some reason, and he's been kidnapped, and there are some people who'll probably never believe it wasn't a put-up job.

Although, Hank had to admit, if the kidnapping business *had* been a ploy, the kid's not taking off in his own car had been a really smart move. Hank had wanted to discuss it with Ainley, but Ainley wasn't in a discussing mood. All he could talk about was the danger to Mark, my God, we have to get Mark back.

Well, of *course* they had to get Mark back. The sooner the better, too. This was going to mess up the Presidential campaign the way things were going. Take the country's attention away from Senator Van Horn's forthcoming (one of these days) Presidential endorsement, and put it back on the continuing soap opera the public seemed to love to make of the Van Horn family.

And they had to get Mark out of danger, too. He didn't need an adviser to tell him *that*. He was the boy's father. Ainley wasn't.

Things were a little better once the kidnappers got in touch with Hank, since the FBI had been monitoring the phone, and they vouched for the message's being genuine.

The message hadn't said much—your son is unharmed, you will hear from us again. The voice was clear and unaccented, and didn't sound like anyone Hank or Ainley knew. The FBI had said they'd play the tape for some people who got around in different circles, and Hank had said that would be fine.

In a way, it was kind of *fun* to be innocent.

Now the press was baying, so Ainley (whose nervous dithering in private didn't seem to effect his cool, public efficiency one bit) arranged this press conference in the room the Senate keeps for such things.

As usual, they started screaming the questions the minute Hank showed his face. As usual, every time he moved his head, a new flashgun went off in his eyes. He could handle it. He'd stopped wincing at flashguns long ago—it made for bad photos in the paper.

As for the chaos of voices, he'd been trained to handle that practically since birth. Hold up a hand. Smile—in this case, a little wearily, a little sadly. Say, "One at a time, gentlemen, please." Then call a name.

The questions were easy, nothing he wasn't ready for. Except one, from a good-looking redhead from some paper in Texas. "Senator, have you spoken with Undersecretary Fraser since the incident?"

Hank made his face suitably grave, but inside he was smiling. He thought he might be in love with this young thing who threw such nice fat ones over the plate. He'd have to arrange for her to have a private interview with him at the earliest possible moment.

Lots of things had to be taken care of first though, like answering her question.

Hank sighed. "No," he said sadly. "Actually, I was going to call on him as soon as we were done here, then I was going to go into seclusion while we work on getting Mark back. I know you people have your jobs to do, but can we please try to keep Al Fraser's grief and my concern from becoming a media circus?"

The answer to that turned out to be no. It was beautiful. A media caravan followed Hank's limo to Undersecretary Fraser's house (fortunately, the driver knew where it was). On the way, Ainley congratulated him for handling matters so deftly.

Hank shrugged. "I just thought of what you'd want me to do."

"What's this about seclusion?"

"I thought it would be a good idea to get the press off my back."

"Of course it would, but we can't afford it now. What if the kidnappers call? What if you've got to do something to get Mark back?"

"I'll be in seclusion, not incommunicado. Relax, Ainley, it's all taken care of. Gus Pickett's helicopter is going to pick me up and fly me to his place in Virginia. Instant worldwide communication, and protection you can't beat anywhere."

Ainley thought he was going to argue, but the driver's voice came over the enunciator telling them they were at the Fraser Residence, and Hank was popping out of the car before Ainley had a chance to say anything.

Al Fraser himself opened the door. Apparently an enterprising reporter had phoned ahead to tip the Undersecretary off and to set up a better photo-op. Fraser didn't let them down. The poor guy opened the door with his hair combed crooked and his face puffy from crying. Tears glistened in his eyes at this very moment. Hank, going with the moment, embraced him, and five thousand flashguns went off. This picture would be on every front page in the country, and the tape would run on TV for a week. You couldn't buy that kind of coverage. You couldn't plan it. People would see those images and see what a brave, sensitive guy Hank Van Horn was in a time of crisis. Maybe some of them would decide to forget about Pina Girolamo. Most of them would think better of him than they had, no matter where they were starting from. And in this business, good opinions translated into power. In this business, you could never have too much power.

Hank went inside, and the reporters pitched camp. Hank spent ten minutes listening to Fraser say, "Why? For God's sake, why?" and making soothing noises, and left. The press yelled that it wanted to know what had been said. Hank looked sad and simply said, "Now, come on, folks," in tones of gentle admonition. He got into the limo with Ainley. Ainley had apparently decided not to waste his energy trying to talk Hank out of going to Gus Pickett's place. Ainley had always been smart.

They made it to the heliport just in time. Hank climbed in the bubble of the chopper, the pilot welcomed him and made sure he was safely buckled in, and then they took off.

CHAPTER SIXTEEN

Trotter reflected as he unplugged the miniscrambler and hung up the pay phone that he should have waited a few days before letting his father step back in as head of the Agency. When he was in charge, if he wanted to give permission for a semi-authorized personnel unit (as Rines insisted on referring to a human being) to blow his cover to a totally unauthorized unit, he could just do it. Now that he was back in the ranks, he had to sneak around.

Now it was up to Regina. She'd have to decide how much she trusted Murphy with her fiancé's life. She'd do fine.

Trotter sighed. Stopped talking to her thirty seconds ago, and he missed her already. All right, he told himself. Forget about that now. An operation has started to break. Your audience awaits.

It was late enough in the year now that there was no more spring chill. Trotter walked the six blocks to Fenton Rines Investigations, Inc., and his legs hardly hurt at all.

"Well, son," the Congressman said as Trotter entered the inner office, "it worked. You bagged a big one."

"Save the congratulations." Trotter did not like to be congratulated on the success of operations that ended in innocent people dying, something his father could never understand. Trotter hadn't been a big fan of Helen Fraser's during the few minutes they'd spoken. He'd thought her silly and not too bright. But she didn't deserve to die. Nobody deserved to die for a reason she didn't know and probably wouldn't have understood. Trotter would have liked to be able to believe there was something to the young woman's belief in reincarnation; that even now, she was being born smarter and wiser in some infant's body. It would ease the guilt. But he couldn't.

Even telling himself it was shockingly unprofessional for a kidnap squad to kill a witness in a situation like that didn't get him off the hook.

Trotter had deliberately and consciously provoked one of the most dangerous men in the history of the planet into lashing out. He had *thought* the provocation to be relatively mild; he had *believed* that Borzov's response would be measured.

He was wrong, and Helen Fraser was dead.

Rines was talking.

"What did you say?" Trotter asked.

"I was wondering if you suspected his target would be Van Horn when you set this up."

"Not really. I mean, it was always a possibility, but after the party I discounted it."

Rines nodded. It was almost a rule that when you had someone in deep cover, you never associated with him openly in any way.

"We'll never get Borzov going by the book," the Congressman said. "He wrote the goddam book."

"We weren't after Borzov, Congressman," Trotter said. "We were out to flush his mole."

Rines was shaking his head. "Van Horn. Well, at least they think big. I wonder what's in it for him. It can't be money. It can't be a matter of principle. The Van Horns have never had any."

The Congressman chuckled. "You can take the boy out of the Bureau, but you can't take the Bureau out of the boy."

Rines was stiff. "What's that supposed to mean, Congressman?"

"Just that the Bureau never got along too well with that family."

"There are excellent reasons for that going back to World War Two—"

Trotter cut in. "Can we stop playing 'Be True to Your School' for a minute and address the question? What is in it for Hank Van Horn?"

"Protection," Rines said. "I was leading up to that."

"Borzov's got something on him," the old man added. "You've been figuring that way all along, or you wouldn't have sent Borzov that fake bomb."

"Obviously. But what—"

Trotter stopped. Suddenly he knew what.

"Tapes," he said. "They've got tapes of something bad."

"The girlfriend barbecue," the Congressman suggested.

"Of course! It fits, it all fits. When was that? Can you call that up on the computer, Rines?"

"I don't need to. August 1974. The day before Nixon resigned. The Bureau may hold a grudge, Congressman, but sometimes it pays off."

"Well, you're not in the Bureau anymore."

"Catch me forgetting *that*," Rines said. He turned to Trotter. "Okay, I admit a tape of Senator Van Horn committing murder and arson is one of the few things I can think of that could put any Van Horn in the power of an outsider. And I think it's hilarious that a Van Horn could be screwed by a wiretap, since for years the Bureau has known Ainley Masters has a better file of electronic security people than the secret services of half the world's governments. But is this just an inspiration on your part, or do you have something?"

"I've got twelve dead electronic surveillance men. All active during the right period. All killed during the months before Borzov felt himself moved to visit America for the first time."

"My God," the Congressman said. "My God. That guy in Minneapolis. He was the youngest one, the last one who was in business soon enough to have planted a bug on the Senator."

Rines looked sour. "Why would they kill *all* of them? If they wanted to shut up the one who did the job for them, why didn't they just kill him?"

"Smoke screen," Trotter said. "If they just killed one, somebody like us might dig into it and find something Borzov couldn't afford to have found."

"I'll get people digging on all of them as soon as we're done here," Rines promised.

The Congressman scratched his jaw. "It could be, you know, that Borzov has had to kill all these guys because he doesn't *know* who the right one is."

Trotter nodded. It was embarrassing to admit it, but sometimes a supersecret operation could become *too* secret. An intermediary is told to hire someone to plant a bug. This is done, the tape is sent back to headquarters, and no one, not even the man at the top, knows any more than necessary.

But then, perhaps, the intermediary dies. That was something that happened with remarkable regularity in the spy business. If, after that, it became desirable to find the man who had planted the bug for you, you wouldn't necessarily be able to do it. The better agent the intermediary had been, the less chance there was that he had left any documents behind to help you trace his contacts.

That could leave you with the messy necessity of killing a dozen men to get the one you want.

Trotter shook his head. "What about Jake Feder?"

"What about him?" the old man said.

"He never did any work for the Russians. You know that, and I know that, and Borzov damned well knows that. He couldn't have been on their list."

"They were being subtle," Rines offered. "They didn't want to leave anyone out, or we might ask why, and the fact that Jake Feder worked only for the Congressman would stick out."

"Does it bother you as much as it does me," Trotter asked, "that we never did ask ourselves any of these questions Borzov is supposed to have been afraid we were going to ask?"

"He couldn't take any chances," the Congressman said.

"It also shows what a piss-poor Agency chief I was."

"Rines and I were here, too, son," the Congressman said softly. "We didn't think of it either." He cleared his throat. "Maybe that son of a bitch just decided, while he was at it, to cost us a good man."

A good man, and, Trotter knew, the closest thing to a friend his father had ever had.

"I don't know," Trotter said. He scratched his chin. "I don't like it. It doesn't add up."

He stared at the wood paneling for a second. Then he shook his head as if to clear it.

"Okay, what are we doing now? I assume we've got the Russian Embassy under surveillance."

"We do, but it's just a formality. Borzov isn't there."

"Oh? Where the hell is he?"

Rines was even more sour now. "I don't know. He left the embassy right after he got your little gift. I figured he might be a little goosey, so I didn't have him tailed. The idea at the time was to leave him free to tip off his partner, right?"

Trotter sighed. "Right, right."

"Well, he just never came back."

"You've got someone on Van Horn?"

"Five of them. There are so many reporters around him, we could have a dozen. I should be getting a report any minute. In the meantime, what are we going to do about this?"

Trotter had a few ideas. He lined them out for a while.

The computer on Rines's desk beeped. He hit a few buttons and punched up the report.

"Son of a fucking bitch," said Rines, who never swore. "This clinches it, at least for me."

"What happened?" Trotter demanded.

"The Senator climbed into a private helicopter that is whisking him off to the Virginia estate of Augustus Pickett."

The Congressman laughed. It seemed to Trotter that his laugh had gotten stronger once the old man took his job back.

"Gus Pickett," the Congressman said. "Another one of the Bureau's old favorites."

"A great American," Rines said through his teeth.

"Borzov is playing this like a wild man," Trotter said. "Let's wait a little and see where he goes with it."

CHAPTER SEVENTEEN

Virginia

"If you want your son back," General Dudakov said severely, "you will listen carefully."

Hank Van Horn took a long pull at his Gibson. He was still trying to figure out what the hell the General was doing here.

Things had been happening fast since the helicopter landed. Gus Pickett, all smiles and heartiness, had risked getting his silk smoking jacket drizzled on in order to meet Hank at the landing pad. Gus had put his arm around the Senator and led him inside the house, a big stone palace of a place some tobacco baron had built around the time Gus Pickett had been born.

Gus brought him to the drawing room, showed him to a seat, and asked Hank what he wanted to drink. Then the multibillionaire fixed a pitcher of Gibsons with his own hands and placed it, along with a crystal glass full of pearl onions, on a table at Hank's elbow.

Still smiling, Gus had said, "See you in a minute," and disappeared.

Hank sat and drank Gibsons and tried to decide how many times his library in the town house would fit in this room. A voice over his shoulder broke into his thoughts.

"Senator Van Horn!"

Hank spun around to see the Russian general bearing down on him. He looked a lot less friendly than he had at the party Hank had thrown for him.

Hank was no fool; after a slight start (and anybody would be startled to hear that voice suddenly barking behind him) he realized what was going on. Dudakov was one of the Russians who had something to do with his situation. And obviously, Gus Pickett worked for him. That was kind of funny, but Hank didn't laugh. There had been rumors about Gus for years—he was so chummy with the Russians, he must be on their string *somehow,* was the way the thinking usually went—but he had so much money, only a handful of fanatics really believed anything could be going on. Chalk one up for the fanatics.

And now Dudakov was throwing threats around about Mark.

Hank was thinking hard; when he did that, habits took over. The habit of a politician is to be affable.

"General," he began heartily.

"I said *listen,*" Dudakov snapped.

Hank blinked as his brain jumped out of its groove. "What have you done with my son?" he demanded.

"Your son is safe."

"Why did you kill the girl?"

"Your son may not always be safe. Now be quiet."

Hank closed his mouth. When the general told him to sit, he sat.

Dudakov was calmer, now, but the menace in him was still obvious. "That's better, Senator. Relax."

Hank tried and failed.

"Look around you."

Hank looked around. There was nothing to see but Gus Pickett's enormous room.

"We are alone," the General said. He began to cough, and it took him a long time to catch his breath. He'd done this, Hank remembered, at the party. This wasn't quite as bad. Hank began to rise to help him, but Dudakov raised a hand for him to stop. The old man made his own way to an ornate love seat striped in gold and purple and plopped down on it. He wasn't a good match for it—you might as well put a frog on a velvet cushion, Hank thought—but sitting down seemed to help him. Borzov took a couple of deep breaths and began again.

"We are alone. I am not going to have you beaten or shot. Besides—"

"You have my son."

The General smiled. "I have your son. We must talk about what you have done and what you are going to do."

Hank clasped his hands together in front of him, realized that was weak body language, and let them go. He wished uselessly that Ainley were here. Still, he wasn't as worried as he might have been. As long as they were still talking, he knew everything would be all right.

• • •

Borzov looked at the Senator with disdain. It was an unfortunate fact of his calling that while the weak were the easiest tools to obtain, they were the most difficult to work with. With a whole man, a man with a mind and a soul and convictions (the General's Presidential candidate, for instance), no task was too great. The Senator's mind, if he had one, had been buried under a life of ease and unearned power. His soul contained only arrogance and lust. His only conviction was that the arrogance and lust should not be left unsatisfied.

Even the Senator's concern for his son, the General could see, was a vestigial thing at best. Oh, he was willing to believe that the Senator would prefer that the boy live. But, Borzov believed, the Senator showed outrage because The Public would *expect* him to show outrage, and fear because it would *expect* him to show fear.

In truth, it was Borzov who was afraid. He was a dying man in a wearing business. His mind and soul and convictions had been devoted to the service of his country, and that service was incomplete. Its completion depended in large part on the Senator. The Senator had been saved for just this occasion. And now, on the eve of fruition, Van Horn had done something unexpected. Worse, hostile. To be sure, weak tools often twisted in the hands of the craftsman, but Borzov was the Guild Master of this art. He should not be taken by surprise by such a one as Senator Van Horn.

Borzov had to find out what was wrong, and fix it without ruining his plan. It would take handling, handling made no easier by the bumbling fools who had so needlessly killed the girl when she'd walked in on the kidnapping. That had been foolish—they could simply have taken her along. They had compounded their stupidity by leaving the body there—something that could only send a message of terror to the Senator, and bring a more concerted effort to find the perpetrators.

Borzov shook his head. If this had been done properly, the American authorities need never have known of it.

Enough, he told himself. Time advances.

"Tell me, Senator," he said, "do you not realize the nature of the tape that has been in our possession these many years? Did we not send you a copy of it?"

Van Horn nodded. He had decided to be "reasonable." "Yes," he said. "Yes, you did."

"At any time, we could have destroyed you. We could have changed what is a mere suspicion in the minds of some Americans into a certainty in all of them. But we have not done that, have we?"

"No," Senator Van Horn said.

"And our . . . agreement. You haven't found it particularly onerous, have you? Our requests for your assistance have not been excessive?"

"Not at all," the Senator said.

And well he might, Borzov thought. Except for some minor things during the early days—names of people to recommend for appointments, a few projects to mention in his speeches—they had asked him to do nothing at all. And even those early requests were more tests of the Senator's commitment to the "agreement" than anything important in the way of operations. The Senator was too important a piece to be wasted in the daily play of the game of put-and-take that was international politics.

"Are you so stupid, then, as to think that I possess the only copy of the tape? That if I were to die, my organization and my nation would somehow be powerless to enforce the agreement that has allowed you to live in luxury and power for over a dozen years?"

The Senator scowled. "I—I—"

"Yes?"

"I don't know what you're talking about, General."

"You deny you sent a bomb to me at the embassy?"

"A *what?*"

Borzov looked at him closely. He knew that for all his faults, Senator Henry Van Horn was a man with years of experience in American electoral politics, and therefore, an expert liar. But Borzov considered himself to be an expert at detecting liars, and the Senator did not seem to him to be lying.

"I don't even know how to *make* a bomb!" Van Horn protested.

"This device was the work of a clumsy amateur. It was exactly the sort of thing a man who did not know how to make a bomb might attempt to send me."

"Anyway, how do I even know there was a bomb? I didn't hear anything about an explosion at the embassy."

"There was no explosion. It was easily detected. That is not the point. The point is the *attempt*."

"Why pick on me?" The Senator was petulant. "There are lots of nuts running around who hate Russians."

"That is true. You, however, are a man who may have decided he has a reason to want me dead. And you are known to be a man who panics and resorts to violence under pressure."

It was obvious from Van Horn's face that he didn't like that, but he let it go. Instead he said, "Besides, I'm not a total idiot. My grandfather was ambassador to Germany, you know. I know how embassies work. You don't open your own mail. Don't you think I know that?"

Borzov took a deep breath, which for once did not cause a coughing fit. "Yes, Senator. I am aware you know that. But I am also aware that you depend on your staff for assistance in most of your endeavors."

Now the fool's feelings were hurt. "Every Senator does," he said. "We couldn't function efficiently otherwise."

"Of course, Senator. It was not a criticism. I, too, have a staff. My point is, that the nature of our agreement cuts you off from their counsel and assistance. You might have recruited some other help, someone, say, willing to act on vague instructions to 'take care' of me in some way."

"And saddle myself for life with a blackmailer. Come on, General."

"Very well. I accept that. It was something that had to be checked."

"It had to be checked," Van Horn echoed. "You kidnapped my son and killed that girl because it had to be checked."

"We are working for the good of the world. Over five billion lives, Senator. Almost everyone who was alive yesterday is alive today and will be alive tomorrow. Yet someday, each of us will die. One day, we will be here, the next, gone. One day Helen Fraser was here, the next gone. One day, Josephine Girolamo was here . . ."

"When can I have my son back?"

"He will be released immediately. The word will reach you here, and you will be helicoptered back."

"The sooner the better. I don't think this was one of your better ideas, General."

"The matter is by no means over, Senator. In the coming weeks, you will be watched."

"Help yourself."

"Don't get up, Senator." Borzov took a small plastic box from his pocket and pressed a light-blue button on it. One of Augustus Pickett's mountainous bodyguards entered the room, gun drawn.

"The gun will not be necessary," Borzov said. "Please tell your chief that the bird may fly."

The security man nodded and left. Borzov turned to Van Horn. "Now. We have more to talk about, Senator."

"Now what?"

"The fascinating topic of American Presidential politics. We are going to discuss whom you are going to endorse for your party's nomination, and when and how you are to do it.

"You will notice, Senator, that your son is being released as a gesture of good faith. He will be at your side, if you wish it, all the while you are carrying out your final instructions."

PART THREE
ATROPOS

She who cuts the thread of life . . .

CHAPTER ONE

June—State Capital

The bellboy showed Gus Pickett around his hotel suite. "Sitting room here, shower here, television's in the cabinet, the remote control for it is in the—"

"I'll find it, thanks," Pickett said. He tried to decide if he sounded gruff. Magazine articles about him never failed to include the phrase "the gruff-voiced octogenarian," but Gus never thought he sounded gruff. Gus thought he sounded just fine.

With a skill born of a million stays in a million hotel rooms, Gus had the kid tipped and out of there before he started to lose his patience. He'd been a hard-working man for seventy-two years, now, and he didn't plan to waste what time he had left in small talk with bellboys.

"In town for the primary?" the kid had asked.

"Got business," Gus had replied. "All my trips are business." Then he'd tipped the kid five dollars, or fifty times what the job was worth—okay, at least five times, allowing for inflation—and told him to scoot.

Of course, his business here *was* the primary, but that was nobody's concern. Anybody who wanted to waste his time checking up on old Gus would find that the purpose of this trip to the middle of the Great Plains had been to sell a bunch of wheat that had been sitting out in a bunch of grain elevators not far from here. Gus had been in the wheat business since the fifties. He'd gone into it to make money, of course—Gus was always interested in making money. But he'd also done it because his pal Borzov had foreseen the day when Russia might need more grain than they could grow. It would help to have a friend at the source if a clandestine wheat line had to be established at some point or other.

Then when the time came, the United States just up and sold Russia the wheat as if they were best friends. By the time anybody got the idea to cut off the wheat as a slap on the wrist for the invasion of Afghanistan or some other offense to American sensibilities, America's beloved allies had gotten the idea. They gladly fronted for the Soviets in huge grain purchases. The U.S. Government was perfectly aware of it, of course, but what the hell could they do? If they really clamped down, they'd have the farmers on their throats. So they winked at it, and undercut their own policy. It was things like this that made Gus Pickett sure he had made the right choice all those years ago.

Because the Russians were going to win. Lenin said the capitalists would sell the rope Communists would hang them with. Gus Pickett had never met Lenin; he wished he had. He'd met Stalin, though. Back in the thirties. Gus's father had just died, leaving his son with a Depression-idled mine and foundry. There was little demand at home for what Gus had to sell.

But Europe would be going to war, soon. That was obvious to anyone who could read a newspaper—at least to anyone who didn't have a big, sentimental thing about peace. Gus Pickett was not sentimental about anything. And it took a lot of metal to wage a war.

So he'd scraped together some money and headed overseas. He didn't waste any time with England or France—those idiots were still pretending war was avoidable. Germany didn't need him—Hitler already had the Krupps and the rest of German industry tamed and eating out of his hand.

But the Russians were different. Stalin's five-year plans had gotten a few factories built, but nowhere near what was going to be needed with a war coming up. So they were willing to talk. And while the talking was going on, Gus kept his eyes open. He saw the way the population had been cowed into submission. He heard whispers of the purges; he himself had once seen a man dragged screaming from the lobby of his hotel by three big guys in bad suits and heavy shoes.

And Gus himself had been picked up and interrogated. They didn't rough him up, but they made him plenty uncomfortable—salty food, and no water. Bright lights in the eyes. No sleep. Crude, but effective.

A captain named Borzov was the chief inquisitor. "We know you are spying for the British," he would begin, and Gus would tell him to come off it. After about two and a half days, they'd satisfied themselves that Gus was what he pretended to be, apologized, and invited him to talk business.

Gus had been delighted to. More than delighted, ecstatic. He felt as if he'd come home. Because this was the place that had caught on, this was the system that understood what Gus knew to be the true secret of life.

Power is everything.

Because mankind was just a bunch of animals clawing after the same piece of meat, and it was the nature of man to want the best. The best food. The most comfortable life. The most beautiful women. It didn't matter. The key to happiness was getting exactly what you wanted as soon as you decided you wanted it. And the secret to that was power.

But it was more than that. Capitalists were always being quoted as saying that they did what they did because it was a challenge to them, a game, and the money was just a way to keep score.

That might be true for capitalists. Gus was not a capitalist. He was a survivalist. Not one of these clowns who go off to live in the woods with six rifles and a book of raccoon recipes. A *real* survivalist. Someone who knows that the *real* score is kept in human lives. Do you need to negotiate, or can you crush instead? How many men could you safely have killed? How many families can you reduce to poverty if the whim takes you? In short, how many people owe their lives and livelihoods to the simple fact that they have yet to get on your nerves?

For Stalin, and to a lesser extent for Borzov, the answer to that final question was—and, more important, *rightly should be*—everybody.

A nation run that way *has* to prevail. So Gus went with a winner.

It didn't happen all at once. There was a long period of feeling each other out, and the war offered a certain amount of distraction. But by the late forties, Gus and his war-bloated fortune were at the service of the "Communists." Gus wanted to laugh. As if ideology had anything to do with it, right? Communism was just a convenient label Lenin had seized on (damn, but Gus wished he'd met that guy—they really could have hit it off) to sell the sheep on the idea of volunteering to be lamb chops. At other times, in other places, it had been Fascism or Nationalism or God's will. What it all was was grease on the wheels of the juggernaut that carried those with brains and guts enough to the seats of power.

Gus had known all along that he might not live to see his work finished, to see America brought under the control of one strong man. But here he was, by damn, on the verge of making it happen.

Gus had had his doubts about this Project Atropos business—he was never as certain about this thing as Borzov was. Too many things could happen between now and the inauguration. Despite the Party's overwhelming strength, their candidate could still lose. Stranger things had happened in American politics. Or he could have a heart attack or something. Or the sneaky little double-whammy Borzov had built into this thing could backfire. It was brilliant, and it was tricky, but it was hard to guess what two hundred million people would do in the wake of a shock. They might shrug it off, or they might get disgusted enough to turn off on the whole election. That had come close to happening a few times already.

Borzov had planned things so as to minimize the risk, however. By springing it before a key primary, he reduced the number of voters he had to affect to swing the nomination the right way. By planning the big event for today—Friday—and the day after, he left the media just two days to shake the animals' cages before they went to the polls on Tuesday.

Borzov had been running in luck, too. The race for the nomination had stayed close enough that the last few primaries still made a difference. Now there was only this one and the California primary next week, and as far as anybody could tell, it was still a toss-up between Abweg and Babington. It would take something like a big endorsement to swing things. Something, anyway, to make a splash in the headlines.

Gus Pickett smiled. They'd give them a splash, all right. They'd give them such a splash that by the time they'd wiped the water out of their eyes, Borzov's man would be sitting in the White House.

Of course, real luck would have been if Borzov's man had simply had the horses to pick up the nomination on his own. That way, they could have kept Senator Van Horn on the hook for some other purpose. But no matter how much power you grab, you can never overpower time. This was their candidate's moment; the press, party leaders, everyone who shaped the political climate had proclaimed that this year it was going to be Mr. A or Mr. B. If either of them had decided to pass, he would have looked as if he'd chickened out. It would do nothing to enhance his chances four years down the road.

And there was the personal angle. Borzov wouldn't be alive four years down the road. He knew it, Gus knew it; all you had to do was look at him. He'd conceived this operation, had nursed it through long years of Cold War and Detente and whatever the current catch phrase was. Now, with the present Chairman apparently genuinely wimping out with this *perestroika* nonsense, Borzov didn't want to trust his vision to a successor who perhaps shared the Chairman's utopian ideas.

Gus couldn't blame him.

So they would take the shot. If it failed, Gus would be in no worse shape than he was now, and that wasn't too bad. If it worked . . . well, then, things would get interesting. Their boy looked good, and he spoke okay, and he could handle a press conference. But he was so used to taking orders, he was going to need a lot of good advice running the country.

And Augustus T. Pickett was going to be around to see that he got it. Gus would, in fact, more or less run things his way, with the support and cooperation of the Soviet Union. They may have been going soft, but not so soft that when they got handed the United States of America on a silver platter they were gonna give it *back*.

Gus smiled.

I'll do a good job for them, Gus thought. And for me.

Power. Lots of it.

I win, Gus thought.

CHAPTER TWO

Amber waves of grain flanked the interstate. The farther Joe Albright got from the state capital, the more out of place he felt. He'd had the Congressman's research people check it out before he'd left Washington. There were 70,000 black people in this state, and 68,300 of them lived in the capital. Joe wondered how far he could follow Gus Pickett into the middle of a wheat field before he really started to stand out.

Gus Pickett had been Joe Albright's special project since last month. He didn't tail him all the time, of course, but when he wasn't, he was supervising the people who were. He supposed he should have been flattered. Trotter had told Joe that watching Pickett was a job of incalculable importance; that the only reason Trotter wasn't doing it himself was that he was watching Van Horn, disguised as a mild-mannered reporter. The idea there was that Trotter was going to follow the Senator around until he endorsed either Abweg or Babington. After that, he'd think of some other excuse. In the meantime, Joe was to stick to Pickett (who had never met Joe, something that was untrue of practically everybody else in this case, which, Joe suspected, was the real reason he'd drawn this assignment) like a bad reputation and to keep his eyes and ears open.

Joe looked at the car in front of him, a white Ford Taurus, personally rented by Augustus T. Pickett, eighty-some-odd-year-old jillionaire, at a Thrifty Car Rental office nine blocks from his hotel. Joe had seen him walk by three other places. They probably charged an extra three cents a mile or something.

The old bastard was driving himself, too. Not badly, either. Joe hoped Pickett was concentrating mightily on the road ahead of him, mainly because he didn't want him thinking too much about the road behind him. The Bureau could teach you a lot of useful things about tailing another car, but they had yet to come up with a technique to let you avoid detection when you and another car are on a perfectly straight road in the middle of perfectly flat land. The wheat wasn't even tall enough yet to hide in. Joe's mother frequently said something was "as obvious as a bug on a plate." Now he knew how the bug felt. It was beginning to be a pain in the ass.

Because Uncle Gus was full of surprises. When he'd left his farm in Virginia this morning (the one Hank Van Horn had been spirited off to) there was no indication that he was going anywhere. No luggage, none of the servants saying, "See you next week, Mr. Pickett, have a nice trip." The FBI operative who'd been watching overnight (they were using Rines's people in the D.C. area) had had a hunch and enough self-confidence to share it. He'd decided that from the roads Pickett's limo had been taking, they were on their way to Baltimore-Washington Airport instead of the more convenient Dulles.

Joe didn't put much store in hunches, at least not in other people's, but he couldn't afford for this kid to be right and himself to have done nothing about it. He hauled himself out of bed and made it to Balt-Wash just in time to spot Pickett's arrival. He made a mental note to recommend the kid for a raise.

When the old man got out of the car, he had a suitcase. Obviously packed the night before and stuffed in the trunk of the limo while it was still in the garage. Joe wasn't a Special Agent for nothing.

Pickett carried his own bag through the airport. That was either for extra security (to keep the number of people who knew he'd come to the airport to a minimum) or because Pickett was too cheap to tip a redcap. Considering how famous the man was, Joe leaned toward the latter.

Joe got close enough to the check-in desk to find out where Pickett was going. He let the old man get out of earshot, then talked his way onto the same plane without having to pull his badge. The flight itself was uneventful, though there was a tense moment at O'Hare, between connecting flights, when Pickett seemed to disappear. Joe was trying to work out a plan that would let one man search an entire terminal by himself when he spotted Pickett coming out of the men's room. Obviously one of those people who didn't like to use the johns on the plane.

At their destination, Joe eavesdropped again, this time as Pickett told a taxi driver where to take him. Joe ran back into the airport to the Hertz desk, and arranged for a car to be left for him at the same hotel. It was a breeze to find out what room Pickett had at the hotel—he just asked. So much for the high-security scenario.

Joe checked in himself, but didn't go to his room right away. Instead, he walked up to Pickett's to get a fix on where it was in the building. That done, Joe would go up to his own room, phone home for help, get Pickett staked out, get a meal and go to sleep. This would, of course, entail leaving

Pickett unguarded (Joe would knock on the door to make sure Pickett was in, if he had to) for a few minutes, but a one-man surveillance was an impossibility anyway. The best time to leave a man unattended was when he'd just settled in after a long plane flight. Sometimes you just had to take a chance.

And sometimes fate arranged it so that you never got the opportunity to take a chance.

Joe was just getting off the elevator when he ran into Pickett getting on. The old bastard was *never* going to give him a chance to get any rest. He was still carrying the little overnight bag. Joe sprinted for the stairs and made it to the lobby first. The desk clerk called him over, handed him a set of keys, and pointed to a red Chevy Camaro parked outside.

"Thanks," Joe said.

"We'd appreciate it if you'd move it as soon as possible," the desk clerk said. "It's a no-parking area."

"Just a couple of minutes," Joe said. The elevator arrived and let Gus Pickett and a bunch of people wearing Babington buttons out into the lobby.

"We'd appreciate it," the desk clerk said again.

Joe looked at the desk clerk, fighting mightily against the urge to turn around to see where that peripatetic old bastard was headed now. Gus Pickett had seen altogether too much of Joe's face in the last few hours.

"Yeah. Well, I'm going out right now; I'll move it."

"The hotel has an excellent garage just around the corner on Marshall Street."

Joe picked up his quarry with his peripheral vision. He was going out the front door, right past Joe's car, in fact.

Joe renewed his promises to the desk clerk and beat it. Outside, he squinted in the bright midwestern sunshine as he looked around for Pickett. There he was, down the block, just about to cross the street.

If Joe had had to make a U-turn to follow him, he would have forgotten all about his promises to the desk clerk and taken off after Pickett on foot. Since the old man was walking in the same direction the car was pointed, Joe hopped behind the wheel and started up. Besides, even though the billionaire was on foot right now, there was the possibility that he could hail a taxi at any second, or be scooped up in a car he had arranged to have meet him.

But no. He just walked until he found a car-rental place with a price he liked. Joe found a parking place (smaller cities did have some advantages) and waited until he saw Pickett's white hair and rimless glasses behind the wheel of the Taurus.

That had been over an hour ago. Joe was getting hungry. He should have thrown some potato chips or something into his little go-to-hell bag while he was at it. A couple of cans of soda.

They had left the interstate now. Joe was even more paranoid about being spotted. On the interstate, he could simply have been someone driving to Utah or California. On this road, he could be nothing but someone interested in something that was going on in the wheat fields.

A few miles down the road, Pickett hit his brakes, then signaled for a right turn. He was headed, apparently, to a group of gray-white buildings set about a half mile back off the road. It looked like a landing field for UFOs, but, in another flash of brilliance, Joe deduced that they were grain elevators. When the wind blew the wheat aside, Joe could just make out the tops of trucks and the plumes of their diesel smoke. Some of these were undoubtedly the trucks that had passed him and Pickett on the road.

Joe drove by the place where Pickett had turned off. There was a two-lane blacktop road with a cloud of truck-raised dust rising five feet above it, and a sign that said "SkyGrain, Inc.—A Division of ATP Industries."

Oh, great, Joe thought. I've tailed this guy through a night and a day and traveled over a thousand miles to see him go to work.

Still, he was a trained and dedicated agent, and he knew he had to hang around to see if he could learn something. He played with the steering wheel a little to make it look good, then pulled his car off the road. He hurried to the front of the car, pantomiming anger. He knelt by the right front tire, slipped a knife out of his pocket, and stuck the blade into the tread. Then he cursed loudly, in case anyone was listening. He went around to the trunk and got out the jack and the spare.

Trucks were starting to come away from SkyGrain, Inc. Joe figured they had either picked up or left off truckloads of wheat.

A truck about one-third the size of the others came out, turned in Joe's direction, and stopped. The door opened and a young man got out. "Help you with that tire?" he asked cheerfully.

Mark Van Horn.

In blue jeans and a work shirt. Coming out of the other door, dressed the same way, was Senator Henry Van Horn. The work clothes suited the Senator as well as spats would a rooster.

Joe decided to stay and play it out. He'd been at their party, but they might not remember him. He'd talked to the Senator, but there he'd been a Congressman's nurse; he'd been wearing a tuxedo; and he hadn't been talking like Aunt Jemima's favorite nephew, which he intended to start doing in three seconds. There was no reason they should recognize him.

Of course, there was no reason for them to have stopped, either. Joe banished the thought from his mind.

"Man, I sho could. Thank you, mistuh." Joe was making himself sick. He told himself not to be an asshole. He'd make it up to black people everywhere some other time. Right now, he had to get out of this.

Joe wiped his brow. "I swear," he said. "Hot enough to cook aigs inside the hen, today."

"Well," Mark Van Horn said, "we'll have you out of here soon enough. Where's that jack?"

They put the jack together and spun lug nuts. Mark Van Horn lifted the car while Joe got the spare from the Senator and lined it up. They got the new tire on, Mark lowered the car, and the Senator tightened the connections while Joe put the punctured tire in the trunk.

"That ought to take care of it."

"It sho should. I do thank you. Get that tire fixed right away," Joe said.

Joe was suppressing a grin. Not only had he gotten out of it, but he'd conned two members of perhaps the most powerful family in America into helping him change a tire. Now all he had to do was get the trunk closed and get back to Washington with the news that the Senator and his son, wearing clothes that amounted to a half-assed disguise, and driving a truck that only added to it, were meeting with Gus Pickett in the middle of nowhere.

Then Mark Van Horn said, "How about it, Dad?"

"I *think* so," the Senator said. "I can't be sure."

"Think hard, we can't take any chances."

To hell with the trunk. Joe started making for the driver's-side door. Slowly. Unobtrusively, he hoped.

"Sorry, son, I've done the best I can."

"Shit," Mark Van Horn said.

Joe heard quick movement behind him. He turned around just in time to see the flash of sunlight on the jack handle before it crashed into his head.

Chapter Three

It was a simple matter of fact that Sean Murphy had not crawled into a bottle and pulled the cork in after him in the wake of his talk with Regina Hudson. He had no idea *why* it should be true; it just was.

"It's all right, Sean," she kept saying. "It's all right. I trust him. I know all about him, or at least as much as I want or need to know. So don't worry, it's all right."

"It's all right that he's a spy? It's all right that he's using you?"

"He's not using me."

"Well, he's for goddam sure using the Hudson Group as a cover for whatever he's up to. Is it all right that his very presence here corrupts our journalistic integrity?"

"It's not going to happen that way, Sean," she said. Her voice was unfailingly cool, gentle and kind. If Murphy didn't love her so much, he would have kicked her in the knee.

"What do you *mean*, it's not going to happen? It's happening already! I am now not going to print hot stuff on a suspicious character because you're in love with him."

"I appreciate it, Sean, whatever the reason."

"He told me to talk with you, the bastard, he knew you'd be this way. For two cents I'd walk out on the Hudson Group and bring this to somebody else to publish."

Regina got very serious. "I couldn't stop you, Sean."

"Your fiancé could stop me. Permanently."

"He told me on the phone that nothing was going to happen to you."

"How nice of him," Murphy grumbled. "Anyway, that's not the reason I'm hanging around—if I go, who'll look out for you?"

"Thanks, Sean."

"Yeah, don't mention it." Murphy swallowed a bitter taste in his mouth. It was time to change the subject. "All packed?"

Sources in Washington had said that Senator Van Horn was flying out to the Great Plains for the primary on Tuesday. Since he had stayed away from all of them so far except for the one in his home state, it seemed like a good bet he was finally going to anoint somebody with the patented Van Horn political holy water. This was likely to be the biggest story in a tight campaign; the media would be on it in force. Regina was heading out with the troops because of Murphy's belief that her relationship with Mark Van Horn might give them angles the networks and the other magazines wouldn't be able to get.

Regina had gone along with it quite sweetly, saying something about the importance of using every edge you could get. She might make a newswoman yet.

Then she had a little scoop for him. "Allan is coming, too."

Murphy kept his lips tight together for ten seconds. His brain rejected a hundred possible comments about who was using whom for what. Finally, he just said, "He is, huh?"

Regina laughed, warm and happy. Even though he knew she was kidding herself, he found it impossible not to at least smile when he heard that laughter.

"Don't worry," she said. "This way you'll be able to keep an eye on him."

So here they were, one big happy traveling jug band, about to play a gig in the state capital. The propeller of the plane (Murphy hated prop planes) chopped the light reflected from the capitol building's dome into little pieces of golden glitter as they circled low on the approach to the airport.

The gold leaf on that dome was probably the flashiest thing in that whole state, Murphy thought, but right here, over the next four days, the people in this state who bothered to vote in the primary (less than half of them) would be giving the world a strong nudge in one direction or another for the next four years.

They split up at the airport. Murphy was going to scare up some contacts in the Abweg and Babington campaigns while Regina and Trotter checked in at the headquarters the Hudson Group reporters had established at the building that housed the local Hudson Group paper. The ban on using the local journals to stretch coverage for *Worldwatch* didn't apply to real estate, only personnel. Regina would go there, show the troops the executive colors, give a pep talk, cast aspersions on the networks and the other national newsweeklies, then go to her hotel and wait to see what Murphy had been able to set up with the Van Horn family or any member thereof.

He didn't know what Trotter was going to be doing. He tried not to think of it.

Trotter hadn't done much of anything on the way out here. It was almost as if he had been going out of his way not to get Murphy upset. That was ridiculous. Trotter had already shown he didn't give a damn about Murphy one way or the other. Maybe he was doing it to please Regina. Maybe he was doing it to drive Murphy crazier than he already was.

He was succeeding at both.

Murphy put it out of his mind, just as he put out of his mind what Regina and Trotter were likely to get up to once she got back to the hotel.

The Van Horns were staying at the Ambassador, where Babington had his headquarters. Hudson Group reporters had checked that little fact out for significance, but had found none—Senator Van Horn had actually booked in first. The local Babington organization had apparently moved their rally here from an Elks club outside the city limits when the primary shaped up to be a bigger deal that it had seemed the year before.

Still, it was convenient. Murphy could talk to Van Horn people and Babington people all under the same roof.

In situations like this, Murphy preferred to enter hotels through the service entrance. Altogether too many people made a habit of hanging around hotel lobbies, sometimes even as lookouts posted to warn of approaching journalists. When you used the service entrance, not only did you get to meet a lot of interesting people who worked for the hotel, you usually got to talk to one or two of the people you wanted to talk to before the whole building was aware a reporter was on the premises.

You also, sometimes, got to see things you never expected to see. In this case, what Murphy saw was Senator Hank Van Horn and his son, dressed in work shirts and blue jeans (a phenomenon in itself) slipping into the service entrance just ahead of him, looking around them like two desperate farm boys determined to rob the place.

Murphy wanted to know about this. As quietly and unobtrusively as he could, he followed them past the loading dock and through the kitchen.

Murphy was enjoying himself. He'd risen high in his profession, but in the rising, he hadn't forgotten how much he liked being the savvy street reporter, how much fun all this cloak-and-dagger stuff could be. He wondered for a split second if his hatred for Trotter wasn't heightened by a twinge of jealousy at the realization that for Trotter, the cloak-and-dagger stuff never had to stop.

The Van Horns walked down a gray-enameled hallway to the service elevator. Murphy had to decide whether to let them go or jump on with them and see how they reacted.

In his current mood, it was no contest. The years rolled back, and he was Sean Murphy, street reporter, covering land swindles for the Hudson Group paper in Bemidji, Minnesota. He would dare all, find out all, tell all. He waited until the doors were about to close, then jumped on.

"Senator!" he said happily. "Mark! I was hoping to run into you."

The Van Horns each put on a version of the irresistible Van Horn family smile and stuck out hands to shake. A startled animal falls back on instinct; all the Van Horn instincts, Murphy knew, were political.

"Murphy," the Senator said heartily. "I wouldn't have thought a little thing like a primary would get you out of the office."

Murphy kept his face deadpan. The Senator had made a mistake already. A politician, caught off-guard, should *never* be the first one to mention any matter of substance.

"You make it important by being here, Senator. I don't suppose you're willing to give me a little hint as to whom you'll be endorsing."

Mark Van Horn chuckled. Murphy saw shrewdness in the young man's eyes.

"That's why we're here on the service elevator," Mark said, mock-ruefully. "To avoid questions like that."

"And the work clothes are just a disguise?"

Mark Van Horn laughed; his father followed a split second later. "I suppose in a way they are," the Senator said. "We eastern types never see enough of the farm belt."

"I've never seen it at all," Mark said. "Except from an airplane. That's bad."

"Especially for a young man with connections and political ambitions?" Sean said.

Still smiling, the Senator held up a hand. "Let him finish law school before we get started on questions about political ambitions, shall we?"

"Let's just say it's bad for someone who's concerned for the whole country," Mark offered.

"Right," Murphy said. "I think that answers any questions about political ambitions."

Everybody laughed. Just a rollicking group of pals, Murphy thought, that's us. Well, nobody was going to accuse him of not keeping his end up. "And besides," he said, "more than one politician has come to grief because he didn't know a tractor from a combine."

"He had that explained to him this very day," the Senator said.

Murphy looked at the indicator lights on the wall of the elevator. There weren't many floors left. Time to get serious.

Mark Van Horn wouldn't let him. "How did you come to take the service elevator, Murphy?"

"Oh, I saw you duck into the building. It was obvious you were trying to avoid journalists, so I figured this was a good chance to get you alone."

His pals laughed at that one, too. Murphy went on. "Seriously, Senator, I'd like to get you alone again, for a real interview for *Worldwatch*. Regina Hudson would probably want to sit in."

"I'm giving no interviews until after the primary."

Murphy frowned. "Too late for us. How about right after you make your endorsement?"

"If I make one."

"Of course. If you make one."

"I think that will be all right. Mark, remind me to tell Ainley."

The Senator's son said he would, the elevator stopped, the doors opened, the men got out. Murphy told them he'd gotten what he wanted, and would be heading back down.

As soon as the door closed, Murphy knelt. He ran his fingers along the floor of the elvator and looked at them. Chaff. Bits of stem. Wheat dust. You don't break into journalism in rural Minnesota without learning a lot about wheat. The Van Horns had been more than touring the Great Plains today, they'd been rolling in it. Murphy had been able to smell it on them, see it on their clothes, in their hair.

They looked—well, they looked as if they'd had a wrestling match in a recently emptied silo.

Chapter Four

When they returned to the hotel, Trotter sent Regina upstairs with the bellboy. He stayed behind to use a pay phone in the lobby. He dialed the Agency's 800 number, said a code word ("incipient," as in, "Please hurry, I'm in a pay phone and rain is incipient"). They put him through to Rines.

"Okay," he said. "I'm at the Trent Hotel, Room 636. What do I do now?"

"Anything you want, as long as you stay in touch."

"I was hoping you'd say that."

Rines made a noise in his throat. He really was a prude. "No word from Albright, yet. He booked a room at the same hotel you're at—computer flagged the Agency credit card—but he hasn't called in. Pickett's there, too."

"That was why he was following the man, right?"

"He may still be following him. As far as we can tell, Pickett's out, too. Maybe Albright is on to something."

"Let's hope."

"Right. I'll get you two together as soon as he checks in."

"Right," Trotter said. As he replaced the phone, he was thinking, *just give me an hour or two before you check in, Joe.*

Because Trotter had discovered something almost unbelievable about himself. He was absolutely in love with the idea of having a child with Regina Hudson. Not just having one, *raising* one. Loving one. The idea had turned on a light somewhere inside him that got brighter and brighter as time went on.

It illuminated things he'd never seen before. It used to be that his life consisted of the job, with its roller-coaster mix of terror and exhilaration, pride and disgust—or of emptiness. Now there was something—at least the *possibility* of something (they'd been at this for several months now, without success)—that could supply a better reason than "habit" when he looked for reasons to go on.

The whole project had done wonders for Bash, too. She used to feel the weight of the Hudson Group and of her mother's past like sacks of concrete strapped to her shoulders. Now her attitude was "Screw it—I'm young, I'm rich, and I'm doing the best I can."

She was doing it as often as she could, too. When Trotter got into the room, Regina had already drawn the shades, turned on the air conditioner, and climbed in bed.

"I missed you," she said.

"Business, business, business," Trotter said. He started taking off his clothes.

The air in the room was cool on his skin, cool enough to be an added incentive for him to join the warm woman under the covers. Bright sunlight sneaked in around the edges of the shades and made stripes across the bed. One slash seemed designed to highlight for Trotter some of his favorite places to kiss—the place where her breast began to swell, her throat, her chin and mouth. As if he needed the help.

He slid in under the covers. "You made it cold in here," he said.

"We'll warm it up," she told him, then kissed him.

Bash was right. They had it warmed up in no time. Soon, she was wet and open for him, and he joined with her. Once again they told each other "I love you." And once again Trotter felt the wonder and delight of realizing he really meant it.

Regina said, "Oh," then she said it twice more, then covered Trotter's face with hot, wet kisses. He thought of how happy he was, he thought—but then he was beyond thought, just feeling it surging, exploding, subsiding.

Regina snuggled up next to him. "You think that one did it?"

"Maybe. Let's get married soon. Like next week."

"Even if it didn't," Regina went on, "I'm having just the best time trying—What did you say?"

"I said, let's get married next week. Right after the stupid primary."

"I thought you were saying we'd do it after this job of yours was done."

"I've come to realize that there'll always be another job. You can't wait for things to be perfect before you do anything; you've got to do them when you're ready to, and to hell with everything else."

"And you're ready now?"

"Mmm hmm. How about you?"

"I'm ready. I've been ready. And I never wanted a big wedding, anyway."

They laughed together, for no special reason, then told each other "I love you" in various ways until they drifted off to sleep.

The telephone woke them. Regina gave a little scream, the way she always did when awakened suddenly, then grabbed the phone. She said hello, listened for a second, then extended the receiver to Trotter. "For you," she said. "Rines."

Trotter groaned. "What time is it?" he asked.

"Seven o'clock," Regina said.

"Eight o'clock," said the voice on the phone. "Seven, where you are."

"What's up?" Trotter asked. "You want me to move to another phone and call you back?"

"Don't bother, the line is secure."

Trotter wanted to ask if he was sure, but he had faith in the Agency's communications department. "Besides," he said aloud, "all the people who were good enough to tap us are dead, now."

"Am I supposed to understand what you're talking about?" Rines demanded.

"I don't see how you could. I don't."

"No word from Albright."

"That's bad. Maybe we ought to get some people looking for him."

"Did that two hours ago," Rines said. "I didn't bother telling you because you're not supposed to have any contact with them anyway. I made up a client and sent some of my best young private ops. Happened to have them in Chicago, just winding up a legitimate, money-paying case, so I sent them on to where you are."

"Yeah." Trotter was rubbing the back of his head. "Let me know if they find anything."

"That's what I'm doing."

"Already? I'm impressed. What did they turn up?"

"Albright's rental car. Out in the middle of a wheat field or something. Wide open, trunk up."

"Accident?"

"Not so my people could tell. Battery was dead from the dome light's being on because the door wasn't latched right. Donut tire on the right front, flat in the trunk. And, Trotter?"

"Yeah?"

"My people say the tire was deliberately spiked."

"So Joe found something interesting on the road and wanted an excuse to stop and watch it."

"That's the way I read it."

"And somebody objected."

"No signs of a scuffle. Maybe he ran off."

"You believe that?"

Rines's voice was tight. "No more than you do. The question is, what did they do to him?"

"The question is," Trotter said, "if they took Joe away, whatever shape he was in, why did they leave a car directly traceable to him right out on the open highway?"

"It was open highway, all right. Took my people less than three hours to get onto it. Crop duster spotted it, radioed it in; my boys picked it up on the police radio and got there first. They might as well have tied a red helium balloon to the thing."

"Stupid," Trotter said. "This doesn't make sense. This doesn't seem like Borzov or any of his myrmidons. Just talking about him, I use words like 'myrmidons.' I mean the KGB makes mistakes, but this is amateur night. Just like the killings of the electronics guys."

"You keep coming back to that," Rines said, impatiently.

"Yeah, I do, don't I? I wish to hell I knew why. Listen, Rines, I'm going to hit the bricks and try to see what's going on around here."

"Check in. Frequently."

Trotter promised he would, and hung up.

He turned to Regina. "How much of that did you understand?"

"Enough," she said. "Joe Albright's in trouble, isn't he?" She looked worried. She had gotten to know Albright well over the past year, and she liked him.

"The probability is high. Where's the best place to find Murphy right now?"

"You have to ask? At the paper, Hudson Group's headquarters for the primary."

"Get dressed. That's where we're going."

"Don't I get to eat? I'm starving."

"I've got to talk to Murphy first. Then you can eat." Trotter already had his shorts on, he was reaching for his pants. Regina sighed and got out of bed.

"It was so nice for a while."

Trotter looked at her while she stretched. She was as lithe and unself-conscious as a seal.

"I'm sorry," he said. "I've got to talk to Murphy."

That was a lie. He did not have to talk to Murphy. He had yet, in fact, to decide what he was going to say to Murphy when he caught up with him. What Trotter had to do was to get Regina into the middle of a group of people, especially a group of alert, active, and suspicious people. Like newspaper reporters, for instance. He wanted a lot of eyes open when Regina was around, because he might have to leave to take care of something (you never knew in this business), and someone had already taken Joe Albright, a trained agent.

After that, anything might happen.

Chapter Five

At first, Joe Albright thought the buzzing was in his head. The *pain* was certainly in his head, now a dull throb, now bright bolts of lightning that threatened to hard-boil his eyeballs from the inside.

Joe coughed. He felt as if he wanted to blow his nose, but he didn't think his skull retained enough structural integrity to stand the strain. Every time he took a deep breath, his lungs filled with some kind of airborne crud that made him want to cough some more. He contented himself with shallow breaths.

The buzzing was loud, and consistent. It seemed to be the one thing about his current situation that didn't strengthen or fade each time he moved or thought. The noise was a combination of a whoosh, a whine, and a hum, and the part of Joe's brain that was conscious enough to be aware of it was convinced that, given time, the noise alone would be enough to give him one hell of a headache.

Joe groaned and came a notch closer to full consciousness. "Positively no smoking," he mumbled. *Why the hell did I say that?*

Senator Van Horn's kid had cold-cocked him with the tire iron. That was the last thing he remembered for sure. The Senator and Mark coming out of the silo farm, their pickup truck tiny in the middle of the armada of trucks hauling grain away. *Can we help you fix that tire?* Sure. Wham!

After that it got a little hazy. No. First it got wiped out completely. Then it got a little hazy. He remembered (in a dreamy sort of way) being lowered from the cab of the pickup and being half-carried, half frog-marched somewhere. That must have been when he'd seen those emphatic, red-and-white NO SMOKING warnings. "Danger of explosion or fire," Joe said.

Suddenly, he was wide awake. "Sure!" he said triumphantly, and sat up.

Big mistake. Sitting up hurt his head. Shouting had caused him to take in too much of the dirty air, which made him cough and hurt his head all the more. Joe spent the next five minutes rolling around on the hard floor, holding his head together with his hands, alternately coughing and whining and saying "shit" over and over again.

Finally, the pain diminished. It didn't vanish. It didn't come close to vanishing. It didn't even get back down to where it had been before. But it stopped filling Joe's whole mind with agony; it left him enough brain cells to sustain a coherent train of thought.

Okay, Joe told himself, okay. Take it easy. Don't move around.

A voice inside him sneered. *As if you had a choice. Man, your head been whupped and fucked up good. You better see a doctor.*

Joe told the voice to shut up. Unless there was a doctor's office inside this silo, it was going to be a while before he saw one, and that's all there was to it.

That's where he was, of course. Inside one of those recently emptied silos. The droning he heard was the exhaust system, venting the inevitable particles of chaff and wheat dust that the unloading of one of these things leaves behind. That explained the NO SMOKING signs, too. Fine flammable particles suspended in air in a confined space made a powerful explosive. Every year, a couple of these things went up around the country, sometimes one of the little round deals you saw next to a quaint red barn, less often one of the huge, empty skyscraper-like things that were visible for miles in the middle of the prairie. Joe was sure of all this, but he wondered how he knew it. He decided he'd seen it on "Mr. Wizard" when he was a kid. Sure. Mr. Wizard blew up a tin can with cake flour, and talked about the silo problem. He wasn't sure how big this one was—about medium, he guessed. About the size of a three-story tenement.

All right. So much for where he was. Now, why was he here? Okay, he was here because nobody would think of looking for him in such an insanely dangerous place, but why was anybody *hiding* him?

He had a terrible time with that one until he remembered what brought him to the middle of these amber waves of grain in the first place. He'd been tailing Gus Pickett. He'd followed Gus Pickett, and found Senator Henry Van Horn. And his son. The Van Horns had seen him and, despite his fondest hopes, recognized him from the party they'd thrown.

The Van Horns hadn't wanted it known that they were meeting with Gus Pickett on the eve of what looked to be the decisive primary. Why? Senator Van Horn was known to be a friend of Pickett's. What did they have to hide?

The very fact that they were meeting on the eve of the primary. This close to the Big Endorsement, a meeting with the famed billionaire might lead to questions. Of course, the Senator had sloughed off bigger questions than "Why were you playing farmhand?" and gotten away with it.

So it could be that the reason behind it all was very big; so big they didn't want to risk *any* questions being asked.

What could be that big?

Borzov in the country, right, fool? Man, you in worse shape than I thought.

Right, right, Albright said. God, his head hurt. He wondered who that voice was. He decided it was himself from his blacker-than-thou period as a teenager, the time when he was going to be so tough and smart and cool that the world would just roll over and play dead for him. Joe wished the little snot would go away.

Still, he had a point. Borzov was in the country. Gus Pickett had for years been suspected of fronting for Moscow. And now here was Senator Van Horn sneaking away in a half-assed disguise to meet with Pickett.

Maybe the Senator was selling his endorsement, and therefore, a good shot at the White House.

Joe felt a chill that wasn't caused by the state of his skull. Trotter had said the KGB man was pulling some kind of stunt with the election.

But the Van Horns? The family of millionaires and war heroes and astronauts? What could the Senator be selling out *for?* The Van Horns had more money than God, and they had more power than anybody sane could possibly want. Senator Hank had very likely gotten away with *murder,* for God's sake, what more could Russians give him?

They could refrain from playing a tape one of the dead audio men had made. Just as Trotter had speculated.

So much for that for a while. Try another question.

Like what? the snot wanted to know.

Like why am I still alive? Joe responded silently.

All right, they didn't want me talking about their meeting to whomever I might work for, or to the press. Fine. They went upside my head to keep that from happening. They damn near killed me as it was; one more shot would have done it. Why didn't that blow fall?

Because, fool, they want to find out what you and your friends know already. And they aimin' to find out.

Joe didn't like the snot he had once been, but he had to admit the kid was shrewd. It looked as if there was a lot more unpleasantness ahead.

A big shaft of daylight spilled into the haze of the flour dust as a door slid open about ten feet from Joe. The space was filled by two big men who might have been twins. Both were blond. Both squinted against the dust. Neither smiled.

In a surprisingly gentle voice, one of them said, "Stupid sons of bitches."

The other said, "Come on, now, Ed, what did they know?"

"They might never have known anything, the jerks," Ed said. "Look at him. They threw him in here with hard shoes on, with his belt with a metal buckle. All it takes is one damn spark."

Joe wished he could scramble to his feet and dash past the two men to freedom. He wished he could at least show some kind of fight before they got to him. He couldn't. There was only one thing he could do. He rolled over on his belly and started rubbing his belt buckle against the hard, cold floor.

It might have only taken one spark, but the spark didn't come. Four strong hands lifted Joe from the floor as though he were a toy.

Chapter Six

The Senator's press conference was set for nine o'clock Central time, early enough for the West Coast feeds of the networks' news, but more importantly, in plenty of time to be the front page of all of tomorrow's morning papers. Saturday was usually a slow news day. And the Senator would be available to fly back to Washington in time to do at least one of the Sunday public affairs shows.

Ainley Masters had taken the lead in setting this all up, something Senator Van Horn's press secretary didn't appreciate. But while the press secretary, an aging True Believer who'd been a small-town editor back in the home state, wasn't too bright, he was clever enough to have caught on long ago to the fact that when it came to Van Horn interests, there was no territory forbidden to Ainley Masters.

That, at least, was the way it used to be. Ainley wasn't so sure it still applied. He had the feeling he was being frozen out, not just by the Senator now, but by Mark. Ainley hadn't planned on coming on this rustic jaunt at all until Mark announced his determination to follow his father. Since the kidnapping, Ainley had been loath to let the boy out of his sight. So he came.

He might just as well have stayed in Washington. Since their plane had landed, Ainley had not gotten so much as a hello from either his present or future employer. The only reason he had busied himself at all with the arrangements for Hank's press conference was to have a report to bring them, to have some excuse to lay eyes on them.

A couple of security men lounged casually outside the door of the Van Horn suite. Ainley had arranged for that, too. He wanted to have the Senator and his son (especially his son) attended by full-time bodyguards, but they were having none of it. Reports Ainley had been getting, telling of long, secret trips by the two Van Horns, did nothing to add to his feeling of security.

It was as if being kidnapped, and seeing a young woman murdered in front of his eyes, had had no effect on Mark whatever. Perhaps, God forbid, Mark was more his father's son than Ainley had imagined.

Ainley had taken to carrying a gun himself, a .25 caliber automatic. A little popgun, really, all but worthless for anything otl.er than fighting off a face-to-face attack, but at least it was *something*. He was no hero, but he wasn't a fool, either. He'd taken lessons. If he needed to use the gun, he could. And would, if it meant protecting his own life or that of a Van Horn.

Ainley nodded to one of the security men, who nodded back and told him the Senator and his son had been in their rooms for the last hour and a half or so. Ainley decided to be grateful for small favors. He knocked on the door.

Mark Van Horn said, "Ainley! Come on in."

Ainley looked at him and rolled his eyes. Mark was wrapped in a towel.

Mark grinned. "Caught me again. Dad's in the shower now. Wait a minute while I get dressed."

It wasn't much more than a minute. Mark came back wearing blue jeans and a rugby shirt open at the neck. He looked much younger than his years; he really was a handsome young man.

"I'm glad," Ainley said with some asperity, "that you weren't both showering, or I might not have gotten in at all."

Mark grinned. "We have been kind of busy," he said.

"There was a time when I was trusted to know the Van Horns' business," Ainley said.

Mark was suddenly serious. He came to Ainley, clapped a hand to the older man's shoulder, and left it there. Ainley could feel the weight of it. He could almost imagine he felt its warmth through suit and vest and shirt and underwear. He did not speak.

Mark looked deeply into Ainley's eyes. "Ainley, please, don't worry about this. I know what's bothering you, and I don't blame you. It's just that some things are going on—"

"Going on?"

"Well, being discussed. Things that will change the organization of the family. Things that concern me."

The hand was still on his shoulder. Ainley tried to ignore it. "Things that concern me?"

"If they concern me, Ainley, they concern you. I'd no more think of taking on a responsibility without you to shepherd me through it than I would try to shave with a lawn mower."

Ainley usually had complete control over his emotions, but that was slipping. Right now, he would have been hard-pressed to name *what* he was feeling.

"It's very gratifying to hear that," he said. "But I'd still like to know why I haven't been a party to any of these 'discussions' of 'things.'"

"Ainley, I swear, I'll explain later. It's no reflection on you, I promise. You've got to trust me; stand by me." Mark put his other hand on Ainley's other shoulder and squeezed. "I *need* you, Ainley," he said.

Ainley felt as if he should make some response, but for the first time in his life, he was at a loss for words.

Just then, the Senator walked in, wearing a royal-blue robe. Mark's hands fell from Ainley like dead birds. Ainley himself jumped back, as though he'd been caught doing something shameful.

The Senator, as usual, was oblivious. "Ainley," Hank Van Horn said heartily. "Where the devil have you been keeping yourself?"

Ainley decided to let it pass.

Mark said, "Ainley was just coming to tell you the details of the press conference, Dad."

"Oh. Good work, Ainley."

Just then, Mark winked at him. Ainley found it hard to suppress a grin. "Thank you, Senator," he said. "The conference is set for 9:00 P.M. in the Grand Ballroom on the eleventh floor of this hotel. There will be a brief statement by you, I assume giving your endorsement . . ."

The Senator ignored the hint. Ainley went on. " . . . followed by questions from the press. There will be a buffet and reception afterward, which should put the press in a good mood after the questions."

"It doesn't always work," the Senator said.

Ainley ignored him. "Ordinarily, I would arrange for the endorsee to arrive sometime during the proceedings for photo opportunities—"

"That's a good idea, Ainley. You should do that."

"You have not told me, Senator," Ainley said in a tight voice, "whom you are endorsing."

The Senator was shocked. "I *haven't?*"

Ainley's voice was very quiet. "No, Senator."

At which point, the Senator called himself a fool (a pronouncement on the Senator's part equally remarkable for its rarity and its accuracy) and told Ainley whom he was endorsing. This was followed by an apology so offhanded Ainley suspected it was actually sincere.

"Will you get in touch with his people and ask them to be there?" Mark said.

"I'll handle it," Ainley said. He stood up, shook hands all around, and left feeling much better than he had when he arrived.

CHAPTER SEVEN

The Senator sat down and beamed at his son. He had a feeling of happiness he supposed was parental pride. Hank had to admit to himself that that was a feeling he never expected to experience—he hadn't had that much to do with raising Mark, after all. Still, whatever he'd done, it must have been the right thing. Hank chuckled.

Mark was sitting on the sofa, his legs stretched way out in front of him. He'd been staring at his toenails in apparent fascination, as though they were tiny television screens. Now he lifted his head and looked at his father. "What are you laughing at, Dad?"

"Oh, just a thought I had. This family has had everything but the White House and a motto; I expect you'll take care of the White House."

Now Mark smiled. "One way or another, Dad," he said, "I promise I'll take care of the White House."

"Well, I just came up with the motto—*Whatever we do, it must be right.*"

"I like that," Mark told him. "Nice double meaning and everything."

The Senator frowned. He thought hard for a few seconds, then he got it and grinned. "My God, we might actually be able to use it."

"Well, let's save it for a while, okay, Dad?"

"Whatever you say, son." Hank Van Horn had probably said those words a hundred times over the years, but they were empty things, a way to get the kid off his back. "Whatever you say, son," had really meant "Go bother the housekeeper about it, or your mother, or Ainley, or the driver, or whomever. Don't bother me."

This time, for the first time, he meant the words literally. Hank had thought *he* was smart and tough. Van Horns were *raised* to be smart and tough. But Mark had them all beat—the dead war hero, the dead astronaut, all of them all the way back to the patriarch. What Mark had done was simply—staggering.

And he had done it all for his father.

Hank had found out about what Mark had been up to shortly after the Russians had returned him. They'd gone back to the Van Horn town house for the first of these little father-son chats.

And Mark had told him. *Twelve* of them. His son had killed twelve of the bastards without a second thought. Just to get him out from under, which, as Mark had pointed out, the kidnapping and Helen's murder by the Russians proved it was essential to do.

"They said they'd look out for you, didn't they?" Mark had demanded. "This proves they won't care."

At first, Hank had refused to believe it. But when Mark told him the whole story, beginning with his having cracked the wall safe the Senator had been so careful to have installed, and ending with the death of the last possible wiretapping bastard in Minneapolis, the Senator could do nothing but sit there shaking his head in awe.

He had begun to see why Ainley had always been so gaga over Mark. Hank would ask his son questions, and Mark would deflect him with, "Don't worry, Dad, it's all part of a plan I have," and the Senator wouldn't even mind. For now, Mark said, all they had to do was to follow whatever instructions Gus Pickett passed along from General Dudakov. The General himself had stayed back in Washington. Apparently he wasn't feeling too well, and anyway, it might look a little fishy for a Russian general to follow the band to a key primary.

Since all Hank had been doing was following instructions in any case, Mark's plan was easy to keep to. They had run into a bit of trouble when they'd run into that Albright character, on the way out of the meeting where Gus Pickett had finally told Hank who the hell he was supposed to endorse.

The black man bothered Hank. "I think we ought to finish him, you know," he said to his son.

"Of course, Dad," Mark said. "But we've got to find out who he's working for, and what he might have told them."

"You told me Ed and Jeff don't think he knows anything." Ed and Jeff were muscle that worked for Gus Pickett. Mark hadn't been too impressed with them. He said they got their ideas of how to be smart and tough from reading private-eye novels.

"I'll find out for sure tonight. After your speech, and the interview with Regina Hudson."

"Oh, son, I want you with me during the reception." Hank tried to keep the disappointment out of his voice; he didn't entirely succeed.

Mark shook his head. "As much as I'd like to, Dad, no. This is your night, yours and the candidate's."

"If it's my night, then I should be able to have my son with me if I want to."

Mark shook his head again. "No, Dad, the press would see it as my political 'coming-out' party, and I'm not ready for that, yet. Plus, we don't want to upset the General. He's planned for years and years for you to make just this statement at just this time in such a way that it will make the greatest possible impact. If anything happens to dilute the attention your endorsement is supposed to get, he may be angry. And we're not ready to defy him, yet."

Hank scratched his head. "You're right. Of course, you're right. Should have seen it myself."

"That's okay, Dad," Mark said.

"There's still one thing I don't understand, though."

"Yes?" Was that a trace of impatience in his son's voice? No, couldn't be. No man had ever had more convincing proof that his son loved him.

"I still don't understand *how* taking care of those twelve . . . *people* is going to help. There's still a tape, and you-know-who still has it. What's to stop him from playing it once we do defy him?"

"I told you, Dad, it's all part of the plan. Nobody who hears that tape will believe it, I promise."

"Well, okay, but—"

"Dad, if I work this right, the General won't dare even *play* the tape."

And his son smiled so warmly that the Senator could do nothing but believe him.

Chapter Eight

The word had leaked, as the word always does. An aide brought the news to the candidate at his suite. The aide was controlling his face. The candidate was, too. He put a slight smile on his face, and asked the aide to leave him alone with the news for a while. He'd speak to the whole staff when the news was absolutely official.

The candidate (in lighter moods he liked to think of himself as "The Siberian Candidate," or "The Muscovian Candidate") went into his private bedroom and locked the door behind him. He felt more excited than he had since he was a boy, and had first started on this road. He had to cork his mouth with both hands to prevent unseemly squeals of joy from leaping out.

He could see the headlines now—VAN HORN ENDORSES BABINGTON. The press interviews. The photos—the endorser with his arm around the endorsee. Van Horn perhaps kissing Mrs. Babington. Speculation that the Governor might name Senator Van Horn to the second spot on the ticket, or to a senior Cabinet post when, as seemed likely, he was elected in November.

Well, the candidate thought, this is what I've been promised all along. A greased chute straight to the White House. And when I get there, oh, my friends, history is going to be made. Not the kind of history anybody knows about while it's happening, of course. But future generations, the children of one just and happy socialist world, would know him as the man who devoted his life in secret labor to conquer the People's greatest enemy—and that he did it *without war*.

Tonight was the major step. Tonight, Henry Van Horn's destiny redeemed his crimes. You might say that poor Josephine Girolamo had died in fire so the man in this hotel room, in a city in the middle of a wheat field, could neutralize the only real obstacle to the glowing future he saw for the world. The candidate decided that one day, if it proved to be safe, he would cause some important building to be named after the girl as a memorial. There were already too many things named after the Van Horns.

There was a knock at the door.

"Yes?" the candidate said.

"Phone call for you, Congressman. It's Governor Babington."

The candidate grinned. He wanted to laugh out loud.

"Congressman Abweg?" the aide asked.

"Yes, Gary," Congressman Stephen Abweg said. "I'm here. I'll take the call out there."

Abweg shrugged into his jacket, straightened his shoulders, and left the room.

"I suspect it's about Senator Van Horn's speech tonight, Congressman," Gary said.

"Undoubtedly," Abweg told him.

Congressman Abweg was very conscious of his posture and the look on his face as he walked to the phone. The press would be all over his staff once the story broke for sure; for all he knew, some of these people had already been talking. The Congressman had to make sure the reporters heard he took it all with confidence and dignity. That was important.

He picked up the phone and talked to Babington. The Governor hinted at a Vice-Presidential slot for Abweg if he withdrew from the race after tonight's endorsement. Not in so many words, of course, and couched in terms of the "good of the Party."

Abweg declined confidently, and with dignity. He said he would carry on with his campaign until the convention, and let the assembled multitude decide. He would have had to say that in any case, of course, and Babington must have known it.

Abweg decided that Babington had called merely to gloat.

Abweg walked back to his room with more confident dignity. He was thinking *let the poor bastard enjoy it. It's only going to last a day or so before it all comes crashing down on him.*

Chapter Nine

If Murphy ever wanted concrete proof that I'm not a real journalist, Trotter thought, all he'd have to do is look at me now. Trotter smiled. All around him people were talking loud into telephones, or staring into orange-on-black computer terminals, taking in information and feeding it back to Kirkester.

"Yeah, of course it's going to be lit for photos. Damn TV is going to be there, right?"

"No, this has been one of the best-kept secrets in the history of politics. It's like Van Horn himself didn't know who he was going to endorse . . ."

"Something special?" This was Sean Murphy talking, yelling into the phone as everyone else seemed to be doing. He listened for a few seconds, using the pause to stick a cigarette in his mouth and light it with the beat-up old Zippo. He got one puff in before he was yelling into the phone again. "Yeah. Special. I've got something in the works. Your boss talking with the Senator and his son. At least the son. Maybe a tick-tock on how the decision to endorse went. What? Oh, don't worry about the Babington people—they've practically crawled into our pants, they're so eager to give interviews. Yeah, we're trying to put reporters in limos, but most everybody is staying at the same hotel. So . . ."

And so on.

All this is going on, Trotter thought, and I'm sitting here in front of an old black dial phone that whoever remodeled this unused room in the *Capitol Sentinel* had probably left here out of nostalgia, doodling with a pencil on a stack of letterhead so old the address on it doesn't have a zip code.

The last thing he had written was "CHAFF." It was a sound effect, surrounded by a cloud of smoke streaming from the smokestack of an old-fashioned locomotive.

But it was wheat chaff he was thinking of. Murphy had told him and Bash about his service-elevator encounter with the Van Horns when they'd arrived here about an hour ago. He told Regina to try to work that into any conversation she might have with the Van Horns later. He and Regina went to work trying to set up the interview, and doing the thousands of other things that needed to be done when a possible cover story was about to break.

Meanwhile, Trotter sat in the corner doodling. Thinking. He thought of two patrician easterners like the Van Horns pitching in on the farm, and it didn't wash. Besides, most of the farming done out here was by big, successful agribusiness food-growing factories. No political capital in that. If the Van Horns were going to go rural on anybody, they'd help a small farmer who was about to be foreclosed on. And they damn sure wouldn't do it in secret. Anyway, the whole thing smelled wrong.

The phone worked—Trotter had been checking with Rines every once in a while to see if there'd been any sign of Joe Albright. Nothing.

Trotter stared at the phone.

Since his childhood Trotter had been trained to make connections. Put things together. What did he have here? A missing agent. The Van Horns. Gus Pickett. The two men most likely to be the next President. Wheat.

He wrote the words down on the paper and started drawing lines between them. After about three minutes, he threw down his paper in disgust. It wasn't that the procedure hadn't been any help—it had been *too much* help. There were dozens of possible connections, all of them equally likely. Or unlikely.

Another thing lifelong training had done for Trotter was to make him impossible to sneak up on, but it made Regina nervous when he called her name without looking at her, so he usually let her walk up to him and touch him. Besides, he liked it when she touched him.

Her fingers brushed his shoulder. He looked up and said, "Hello, darlin'."

"Darlin'?"

"Trying to blend in with the locals. How's it going?"

"Okay, I guess. I can't get the Senator tonight, but I can get Mark."

"I thought you didn't want him."

"Ha, ha."

"Okay, just kidding. Will Mark do? For *Worldwatch*'s purpose, I mean?"

"I guess so. Anyway, Sean and I are heading over to the Ambassador now; the rental company finally delivered our car. They say there's been an unexpected demand."

Right, Trotter thought, and one abandoned on the road. He shook off the thought. "Going over already? What time is it?"

"Seven-thirty."

Trotter blew, puffing out his lips. "I *have* been out of it. Listen, is Murphy going with you to see Mark Van Horn?"

"He hadn't planned on it. I'm supposed to meet Mark in the lobby of the Trent right after the speech. I'll watch it on TV in the lobby. Mark said he was going to skip the reception after. We'll go get something to eat, and talk."

"Okay, do me a favor. Will Murphy come with you if you ask him?"

"He probably would, but why should I? You don't have to be afraid of Mark."

"I'm not afraid of Mark, okay? I just want you to be with as many people as possible." He lowered his voice. "There's still no sign of Joe Albright."

Regina said, "Oh. I'm sorry, Allan."

"It's all right. Listen, if not Murphy, then *somebody*. Even two somebodies if you can arrange it. Okay?"

"Okay. I promise."

"Good. Babington—and Abweg, too, for that matter—have the Secret Service looking out for them. I have to do the worrying for us."

"Are you going to be okay?" Regina asked him. He loved the concern in her voice.

"I'm a big boy, Bash."

"I mean, when I'm done, should I meet you here, or back at the hotel, or somewhere else, or what? Are you going to have anything to eat?"

"Call here, then try the hotel. And yes, I will get something to eat. Great steaks in these parts, and a steak house every two hundred feet along the sidewalk. I'll probably stagger into one of those."

"Do you have money?" Before he could answer, she said, "Listen to me, 'do you have money.' I probably sound like your mother."

Trotter, who had never known his mother, said only, "I've got money, Bash."

Murphy's voice came from across the room. "Reg—— Ms. Hudson, we should go now." Keeping up appearances in front of the help. What he'd probably started to say was, "Regina, let's shake it!"

In any case, shake it she did. She bent, kissed Trotter quickly on the lips, said "Bye," and was gone.

Trotter went back to staring at the phone. *Do I have any money,* he thought, and grinned.

Then the grin melted into something shapeless, like a candle left too long in the sun. After a few seconds, his face reset in a frown.

There was a word missing from his list. Money. Spies were just like everybody else who worked for the government in at least one respect—they had a tendency to forget that all their glorious plans would take *money*. The Agency had probably spent a *fortune* on this business, just since Borzov hit these shores. The Russians must have spent even more. But in this case, they had an advantage over most agents operating on foreign soil. They had a local source of money. They had, unless the Congressman and Rines were extremely mistaken, an eccentric billionaire for the quick assist.

Trotter picked up the phone and called Rines.

"It's me," he said.

Rines was getting irritable. "Your father and I are getting sick of you. Every time the phone rings, we think it's Albright."

"That answers my first question."

"Right, still no word."

Then the Congressman's voice came. Trotter wondered how long he'd been there. "You got another question for a change, boy?"

"Yeah. What the hell was the excuse for Gus Pickett to come out here in the first place? There hasn't been a word about him since the last we heard from Joe."

"Ask one of your reporter friends," Rines said. "He's rumored to be going to Babington's reception after the speech."

"Your little private dicks have been very efficient. Where is he now?"

"Sitting in his hotel room, peaceful as a lamb."

"Uh-huh. So did anyone ever catch up with his excuse for sneaking out here?"

"Somebody turned up the cover story . . . here it is. He owns a bunch of grain elevators—you know, he wholesales wheat. He's been holding a huge load of it, waiting for approval for it to be sent to Russia, and today's the day they move it out."

"When did the approval come through?"

"What do you think I've got in this system, God? How do I know?"

"I'll bet it didn't come through yesterday," Trotter said. "I'll bet it didn't come in the middle of the night, to send him scampering out of Virginia like somebody beating a hotel bill. I'll bet the shipment was an excuse arranged in advance to cover a trip out here, if Pickett had to make one."

"What's your point, son?" the Congressman asked.

"I'm going to call you back in a little while. Try to find out about approval for that grain shipment, and find out how you get to Pickett's grain-elevator thing—"

"Skygrain, Inc."

"Right. I think that's where Joe Albright might be."

"I'll arrange backup," Rines said.

"Don't arrange anything, yet." It sounded as if Rines had growled, but that might just have been noise on the line. "I've got some thinking to do. There are ramifications here."

"There's an agent out there who needs us."

Trotter heard the Congressman's lazy drawl. "He needs us to do what's gonna work, Rines. He don't need people runnin' in and gettin' killed. Son?"

"Yes, Congressman."

"I'm gonna get the computer people around here asking some questions about the Senator's boy."

"Like where he was when all those audio men were being killed?"

"Exactly like that."

"I was just about to ask you to. I'm proud of you, Congressman."

"Where the hell do you get off being proud of *me* for being smart? Listen here, boy—"

"I'll call you back soon. Happy hunting."

Trotter was smiling as he hung up the phone. The Congressman was still the best, and had proved it. He wondered how long ago the old man had figured out Borzov's game. Trotter had just seen it a few hours ago. It was worthy of Borzov; almost inevitable once it occurred to you.

But it was time to take a new look at Mark Van Horn, too. Whatever was going on, Mark was in on it, now. Perhaps he'd been in on it all along. If that turned out to be the case, the clean bill of health the Agency's investigation had given Mark's father in the deaths of the surveillance men didn't amount to much.

It answered a lot of questions. The Agency had known the Russians wouldn't have been killing these guys to cover up the taping of Hank Van Horn's touching farewell to little Pina all those years ago. They would only have had to kill one man. And even at that, whoever it was had lived long enough to do plenty of damage to the Russians if he was ever going to.

But the Van Horns. The Van Horns. That family had certainly engaged in enough dirty work over the years to have compiled an exhaustive list of bugging experts. Hell, one might even have been compiled years ago in an attempt to figure out who had helped the Russians get the hammer on the Senator. (The fact that the Russians did have the hammer on the Senator now seemed confirmed beyond all doubt.) In any case, a Van Horn would have no trouble finding these guys if he wanted to.

And the Van Horns *wouldn't know* who the right one was. They couldn't even know for sure which of them had ever worked for the Russians. If they wanted to deprive Borzov of a witness to confirm that the tape was genuine, they'd have to kill them all.

And because ever since the fateful fire the Senator had had to keep his nose very carefully wiped (the voters of Van Horn's home state were extraordinarily forgiving, but that's the sort of privilege one shouldn't abuse), who better to carry out the wastings than his beloved son. In whom he was, no doubt, well pleased.

It was probably the start of some half-assed plan to get out from under Borzov. Borzov could not have been happy. No wonder Borzov had thought that the bomb Trotter had made Bulanin send had come from the Senator. It must have been the last straw.

So Mark Van Horn was kidnapped. Just to sort of underline the message. "No more fucking around, okay?" And Helen Fraser had been killed.

Because of your bright idea, Trotter. Your little chess move. It worked fine—in a way, it led to the break in the logjam. Was the girl's life worth it? Would Bash's life be worth it?

"Shut up," he told himself. Reporters looked around at him. Trotter grinned sheepishly and told them he was sorry.

There were no answers. He knew two things—Helen Fraser would visit him in the dark and trouble his sleep for the rest of his life; and Bash would keep no appointments with Mark Van Horn, tonight or any other night. He'd have to head her off at the pass.

In any case, the kidnapping had undoubtedly brought the Senator back to heel; Jake Feder and the other eleven had died for nothing. Given the usual quality of his thinking (and one had to assume that the shrewd Ainley Masters had been left out of this), this stupid plan seemed typical of what the Senator would consider a bright idea.

But not Mark. Mark was smart. Mark, if Trotter was any judge, was as smart as any Van Horn had ever been, and that was saying something. He'd have seen how useless it would be. Wouldn't he?

Trotter picked up the phone. When Rines answered, he simply said, "Anything?"

"Everything," Rines said. "He was in New York, Phoenix and L.A. under his own name when the murders took place there. Five other places, we've got an airline booking for someone fitting Mark's description traveling as Michael Vincent, all in the right cities at the right times. *Including* Minneapolis. Do you want to quibble about the other four?"

"I've never been much of a quibbler."

"Listen, son, I've been thinking . . ."

"Me, too," Trotter said. "Mark's no fool. He'd *know* he could kill everybody who ever owned a concealable microphone, and it wouldn't make a damned bit of difference as long as the Russians had that tape."

"Unless he could give them a good reason *not to play it*," the old man said. "I can only think of one, how about you?"

"Just one. Probably tonight. Maximum publicity. My only question is, before or after the endorsement?"

"Ask him when you find him. In the meantime you realize, there's no way we can get you any help in time."

"I know."

"If we try to bring in any official police or the Bureau, they'd lock *us* up. We've got enough indications for *us*, but not enough for a local cop to collar one of the holy Van Horns."

"I know that, too. Don't worry. This isn't that big a city."

"Better get moving. It's getting late."

Trotter looked at his watch. Eight-oh-five. The speech was set for nine.

"What are you going to do?" Rines asked.

"I'm going to get right over to the hotel and start looking."

"We'll have people out there by morning," Rines said. "To help you mop up, if nothing else."

"Yeah. Or to mop me up. I'll check in later."

Trotter hung up the phone, yelled across the room to the skeleton crew of journalists that he was leaving (keep up the cover at all costs) and walked out into the deep twilight of the June night.

Chapter Ten

The note was written in crude block letters on hotel stationery with a hotel pen. Mark had written it with his left hand using a pebble-grained fake leather phone-book cover as backing. There was no way the handwriting could ever be traced. The Senator would believe it only because Mark was going to deliver it in person.

He was waiting outside the stage entrance of the Grand Ballroom as his father walked next to Governor Babington, laughing and smiling and ignoring the inner shell of Secret Service men and the outer shell of journalists that surrounded them.

Mark managed to filter through. The Secret Service men were going to stop him, but Babington recognized Mark and told his guards to let the young man through. Mark had been counting on that. The Governor was too experienced an operator to take a chance on offending the Senator, especially when he was just minutes away from delivering the endorsement that would all but ensure the nomination and probably the White House.

"Governor," Mark said. "Congratulations! I couldn't be happier. I won't be able to stick around, so I'm getting my best wishes in now."

Babington stuck out his hand. Mark had been expecting that, too. The note rested securely in his left palm. Mark took the Governor's hand, dropped it, then turned to his father. "You, too, Dad," he said. He brought his hands together and shifted the note. "You made the best-possible choice."

The Senator flashed his famous smile for the cameras. "Glad he said that—Mark's got the best political mind in the family." The press, or at least enough of them to gratify the Senator, laughed dutifully. Still playing to the cameras, the Senator shook hands with his son. Mark gave his father a significant look as he passed him the note. The Senator returned the look, then smiled again.

As Mark walked away, he was surprised to realize that he could not remember ever shaking hands with his father before. He must have, he was sure, he just couldn't remember it. It didn't really matter.

The procession entered the Grand Ballroom, leaving silence in its wake. Mark walked about forty yards in the opposite direction. He turned the corner, then stopped at the fire-hose installation. He opened the glass and took a brown paper bag from behind the hose itself. Then he carefully closed the glass, and wiped the handle with his sleeve.

He walked back to the Grand Ballroom. The guard at the door was an amateur. The Secret Service would draw their perimeter closer to Babington, and Mark had no intention of getting anywhere near Governor Babington. This guy remembered Mark from the crowd that had come by before, and waved him right in.

There was a row of dressing rooms in back of the ballroom, accommodations for the second-rate singers and washed-up TV stars that appeared at "The State Capital's Number-One Night Spot!" as the posters in the elevator had it. Mark had been all around here this afternoon. He'd decided on dressing room "D."

Dressing room "D" was farthest from the ballroom itself, closest to the fire stairs. If Babington or Mark's father were to use anything at all, they wouldn't go any farther than room "A."

There was only one chair in the room, a bench, really, stuck in front of a tacky, pinkish-beige lighted makeup mirror. Mark went to it and sat down. There were about ten feet of gray carpet between him and the door. Mark toyed with the idea of facing the mirror, of greeting his father with his back to him, but he decided against it. There was no need to be theatrical. This was far too serious.

And it would go on being serious, even afterward. Even after Senator Henry Van Horn joined the ranks of martyred Van Horn heroes, when no one would dare whisper the name of Pina Girolamo, let alone play so-called "incriminating" tapes of the incident *(what's the matter with you people, have you no sense of dignity at all?)*, when the mantle of holiness, enhanced by the blood of yet another Van Horn, descended on the waiting shoulders of the grieving son, Mark Van Horn would still be in danger.

Because people would know. Not many, but important ones. Ainley Masters, for instance. Ainley could hardly fail to figure it out—Mark, after all, had practically warned him it was coming. But Ainley had winked at murder before, when the power of the Van Horns had been in danger. Who was more aware than Ainley that the greatest danger the family had ever faced was the stupidity of its current head? What would he say if he knew Hank had delivered the power of the Van Horns into the hands of the Russians? Mark would make sure he did know.

Ainley would squirm; he might balk at first. But he'd come along. If things really got desperate, Mark could probably force himself to cozy up to Ainley in a physical way. It had been obvious to Mark since he was twelve that Ainley had it bad for him. Sometimes, Mark wondered if Ainley himself knew.

If that didn't work, Ainley would have to go. It would be a shame. The road ahead would have lots of hidden turns, and there was no better guide through that sort of territory than Ainley Masters.

But in the long run, Ainley didn't matter. Ainley could be taken care of.

The Russians would know, too. General Dudakov, or whatever his real name was.

Mark figured he would have a year, maybe two, before the Russians came after him. They had their own tricky game on, and the death of yet another Van Horn would be a wild card that could cost them the whole thing. They'd take things nice and easy, and secure the White House for Babington before they made any move against Mark.

That, at least, was the way Mark had to play it. That was why he had decided to do this *after* the endorsement speech. Let the Russians have their fun. Their success would be Mark's own.

Because Mark would be in the next Congress—he was over twenty-five, and even now, no power on earth could keep a Van Horn from winning an election in the home state. After Hank was dead, the voters back home would gladly elect him God, if the Constitution allowed it.

But he would be different from all other freshman congressmen. Mark Van Horn would know for a fact that the President of the United States was a Russian agent. And he would have the media access and the clout to get that assertion thoroughly investigated, if not instantly believed, should he choose to make it.

Not that he planned to so choose. It was just that he intended to make sure the White House was very friendly to any legislation he might propose. The legislation, of course, would all be carefully designed to aid and ennoble the American People. It would be even more carefully designed to add to the power and riches of the Van Horn family, as represented by heroic young Mark Van Horn.

His plan was to make himself indispensable. Being on the inside, he could be a great help in furthering General Dudakov's plans, whatever they might be. For a time. After all, Babington couldn't be President forever.

Time would tell. All he could do was to continue to act boldly. He was having a lot of fun in the meantime.

Mark grinned at the door and waited for his father.

CHAPTER ELEVEN

Hank didn't get a chance to read Mark's note until he was actually at the rostrum, about to deliver his endorsement. It wasn't really a problem. He just mixed it in with his prepared statement, and took a moment to look it over before he raised his head to speak.

It was all in a sort of scribbly block printing, but it was legible enough. It read:

IMPORTANT. SEE ME IMMEDIATELY AFTER SPEECH, DRESSING ROOM D BEHIND CURTAIN, STRAIGHT BACK, 3RD DOOR ON RIGHT. TELL NO ONE.

Tell no one. All right. He crumpled the note tightly in his hand, and looked upon the assembled journalists. "I want to get this absolutely right," he said.

He then proceeded to endorse Governor Babington in terms both glowing and vague. It was the best he could do—he hardly knew the fellow. He *did* know Abweg, curiously enough. Things might be a little cool between him and Stephen back under the dome, but that was politics. Nothing personal. Stephen would come to see that in time.

He went on to say that all of the candidates were fine men (though most of them had dropped out after New Hampshire) but that he had decided to lend his support to Governor Babington because of his experience as a chief executive and because of his vision of a greater America.

Hank was an experienced speaker, especially experienced in talking to the press. He could tell when what he was selling was going across. This was going surprisingly well, considering that if anyone thought about it for thirty seconds they would see that he could be delivering exactly the same speech in endorsing Abweg. The only difference would have been that he was backing Abweg for his "experience in the workings of the Nation's Capital" in addition to his vision of a greater America.

This further told Hank that he truly was riding the coattails of history, that the press had been pulling for Abweg all along. Hank had been amazed to discover, years ago, that a lot of reporters honestly believed that the press didn't have a collective favorite it steered toward nomination. After that, they had never worried him again.

Hank finished his speech, and posed for pictures with Babington and his wife. The press hollered questions. Would there perhaps be a job for you in a Babington administration, Senator? "I think I could be of more help in the Senate." What specific programs of the Governor's are you most enthusiastic about, Senator? "It's not the specific programs, fine as they are, that have claimed my support; it's the Governor's *vision* of a greater *America*, as evidenced by those programs, that has led me to back him, as I urge all my fellow Americans to do." Then, with one question answered and one question successfully ducked, he smiled and waved his way to the back of the stage. He took a quick look around. The mob had descended on the candidate; the Secret Service was closing in to protect him. Hank slipped quietly through the blue-green satin curtain.

It was easy enough to find the corridor where the dressing rooms were. Hank looked down the hallway and saw light leaking through a crack at the bottom of one of the doors. He walked over to it. Dressing room "D."

The Senator knocked on the door.

"Come in." It was Mark's voice. The Senator let his breath go. He hadn't realized he'd been holding it.

He stepped inside a small room. Mark was sitting at a makeup table at the other end, facing the door. He had a brown paper bag in his lap.

"Hello, son."

"Hi, Dad." Mark's voice was dead. Hank wondered what was wrong.

"What's up? Anything wrong?"

Mark said nothing. His hand went inside the bag and came out again. It was holding a silenced automatic.

Hank felt something thump against his chest. It was like being hit with a line drive. He tasted dirt in his mouth before he even knew he was falling. His eyes happened to be pointed in the right direction, so he saw Mark stand up and begin to walk toward him.

Hank tried to get up. Failed. Tried to crawl for the door. Mark reached across the top of him and slammed it shut. Painfully, Hank turned over and looked at his son. He wanted to ask why, wanted to ask Mark if he'd gone crazy, but he seemed to be able to make only gurgling noises. Wetness fell down his chin.

Mark said, "Sorry, Dad." The gun coughed again.

Hank hardly felt it. He was thinking, *you didn't have to be so cruel about it.* Hell, I was nicer to Pina; I was, she didn't suffer at all.

As he lost consciousness, he was wondering if maybe Pina would be waiting for him somewhere. And if she held a grudge.

Chapter Twelve

Trotter's luck had been running bad since he'd hit the hotel. He wanted to find Bash in the lobby and tell her her meeting with Mark Van Horn was off. She wasn't in the lobby, and she wasn't in the bar off the lobby. He didn't have time to look anywhere else. The TV in the bar was tuned to CNN, which was carrying Senator Van Horn's speech live from upstairs.

"Screw this," somebody said. "Ain't the Royals playing or something?"

"For Christ's sake, Dave," the bartender told him. "This is history in the goddam making under this very roof."

"Yeah, but it's politics. I don't get politics. I get baseball."

Trotter walked out before the issue was decided.

He made a beeline for the elevators and the Grand Ballroom. This is what I get, he thought, for waiting so long to have my brainstorm.

What he'd wanted to do was to find Mark Van Horn and take him out of circulation quietly, take him somewhere private where he could be made to answer some important questions, such as, was Joe Albright indeed at SkyGrain, and if so, exactly where, and who was watching him? More elaborate questioning could wait until later.

There might not be time for that. The only place Trotter could be sure Mark Van Horn was going to show up was in the vicinity of his father. Mark didn't seem to be the bomb-planting type—he struck Trotter as more the in-your-face kind of killer—but of course you never knew, and wasn't that a jolly thought?

Trotter would have to attach himself to the Senator and wait for Mark to show up, with or without lethal intent. This could be embarrassingly public, not to say dangerous.

Trotter's Hudson Group press credentials got him inside the Grand Ballroom just at the end of the Senator's remarks. Governor Babington was beaming. Trotter had seen thousands of politicians up close, and they invariably beamed brighter the closer they got to the Presidency. He had wondered more than once what kind of psyche it took to rush toward the responsibility for preserving or destroying the world and every living thing on it with a huge smile on your face.

Trotter's gaze passed from Babington to Senator Van Horn. The Senator was beaming, too, but he was doing something else, something rare for any politician and unheard of for a Van Horn. He was effacing himself, almost *willing* himself not to be noticed. Doing a good job of it, too. He posed for pictures, hugging the Governor, shaking hands with the Governor, thumbs-up with the Governor, and then he just sort of backed away from the attention. Trotter might well have been the only person watching him as he slipped through the curtain and off the stage.

If Trotter expected to catch up to him, he had to get moving. There was no chance of duplicating the Senator's route, not unless he wanted to risk being detained, roughed up—or worse—by the Secret Service. Trotter left the same way he'd come in, moving just shy of a speed that would have attracted attention.

As soon as he hit the corner of the corridor, he burst into a sprint. And pulled up to a walk again when he saw the guard at the stage door.

Trotter didn't want to take the time to find another way to get backstage; he would have to take this guy out. The question was, how hard? The kind of measures he'd have to use against a Secret Service man might kill a hapless rent-a-cop. The only thing worse than that would be getting killed himself by someone he failed to take seriously enough.

This guy didn't look Secret Service. Too fidgety, too openly bored. To play safe, Trotter decided to assume the guy was a highly trained state- or city-level cop.

Trotter put on an innocent face and approached the man. "Ah . . . I wonder if you can help me?" Trotter scratched his head.

"What's the problem?" Now Trotter knew he wasn't Secret Service. A Secret Service man would simply have told him to keep moving.

Trotter brought the scratching hand down from his head in a hard chop to the man's neck. He poked stiff fingers of the other hand into his solar plexus. As the guard sank, Trotter grabbed him, reached for his neck, and pinched the carotid until the man's eyes rolled up.

Trotter dragged him through the door and propped him up gently on the other side. He waited a second (he could spare one second) to make sure the man was breathing normally before moving on.

Trotter was standing at the mouth of the short hall that held the dressing rooms when he heard the coughing noise. He knew instantly what it was.

Most Americans, as opposed to, say, most Lebanese, are not familiar with the sound of real gunfire. Compared to the apocalyptic explosions furnished by TV and movie sound-effects men, the sharp pop of a real firearm sounds almost harmless. Even fewer Americans are familiar with the sound of a real-life silenced handgun, but Trotter was one of them.

Damn it! Trotter thought. Damn it to hell. Too late. Silenced gunshot, body falls, mumbles, footsteps, silenced gunshot. That last one had to be the finisher.

Not that Senator Henry Van Horn was any great loss. It might have been fun hauling him in and debriefing him, finding out just what little favors he'd been doing for the Russians through the years, but it wasn't essential. What really bothered Trotter was that he had set out to stop Mark before things got nasty tonight, and he had failed by seconds.

What he did know was that Mark Van Horn was in one of these rooms with a gun, and he'd be coming out any second. Trotter considered waiting for him out of sight just this side of the entrance of the hallway. He thought about it for maybe three seconds before rejecting it. From the layout of the building, there had to be a fire exit at the other end of the corridor.

There was no choice. He had to be right outside the door of the right room (Trotter could see the light under the door) when Mark Van Horn made his exit. The only thing Trotter had going for him was surprise, and that wouldn't last long. The closer Mark got to where he could expect to see people, the warier he'd become.

Trotter tiptoed down the hallway, walking as close to the wall as possible to reduce the chances of his being given away by a creaking floorboard. This would be the worst five seconds—if Mark poked his nose out now, there was nothing Trotter would be able to do but take a bullet.

He made it to the side of the door. He wanted to let go a deep sigh of relief but didn't dare.

Just as well. At that moment, Mark Van Horn came sauntering through the door. Trotter put the energy of his pent-up breath behind a left hook to Mark's face.

Mark staggered backward. He tripped over his father's body and went down. While the Senator's son was still wondering what had hit him, Trotter bent over and picked up the gun. He pointed it a little above Mark's navel.

"Just lie there," he said. "I know how dangerous you are. Daddy makes an even baker's dozen, right? The audio men and the Senator."

"I have no idea what you're talking about. You must be crazy."

"Somebody must," Trotter admitted. "You have *no* idea what I'm talking about? This isn't the dead body of Senator Henry Van Horn behind me on the floor? Isn't he your father? You must understand that much of what I'm telling you."

Mark took a breath as if to speak, then subsided.

Trotter smiled. "That's right, remember the gun. The trouble with screwing a silencer onto an automatic is that you can only get off one shot at a time. You had to reset the gun to shoot the Senator again, didn't you?"

"You need help, Trotter."

"And I plan to get it. I give you credit for guts, Mark. And luck. You could use better brains. If I need help to find out what I need to find out from you, I'm going to get it. Right now, I don't know whether to shoot you or pin a medal on you."

That brought a reaction. "A medal?"

"That's right. By killing your father here and now, you ruined a plan that Borzov—I guess you know him as Dudakov—has been nursing along since your father killed that girl."

"*Ruined* it? What the hell are you talking about? Does Regina know you're here?"

Trotter chuckled. "She knows a good journalist is wherever he's supposed to be."

Mark was almost petulant. "You're no journalist."

"I've got a press card."

Mark licked his lips. A good sign. Nerves were starting to tighten. "What did I ruin?" he demanded.

"The plan to take the White House. Or at least to fuck up the election so bad the country would be hopelessly weakened."

"You're sick, Trotter. You're in a lot of trouble once I get out of here."

"I'll worry about that after you get out of here. Bet you I won't need more than one shot. But you still don't get it, do you? *Abweg* is the deep-cover man. *Abweg* is the one they want in the White House. They made your father endorse Babington tonight; in a day or so, the tape leaks, the one that has the sounds of your father killing a young girl all those years ago. It's the only way it makes sense—Borzov isn't the type to leave a potentially dangerous tool around after he's used it. This way, your father is destroyed, and so is Babington. Abweg promises to appoint a special prosecutor as soon as he's in office, and similar baloney." Trotter looked at him. "What do you think?"

Trotter knew what *he* thought. He thought Borzov was a genius. He set U.S. Intelligence up to be looking for a Russian agent seeking the White House, then planned to give them the innocent Babington on a platter. If Mark hadn't started killing audio men the Agency probably wouldn't even have come in on this case until now.

Mark Van Horn dropped the pose of anger and bewilderment. He raised himself up on his elbows, brought his feet up flat to the floor and spread his knees. "How did you know about the tape?" he asked.

This was, of course, the first confirmation Trotter had that there actually was a tape. "Don't worry about that," Trotter said. "The only thing you have to worry about is telling me where Joe Albright is, and how to get him out of there."

"You're a friend of this Albright character? He's the black guy, isn't he?"

"Don't try to stall me, Mark."

"You want him?"

"Badly."

"What do I get out of this?"

Without a word, Trotter kicked him in the groin. Hard. Mark wanted to scream, but he choked on it, producing something between a cough and a gurgle. His face turned red and he rolled on the floor.

"Go ahead and scream," Trotter told him. "Don't hold down the noise on my account. The guard is unconscious, and Babington has undoubtedly already left the ballroom by now. Where he goes, the Secret Service goes. It's just us, my friend."

Mark whined. Trotter leaned over him, grabbed his shirt and pulled him face-up again. He leaned his face close against Mark's. The Senator's son cowered.

"Listen, you stupid little jerk. This isn't a *game*. You don't get to fuck around with the fate of the world because your name is Van Horn. You are in deep shit, and I hold the flush handle. You want to know what you get out of this? You get to keep your balls. If you make me happy."

Trotter threw him back to the floor. "Now. I'm going to ask you again. Where is Joe Albright, and how do I get him out of there?"

There were a few rasping sobs as Mark tried to get his breath back.

"Just one thing before you answer. You are coming with me, every step of the way, and the first time we find something that doesn't match with what you told me, you're going to get something that will make the kick I just gave you seem like a pleasant memory."

Mark told him. He gagged on the words, but he told him. Trotter was surprised that Mark hadn't had to throw up yet—he must not have kicked him as hard as he thought he did.

"SkyGrain, Inc. Out on Highway 41. In one of the silos. Number 16. It's just been emptied."

So far, so good, Trotter thought. "How many guards?"

"Just—just two."

"Names?"

"Jeff and Ed. Jeff's in charge."

"How do we get in?"

"Flash headlights three times at the gate. Then drive to the sign that says 16, leave the car and walk."

"Wonderful. Can you?"

"Can I what?"

"Walk?"

"I don't know."

"Well, let's find out." Trotter grabbed Mark by the shirt again, began dragging him to his feet.

Behind him, the door shot open.

Trotter spun to see who it was. That was a mistake; he should have hit the floor. The figure in the doorway had a gun, and used it. A small-caliber bullet took Trotter in the right arm, stinging him like a hot needle. The silenced automatic fell from Trotter's hand. The man in the door—Ainley Masters, Trotter thought, Jesus, how humiliating—fired twice more. One bullet took Trotter below the ribcage, the other in the chest.

Trotter sank to his knees.

Masters fired again. The gun made a sharp little pop, undramatic and unremarkable. This time, the bullet missed. Either that, or Trotter was past feeling it.

No, Trotter thought. *This is wrong. I'm not supposed to die now. I want to live.* He wished he could figure out how he was going to manage it.

Trotter sprawled out on the floor across the body of Senator Henry Van Horn.

CHAPTER THIRTEEN

Ainley Masters stood there, experiencing a new sensation. He had never been shocked before, least of all by himself. If you'd asked him, he would have said he'd seen too much, been a part of too much, to be able to feel the emotion.

He was shocked now. True, he had bought the gun, and had practiced with it. But that was mental, that was precaution. To think that he had actually had to *use* the gun, that he had used it *successfully*, that he had succeeded in *killing* a man, boggled the mind.

A boggled mind, Ainley was learning, had trouble taking in details. Now an appreciation of just what he had walked into was seeping into his brain. The Senator dead. Mark threatened with death.

"Ainley," Mark said. His voice sounded strange. "You're a hero!"

"This is terrible. Are you all right?"

Mark burst out laughing. "Not a game," he said, and laughed harder. Hysterical, of course. Ainley thought of slapping Mark's face, but Mark brought himself under control.

"I'm sorry, Ainley," he said. "Shock, I guess." Ainley understood perfectly. "Dad's dead," Mark went on.

"Who—who did I . . . ?"

"Who did you kill? Trotter. Regina Hudson's fiancé. He was after me—Dad stepped in front of the bullet."

Ainley thought, at least Hank *died* like a Van Horn. He said, "But why would this Trotter want to—"

"Who knows? Maybe he couldn't stand it that I had been with his girlfriend before. I just hope he hasn't done anything to her." Mark's face showed sober concern, but his eyes were very bright.

"Listen, Ainley," Mark went on. "I've got to go get the police. You stay here and watch things."

"I should handle that," Ainley said. "It's my job."

"You've handled this part fine, so far." Mark bent over and picked up a gun larger than Ainley's. He held it gingerly, by the trigger guard. "I want to get this safely in the hands of the police—it's the gun that killed my father. It's evidence. You just stay here and make sure nothing gets disturbed."

It made perfect sense, but Ainley wasn't sure he liked it. "What if—what if he's not really dead?"

"Who, Trotter?"

"Yes."

"You got him twice in the chest, Ainley. He's dead. If you're nervous about it, put another bullet or two into him."

Ainley shuddered.

"You'd be perfectly justified." Ainley closed his eyes. "Are you going to be all right?" Mark asked.

Ainley ran his hand over his chin. "Yes. Yes, Mark, I'll be fine. I saw the Senator leave the ballroom, go through the curtain, you know, and I wondered what he was up to, especially since it was obvious he didn't *want* to be noticed. I went around to the stage door, and found the guard unconscious. So I took out my gun and came in. I heard some strange sounds, and I found that room and you—"

"All right, Ainley. Save it for the police. I'll be right back."

Mark clapped him on the shoulder, then left. Ainley still worried about him, though. As soon as he was out of sight, Mark had made a sound that was quite like laughter.

• • •

Regina Hudson was standing in the lobby of the hotel, losing her temper by inches. The Senator's endorsement and Babington's appreciation of it had been over for twenty minutes now. Mark was supposed to meet her *immediately* after. She did not like being stood up, even by a Van Horn.

But it was more than that, more than who Mark was or what he and Regina had been to each other (whatever that was). Most of her anger was directed at herself. She had agreed to this. She was *supposed* to be the publisher of the nation's most powerful newspapers, and here she was, waiting in a hotel lobby like a blind date. Or at best, a cub reporter.

To hell with it, she decided. *Worldwatch* will live without the interview. I'll get to a pay phone, she thought, I saw one just outside the ladies' room while the Senator was making his speech, find out where Allan is, and spend the night with him the way I spent the afternoon. I'm an executive. I hire competent people. Let them get on with it.

She'd taken two steps in the direction of the ladies' room when the elevator opened, and Mark Van Horn stepped out. Dammit, she thought.

"Regina," Mark said. He was a little breathless, and he seemed to be walking strangely, but he appeared ridiculously happy to see her. He wore no tie, and was carrying his jacket over his arm. "I'm sorry I'm late. I ran into some people."

Regina sighed. "Oh, it's all right. Nice speech."

"What?"

"Your father made a nice speech."

"He always does. He's good at it. I suppose you want the family angle."

Regina smiled in spite of herself. The Van Horns probably had a gene for knowing what the press wanted and giving it to them. "Where do you want to eat? We'll go as soon as Sean Murphy gets here. He went to check our coverage of the party. There's a pretty good steak house down the street, I understand."

"Do you have a car with you?"

"Well, yes, I do. But I don't really want to drive anywhere, Mark—"

"Yes, you do."

"—I mean we're right in the middle of town, there must be a dozen places that . . . What did you say?"

"I said, 'Yes, you do.'"

Regina felt something poke her in the ribs. She looked down. Mark lifted the jacket over his arm enough to show her the gun.

"Yes, you do," he said again.

• • •

Mark looked at Regina as she drove. Her chin was firm; she kept her eyes on the road. The little bitch had guts. If she'd been less inhibited in her love life, they could have done great things together.

"Take the ramp for the highway," Mark told her. A little bit of pink tongue flicked across her upper lip. "Oh," Mark went on. "If you're thinking of flooring it and threatening to crack us up if I don't get rid of the gun, go ahead and do it. You won't live past seventy-five miles per hour. Right now, Regina, I'm a man with nothing to lose. The police and the KGB and God knows what else is after me. You are alive only because I'm betting that not even the KGB would want to monkey with the American press. Got it?"

Mark wondered how much of that he meant. He was sure the KGB would be on his ass—all the reasons he'd postulated for their keeping him alive went out the window once you bought the idea that the Russians' plan had been to deliver Dad to the wrong candidate, then destroy them both. And Mark did buy it. It was beautiful, it was safe, and it was nasty. It was exactly the kind of thing he might have thought of himself.

Then why hadn't he?

He told himself to shut up. He couldn't think of every goddam thing, could he? The thing he had to think of was what he was going to do now.

"What are you going to do now?" Regina asked. The bitch had been reading his mind.

"Shut up and drive."

"I mean, you're obviously in trouble, Mark. But you can't be in worse trouble than my mother was. Allan Trotter helped her; maybe he could help you."

Mark had to laugh. "I doubt it," he said. "Trotter's dead."

Regina gave a little gasp at that. She said nothing more, but her chin was trembling now. Mark derived an obscure satisfaction from watching it.

But what am I going to do? Well, Ainley had probably gotten tired of waiting for the police by now. He was undoubtedly telling them that Trotter had killed the Senator in an attempt to get Mark. He would tell them that there might be reason to believe something bad had befallen Regina Hudson, too. And what had happened to Mark? Could Trotter have had an accomplice?

It might not have been the best idea to plant all that for Ainley to recite—for one thing, it would make him and Regina the subject of a police search. Still, it was a good story for later.

And all Mark could do now would be to do his best to make it stand up. He had to tie off loose ends—the girl, Albright, Jeff and Ed—then convince the cops the three men had been Trotter's accomplices and that they'd killed Regina. If the fact that Jeff and Ed worked for Gus Pickett tainted that old bastard, too, Mark wouldn't cry about it.

After that, he'd show up at the police station like a good boy, yet another Van Horn hero. That would take care of the police.

Then he'd gather up Ainley Masters and go back to the home state, to the home compound, triple the security, and stay there as many months or as many years as it took to get the KGB off his tail.

He'd do it. The Van Horn brains, skill, and luck might have skipped his father, the poor dumb bastard, but Mark had them in full measure. Trotter had thought he was finished, but Trotter was wrong.

Mark was beginning to realize that for Mark Van Horn, there were no defeats, only temporary setbacks. *Whatever we do, it must be right.*

Chapter Fourteen

Don't moan, dammit! Whatever you do, don't moan.

Trotter kept telling that to himself, shouting, *screaming* it over and over silently in his mind. Lying there on the floor of that godforsaken dressing room without moaning was the second-hardest thing he'd ever done.

The hardest was not reacting when Mark Van Horn casually suggested that Ainley Masters put another bullet or two into him. That wouldn't have been a moan—it would have been a cry of rage, or a whimper.

Sooner or later, he would have to make some kind of noise—it was inevitable. When he did, he'd also have to make a move, because Ainley Masters was still there, about three feet away from him, still holding the gun.

Trotter couldn't see him. He'd blacked out temporarily when the third slug hit, and landed with his eyes closed. He didn't dare open them—what if Masters was looking at him when he did? He could feel his back muscles tighten at the idea of the bullet that would crash his spine and finish the job.

He forced himself to relax; to take shallow, almost imperceptible breaths through his nose. You've been trained for this, he told himself. You've been trained for everything. Use it.

All right. All right.

For starters, he was alive. That alone put him ahead of the game. Three slugs at that range, even with a little popgun like Masters's .25, could very easily have been lethal. Mark Van Horn had been positive that they were—that branded him an amateur. All Mark's shooting had been done with heavier guns.

Trotter was in a lot of pain, but there was no blood in his mouth or nose.

That meant that the bullets had missed his lungs. His right arm was killing him, he doubted if it would be any good at all; his chest felt as if he were lying face-down on rocks.

Trotter had to make his move soon. Now. He didn't like what he'd heard them saying about Regina. Not at all. Van Horn could use her to—

Trotter made himself stop. He couldn't afford to worry about that until he got out of there. He couldn't get out of there without thinking.

It was easy to see what was working against him—unarmed, wounded, possibly unable to move at all—either or both of the bullets that hit his torso could be lodged in his spine, in which case this entire train of thought became academic. So forget about that, too. Either he could move, or he couldn't. He'd find out soon enough.

All right. Assuming he *could* move, what did he have going *for* him? Two things. Surprise, for one. If Trotter could do anything at all, it was a lot more than Ainley Masters would be expecting from a dead man.

Trotter's other advantage was experience, or rather Ainley Masters's lack of experience. If Masters had any idea of what he was doing, he would have sat down in that chair in front of the dressing table so that he'd be able to sight a straight line past Trotter's (and the Senator's) body to the hall. That way, he could correct Trotter's condition if he showed unwelcome signs of life, and he could make sure that anybody who wanted to enter the room was a friend.

Instead, Masters was pacing back and forth, muttering little prayers asking that the police get there soon, that Mark should hurry up, that he didn't like this, and what was the press going to say?

Every third or fourth trip past Trotter, Masters would open the door and look out, then walk back toward the makeup table. That was the time. He came within three feet of Trotter, he was facing away from him, and he had his mind on other things.

Trotter listened. Step, step, step, step. Door opens. Masters's curses. Door closes. Step, step, step, step, step.

Now.

Trotter opened his eyes to gauge the range, then, with a sudden effort, whipped his legs around as hard as he could. The effort made him scream—a high, almost voiceless scream that sounded inhuman to him even through the pain that had caused it.

But the maneuver had worked. Trotter's shins caught Masters just above the ankles and tore his legs out from under him. The gun went flying as Masters hit the ground.

Pushing with his legs and his good left arm, Trotter half-crawled, half-sprang on top of Masters. He pinned the smaller man with his weight and smashed his face with his left fist until Masters lost consciousness.

Then Trotter collapsed on top of him. He heard Masters's breath rasping in his ear, and was vaguely glad he hadn't killed him.

Now, Trotter could moan. And whimper, and scream. Which he did until he decided that not only wasn't it getting him anywhere, it didn't even seem to reduce the pain much.

Well, he thought, *at least I'm not paralyzed*. Then he laughed, but that hurt, too.

Trotter took a deep breath. I have to stand up, now, he thought. He thought it five times before he actually tried it. In a way, it was worse than jumping Masters. He'd *had* to do that. This was a matter of choice.

He struggled to his feet, staggered, then almost went down again as a wave of nausea washed over him. There was a small sink in a corner of the dressing room; Trotter made it in time to throw up. He stood there retching long after his stomach was empty. He felt as if he were being torn in half.

Finally, it stopped. "Jesus," he said. He looked into the sink. No blood in the vomit. My lucky day, he thought. Shot twice in the chest, didn't get shot in the heart, lungs or stomach. If he could get these holes in him covered up, he could live for hours yet before he bled to death, or died of gangrene or peritonitis. Hours would probably be enough. By tomorrow, expert help would be there, and he could take it easy in the hospital.

There were towels on a shelf above the sink. Half of them looked clean enough; the other half, though folded, had smears of stage makeup on them.

Trotter turned on the cold water, took off his glasses and splashed his face over and over. He soaked his jacket and shirt in the process, but he was going to lose them, anyway.

He put his glasses back on and struggled out of the wet clothes. He assessed the damage in the mirror.

There were two holes in his arm. That meant the bullet had passed right through. That wound could be ignored, except for the fact that it hurt like a son of a bitch. There was a hole just to the right side of his sternum, and a bluish lump under his skin halfway between the hole and his armpit. That was the third bullet, the one that had hit him as he was going down. Thank God for luck and small-caliber weapons, Trotter thought. The bullet had hit a rib and skidded along it under the skin, not piercing the chest cavity at all. It had also fucked up any motion of his right arm that the first bullet might have left him, but you can't have everything.

The second bullet was the joker. That one had entered just below the rib cage, and was still in there, somewhere. Blood oozed from the wound freely, and when he moved it opened and closed like a tiny mouth. Trotter was almost sick again, looking at it. Instead, he covered the two holes in his chest with a clean, folded towel, tying it in place with strips cut off another towel with his pocketknife. He had to lean against the edge of the sink to get his arm to bend enough to get his right hand into play, an effort that brought tears to his eyes, but he got it done. Then he cut a wider strip, and with his left hand and teeth tied it around his arm. He picked up the .25, closed his eyes, swallowed twice, and left the room.

The air was cold on his bare chest. That was bad; a sign of loss of blood. Couldn't stop to worry about it. What he needed now was clothes. Ainley Masters's were hopeless, the man was much too small. The Senator's shirt and jacket would be no improvement over his own bloody and bullet-riddled stuff. That left the security guard.

The man was moaning when Trotter got to him; Trotter put him back under, hoping as he did that he wasn't giving the poor bastard brain damage. Trotter rolled him out of his jacket and shirt and struggled into them. They were a bit tight, especially with the improvised bandage underneath them, but they'd do. Trotter kept the jacket buttoned in the hallway to hide the blood that was even now soaking its way through the towel.

He took the elevator to the lobby. A phone, he thought. Got to get to a phone. As he crossed the lobby, he supposed he was walking all right. Certainly no worse than a man who'd had a few drinks. He was glad now for all the exercises he'd done to strengthen his legs.

A voice behind him said, "Trotter!"

Trotter almost drilled him with the automatic. His left hand was on its way out of the jacket pocket with the gun when he recognized the voice as that of Sean Murphy.

"Murphy," Trotter said. "What are you doing here?"

"I was going to ask you the same thing. What's the matter with you, you look like hell."

"Murphy, I've got no time for this. What are you doing here, some kind of story?"

"Might be. Though I actually came to meet Regina. Babington's party has moved to his campaign headquarters suite, and Senator Van Horn isn't there. I thought it might interest our readers to know where he is. Especially if he's shacked up with a bimbo."

"He's not," Trotter said. "You got any aspirin?"

"In my car. You sound like you know where Van Horn is."

"When was the last time you spoke to Regina?"

"Right after we got here. We had jobs to do, you know. She's doing hers. A guy from the local paper saw her go off in a car with Mark Van Horn about fifteen minutes ago. I wonder why she didn't wait for me."

"Son of a *bitch!*" Trotter said.

Murphy smiled at him. "What's the matter? Jealous?"

"Where's your car?"

"What do you mean, where's my car?"

Trotter's left hand grabbed a handful of Murphy's shirt. "I mean, where's your goddam car? Because we're going there *right now.*"

"Okay, okay," Murphy said. The reporter cursed himself. Trotter looked at least two-thirds dead, and Murphy was *still* scared shitless of him.

"I'm sorry," Trotter told him. "Really."

"It's all right." Murphy certainly *hoped* it was all right. "Is this about Regina?"

"Oh, yeah. I'm going to need your help. And I'm really going to need that aspirin."

Chapter Fifteen

And the next thing that happens, Sean Murphy told himself, is that a big tornado comes along and blows me to Oz.

Unless, of course, I'm already there.

Murphy sat in the front seat of the Acura Legend he had borrowed from the publisher of the local paper, wondering what Trotter's blood would do to the custom interior. Trotter had spent the whole trip out here to SkyGrain, Inc., talking, eating aspirins like M&Ms, and bleeding on the publisher's leather upholstery.

If Murphy looked really hard into the rearview mirror, he might convince himself he could still see Trotter making his slow, agonizing way toward the silver-gray building known as Silo 16. Trotter had avoided the access road, but there was enough moon to light his way.

Murphy was looking in the rearview mirror because Trotter had given him instructions—he'd given him *tons* of instructions, the last of which was "turn the horses for home"—in other words, have the car pointing in the right direction so as not to waste a second if he had to get the hell out of there in a hurry.

Murphy had a gun in his hand—a .25 automatic, according to Trotter. Trotter had insisted that he take it.

"I know nothing about guns," Murphy had protested.

"Nothing to it," Trotter had said, in the dreamy voice he had spoken in for their entire trip out there. "Are you right-handed?"

"Yes."

"Good. This gun was made for you. Point. Press this lever with your thumb. Pull the trigger. Bang. If you don't press the lever, the trigger won't pull. If anybody gives you any shit trying to get out of there, shoot him."

"You shoot him. You're the professional."

"My right arm doesn't work. Can't use this gun lefty. Give me your lighter."

"My what?"

"That goddam Zippo you're always waving around. You've lit three cigarettes with it since we got on the road."

Murphy had taken his eyes off the road to look at Trotter. A mistake. The man looked like a corpse, except corpses don't ooze blood through their clothes. "Why do you want my lighter? I've had this thing through two wars."

"Because I *can* use it lefty. Come on, Murphy. Lives are at stake here. I need your lighter, and I'm too weak to take it from you."

Murphy handed it over. Trotter began to tell him a story about international politics and espionage, about cowardice and betrayal, about sex and murder and the future of the world.

Murphy refused to believe it. "You're bullshitting me to keep yourself awake."

"Murphy, I have probably told you fewer lies than anybody I ever met in my life. Lies I expected to be believed, anyway. I'm not lying now."

Murphy saw Trotter close his eyes and swallow. He looked like a man who'd stayed awake since the beginning of time to record all of human folly. Murphy didn't doubt anymore.

"Why did you tell me this?" Murphy asked.

"If Regina or I or a black guy named Joe Albright doesn't join you within twenty minutes of the time I leave the car, I want you to haul ass to the nearest typewriter, write this up, and print it."

"Print it? All this secret stuff?"

"Print it. I'll be past giving a damn, and the novelty of it alone should make it effective. We've tried every other goddam thing; let's try the truth."

"What if you do come back?"

"We'll talk about it."

"That sounds more like you."

Trotter chuckled, then groaned. "Don't make me laugh," he said. "It hurts."

Then they were at SkyGrain's main gate. When, following Trotter's instructions, Murphy flashed the car's headlights three times, the guard at the gate waved them right through.

"The little bastard told the truth about that much, at least," Trotter muttered.

They'd followed signs on the access road for about five minutes when Trotter told him to stop. He'd given final instructions, then said, "I still like you, Murphy."

Murphy said, "Just get her out safe, okay?"

Trotter's face twisted into something that was probably supposed to be a grin, and he slunk off into the night. Murphy watched in the mirror, every so often managing to believe he saw Trotter making his way to the silo Mark Van Horn had said contained Joe Albright. Trotter was sure he'd brought Regina there too, because Mark had to finish off Albright before he did anything else.

Murphy hoped Trotter was right. He hoped they weren't too late.

And he wondered why he, sound and healthy in every limb, was sitting in a bloodstained car seat shitting bricks, while a badly wounded man went off to try to rescue the woman they both loved, armed only with a cigarette lighter.

Because Trotter was a professional and he wasn't. That's all. Murphy just wished he could get that swallowed and keep it down.

He looked in the mirror again. A small rectangle of light appeared at the base of Silo 16, then disappeared.

Trotter had made it. He was inside.

Now there was nothing to do but wait.

Chapter Sixteen

Regina was sitting with Joe Albright, listening to Mark trying to convince the two big blond men to kill them both.

"It's got to be done, right away," Mark insisted.

"Not in here," the one called Jeff said. "Especially not with a gun. How many times do I have to tell you, we're walking around inside a bomb in here. Will be for another day and a half."

"We're not going to be here for another day and a half," Mark said. "And you don't have to do it here. In fact, I'd rather do it somewhere else. Let's just please get going."

"Should have taken his damn gun away from him the way we took the belt and shoes from the nigger," Ed said. He was distinguishable from Jeff only in that he had a mustache.

"Anyway," Jeff went on. "We don't work for you, we work for Mr. Pickett."

"And Mr. Pickett told you to follow my orders, didn't he?"

"He said find out what the nigger knows. He didn't say anything about killing anybody. Neither did you, till you walked through the door with this girl I never heard of and want her killed, too. Do you think it comes cheaper in job lots or something?"

Ed laughed. So did Regina.

Mark looked at her, and Regina laughed harder. "I'm sorry," she said. "It's you. You've got all sorts of plans to run the country, run the world, and it turns out you can't even run two thugs." Her laugh turned into a cough. They were all coughing. It's probably very unhealthy to be here, she thought, and that started her laughing again.

Mark told her, angrily, to shut up.

"I'll shut up when you kill me, Mark. And even then, you'll know I died laughing at you."

"You tell him, Bash," Joe Albright said. His voice was weak, but he was grinning. They had hurt him badly—his brown skin was purple-black where they had beaten him. Trying to get him to talk, God knows about what.

This was Allan's world. Had been, she reminded herself. Allan was dead. He'd tried to compromise between his world and hers (so had she) and now they were both going to die.

Mark was getting impatient. "Look, I'll get them out of here if you don't have balls enough to do it. Are you going to help me, or not?"

A voice said, "Not." Allan's voice.

• • •

Trotter closed the small door behind him, then raised his left hand to show them Murphy's lighter. Two bruisers, who had to be Jeff and Ed, stopped in their tracks.

"How nice to see everybody here," he said. "Thanks especially to you, Mark. Now I know what it takes to make a Van Horn honest—scare him to death."

Mark was still goggling at him.

"You've led too lucky a life, Mark. You take it for granted. The Van Horn luck would dictate that Ainley killed me, so that was the way it had to be. You didn't even feel my pulse. Not smart."

A fat drop of blood rolled off the tips of the fingers of Trotter's right hand and splattered on the floor of the silo.

One of the muscle, the one with a mustache, spoke for the first time. "You may not be dead, mister, but you're in a bad way."

Trotter winced, and grinned at him. "You're right," he said. "Absolutely right." Trotter backed up to the wall just to the side of the door he'd entered by. He put his back against the wall, and slid slowly to the floor. With his thumb, he flipped back the top of the zippo.

"Absolutely right," he said again. "I've lost some blood, and I feel a little sick and light-headed and weak. But all I need is enough strength to light this lighter. Not even. To spin the wheel and make a spark. Do I need to explain to you gentlemen the explosive properties of recently emptied grain-storage facilities?"

"Christ, no," said Ed reverently. "We've been trying to tell him."

"Regina," Trotter said.

"Yes, Allan."

"Good to hear your voice, Bash."

"Yours too."

"Joe, can you walk?"

"I haven't tried for a long time. I could probably stagger. How bad are you hurt?"

"We'll have a contest later. Regina, get Joe out of here."

"But Allan—"

"Move! There's a car waiting about a hundred yards down the road. Get in it and get moving. If you see a cop, stop one. If you don't, get to the nearest phone and get reinforcements. I'll make sure our company stays here."

"Nobody leaves," Mark said. "What kind of bullshit is this?"

"Mark," Trotter said, "we are three people with nothing to lose. Jeff and Ed, too, unless they haven't figured out you plan to kill them. You can't afford to leave anybody behind who knows what you've been up to, can you?"

"Shut up."

"Get moving," Trotter told Regina. He could see from her face she didn't like it, but she helped Joe to his feet and brought him toward the door.

"Allan," she said.

"Everything will be fine. Go as fast as you can. Joe, you know what to do, right?"

Albright met his eyes. "I know what to do," he said.

"Stop!" Mark said.

Regina didn't even hesitate. Trotter loved her more than ever.

"Close the door behind you," he said as she left. "I love you, Bash."

• • •

Joe Albright was shaky on his feet, but they moved steadily along the access road. About ten yards down the road, Albright stopped. He put his face close to hers. He looked terrible—one eye was swollen closed, and he seemed to be having trouble focusing the other one.

"Joe, are you all right?"

"So far," he said. "Make me a promise. If I tell you to, you promise me you'll drop me like a bad habit and run like hell for the car."

"No. *No!* It's bad enough I have to leave Allan."

"He knows what he's doing. He—what was I saying—" They were walking again, now, and Joe seemed to have trouble concentrating. "Right. He knows what he's doing. He had to stay because I'm concussed; I keep drifting in and out, the way I just did. If something happens, if I slow you down so none of us gets away, it will all be wasted."

Regina said nothing.

"Promise me," Joe said.

"All right, I promise. Are you happy? Now shut up and save your strength."

It took maybe three minutes to reach the car. It seemed like lifetimes, generations of lifetimes, all of them filled with terror. Regina felt a vast surge of relief when Sean Murphy popped out of the car and practically carried Joe Albright the rest of the way to the vehicle. Joe passed out as soon as they got him inside the car, kneeling over sideways like a cowboy shot from the saddle. Regina got in the back seat with him and held him up. Sean started the engine and floored it.

• • •

"That's it," Trotter said when Regina and Albright had left. "Now we wait for the cops."

"You ain't never gonna stay conscious long enough for any cops to get here, mister," the one with the mustache said.

Trotter felt a dopey little smile form on his face. "Maybe not. But I can stay awake long enough to make sure my friends get away. And I can blow us all to ground round if I feel myself start to drift off."

Mark Van Horn made a sound somewhere between a scream and a growl.

Trotter's grin broadened. "Yes, here I am again, Mark, kicking you in the nuts. You're through. The KGB plan is through. The Van Horns are through fucking around with the United States of America like it was their own private plantation."

Mark sniffed. "The Van Horns *made* this country."

"Made it *what*, Mark?" Trotter heard his own voice and realized to his shock that he knew what he was doing. Mark Van Horn must never be seen again by human eyes—the situation was too confused, too delicate for this precocious little grabber to be allowed to live. A Mark Van Horn who came through this alive and able to lie—to anybody—would be too dangerous to be tolerated. He had been ready—even determined—to hand the country over to the Russians. Only Mark's own stupidity had prevented it from happening. With a new Van Horn martyr behind him, Mark would be, in the eyes of many, even less capable of doing wrong than the late Hank had been.

No. Mark had to die.

And all Trotter had to do was kill him. It was so simple. Flick an emery wheel against a flint, and the curtain comes down for both of us.

So why don't you do it? he asked himself.

Shh, he told himself cunningly. I'm giving Bash more time to get to safety. Besides, I might think of something by the time the cops get here. The cops, he reminded himself, who by now were undoubtedly looking for him as the murderer of Senator Van Horn.

Trotter sighed inwardly.

So let Mark do it, he thought. He's been responsible for so many deaths, let him be responsible for his own. And mine, I suppose. Though I don't know if I'm going to make it in any case.

So he taunted Mark. Tried to make him forget the situation and fire the gun.

"Made it what?" he said again. "All you've managed to do is make it stink."

And that did it. Mark growled something that sounded like "You bastard," and the gun came up.

And Ed had to be a hero. "No!" the thug screamed, and threw himself on Mark's arm. Mark had taken the silencer off long ago, but the blast was considerably muzzled.

Ed fell, blood spurting from his chest. He'd be dead in seconds.

The silo was still standing.

"'Walking around inside a bomb,'" Mark sneered.

"The only reason it didn't go up," Trotter said reasonably, "was that Ed's body covered all the muzzle-flash."

The whole thing was just beginning to dawn on Jeff. He walked to Mark and looked at his friend's body with eyes and mouth wide open.

"Don't bullshit me, Trotter. Now I know that lighter doesn't mean anything. Good-bye and good riddance."

He started to raise the gun again. This time Jeff jumped him.

"You stupid son of a bitch!" he yelled, and hit Mark in the mouth. Mark went down and dropped the gun.

Logic still told Trotter that Mark had to die tonight, but self-preservation told him there was no reason Trotter had to go up with him. All he had to do was stand up and get out the door right next to him.

His legs were asleep. His blood pressure had dropped to the point where the muscles in his extremities weren't getting enough oxygen. Sitting in one position on a hard floor had only made matters worse. Trotter cursed and watched Jeff and Mark rolling on the floor. Jeff was bigger, but Mark was dirtier. It looked like anybody's fight, but it didn't look as if it would last too long.

Trotter dropped the lighter, making a promise to get Murphy a new one, if he insisted, buy him the whole Zippo factory, if he could get out of here alive. He licked his left hand, then smacked the palm of it hard against the wall behind him. He pushed straight down and willed his legs to move. The pain came back. It had no locality—his whole body was a throbbing wound.

Trotter managed to get his right leg bent, his right foot flat on the floor. That, and some patience, was all it took. If they could just keep fighting long enough . . .

But no. Mark had Jeff by the throat and wasn't letting go. It would be over in seconds.

With one last effort, Trotter fought to his feet. He had his hand on the doorknob when Mark threw Jeff away and picked up his gun.

• • •

The light came like a sudden dawn behind them just as the Acura was clearing the front gate. Murphy had wondered what he was going to do about the guard. It turned out he didn't have to do anything. He, like everyone for miles around, was looking at the fireball.

The noise came just behind the light, a sharp crack, then a low rumble like thunder. Joe Albright stirred. "What was that?" he asked.

"Shh," Regina said. "Just a storm, Joe. Try to stay awake. We're getting help for you."

Murphy said, "Regina . . ."

"I'm all right, Sean. Keep moving."

"I—"

"Let's talk later, Sean, okay?"

He left her alone. Regina Hudson's tears rolled fat down her cheeks. They fell unheeded from her face, and mixed with a pool of Allan Trotter's blood on the floor of the Legend.

EPILOGUE
CLOTHO

She who spins the thread of life . . .

Chapter One

June—Maryland

Aside from the toilet, this was the first place the Congressman had gone by himself since his stroke. It wasn't his idea. He'd been asked for.

Borzov had asked for him. As soon as he had heard what had happened out there on the Great Plains, the Congressman had begun making plans—foolish, desperate plans—to keep Borzov in the United States, so that he could get his hands on the bastard.

The plans hadn't been necessary. Borzov's illness had taken care of that. There was an infirmary in the Soviet Embassy, but that wasn't good enough for the General. Knowing the state of Soviet medical care, the Congressman was not surprised.

Instead, the Ambassador had engaged an entire floor of a small but superior private hospital in Maryland, just outside the D.C. line. The word was (and the Congressman had always made it a point to get the best available word) that "General Dudakov" might die at any minute.

Then the Congressman had received a personal telephone call from the Soviet Ambassador. It was the General's strong wish—the Ambassador did not say "last wish," though he might as well have—to see his old comrade-in-arms for the last time.

The Congressman had played it cagey, delaying a decision by pleading his own ill health. It was all too possible that this was some kind of scam to finger him as the head of the Agency, to reveal that the Agency existed. Borzov could be trying to put his thumb in the Congressman's eye one last time before he went.

The Congressman grieved for his son. His loss left him empty, an emptiness made all the more barren by the knowledge that "Allan Trotter" would not be simply ignored by history, but would go down as the brutal assassin of Senator Henry Van Horn and his son.

The Congressman's head, however, had not emptied. This was still his game; he was still the master of all the moves. He wanted to see Borzov, but he didn't want anybody putting anything over on him.

The first thing he did was to get the State Department to sign off on his visit to the General.

"Go, by all means," they had said. "It will be good for international relations."

Fine. As good a cover as any. He went.

The Congressman was frisked twice, once by a Soviet guard, and once by an American. He didn't know what the American was guarding, unless it was the Soviet guard. They didn't let him keep his walking stick. The Soviet guard ushered him into Borzov's room. And stayed there.

Borzov was a white lump on a hospital bed. Tubes emerged from unlikely places, flowing with liquids of various unappetizing colors. The face above the sheet was as gray as the implausibly tidy hair on Borzov's head. Someone, the Congressman thought, must have come in every twenty minutes to comb it.

Borzov said something that was muffled by the oxygen tube across his upper lip. The Congressman got closer to the bed. The guard's face said he didn't like that, but he made no move to stop him.

"He speaks English," Borzov said. His voice was a whisper, barely audible above the beeping of the heart monitor.

"Who does?"

Borzov rolled his eyes in the direction of the guard. *"Français, alors, bien?"*

The Congressman smiled and switched to French. "It is a very Imperial habit, for a Russian to be speaking French. You may be in trouble."

"I am already in trouble. I am kept alive only so that they may bring me back to Moscow for trial. You have killed me at last, my friend."

"You climbed the horse's back yourself. Don't complain because he threw you."

"Very good. Besides, I shall win after all. I shall die in this hospital, then I will be celebrated a hero."

"You will forgive me if I harbor doubt about your disgrace."

"I failed. Under a previous regime, that would have been enough. But going ahead with my plan without proper clearance was a crime against *glasnost*, of the new spirit of cooperation. It seems, my friend, that the Chairman truly means it."

"From your mouth to God's ears," the Congressman said.

"Even words addressed to God's ears are tolerated these days. Do you believe in Fate, my friend?"

"I don't know."

"I believe in Fate. You and I have been fated to contest a war the world would not have been able to survive if it had been fought with armies and missiles. We have killed and lied and cheated and perverted the workings of our own and foreign governments. We—it was our fate that we do so. Perhaps if we had been less evenly matched, one of our countries would have found it necessary to trigger the end."

"This whole conversation is probably being recorded," the Congressman said. "Whether the guard speaks French or not. I have no idea what you're talking about."

"For the record, of course." The General took a deep pull of oxygen from the tube in his nostrils, coughed once, and went on. "For the record, you are humoring the vaporings of a dying man, all right?"

"Talk."

"Perhaps Fate has decided that we old men now move aside. Perhaps it is indeed time for the long, half-secret war between our nations to be over."

There were many sad things about war, the Congressman thought, but this was the saddest—as a matter of survival, you *must* descend to the level of the enemy. Not constantly, and not in every way, but in some way at least some of the time. In fighting Borzov and the men like him, the Congressman had in fact *become* like him. He preferred to think he had done it—sacrificed his humanity, if you wanted to put it that way—for a noble cause. But he would have preferred much more to have lived in a world where careers such as his would not have been necessary.

"Perhaps," the Congressman said. "But perhaps not. That is why men like you and I—humoring you, as you say—men like you and I will always be required."

"A sad thought."

"A sad thought indeed. I hate to leave you with one, but—"

"The Van Horns are *all* dead?"

The Congressman wanted to laugh. He was tempted to let Borzov die thinking he had Mark Van Horn tied up somewhere, spilling his guts about Borzov's little project to steal the White House.

He decided against it. The Congressman never lied for fun, only for advantage. "Yes, all. They found the son's—Mark Van Horn's—head in a field about a quarter of a mile away. It was badly burned, but the identification through dental records is positive. At least two others, probably three, died in the blast."

"And the assassin, this Trotter, is he dead, too?"

"According to the witnesses, there was no way he could have gotten out."

"He was at the party Senator Van Horn threw for me. You must have met him."

"I don't recall."

"Miss Hudson—she must be taking this badly."

"She's in seclusion."

"And Ainley Masters, the hero of the affair?"

"He's joined my staff." The Congressman grinned as he recalled his little talk with Ainley Masters. It would take years to unravel the mess the Van Horns had helped make of American politics; with Ainley Masters's knowledge, it might take fewer of them. Ainley was given to understand that he didn't have a choice in the matter. He signed on—what the hell, he'd been out of a job, anyway.

"A wise decision on your part. I suppose now Babington will be President."

"It's a safe assumption. He's acquired the holiness of the Van Horns by osmosis. And Abweg's suicide seemed to remove any doubt."

"It seems unusual for an American politician to take a loss so hard."

Or so messily, the Congressman thought, jumping off the roof of his hotel like that the day after the fateful endorsement. The Congressman wondered if Borzov thought he was fooling anyone. Still, one of the pleasures of the Congressman's job would be to tell the new President exactly how he got to *be* President. Another would be dealing with Gus Pickett. The Congressman had big plans for Gus Pickett.

"Time is up now," the guard said. He must have gotten tired of pretending he understood French, the Congressman thought.

"Help me up," the Congressman said. "Or give me back my cane."

But Borzov had one more question. He beckoned the Congressman closer. "He was your son, wasn't he? I am so sorry, my friend."

The Congressman stared at him for a few seconds. Then he swallowed, said, "Good-bye, General," and gave his arm to the guard.

They had just stepped into the hallway when the Congressman heard the intermittent beeps of the hospital monitor become a sustained note. Doctors and nurses bustled down the hall, nearly knocking him over. The Soviet guard handed him off to an American guard, who gave him his cane back and pointed him to the door.

The Congressman didn't leave. He waited some hours, until a doctor came and told him General Dudakov was dead. He waited more hours before they finally let him see with his own eyes the body of his comrade in the war against Hitler, his enemy ever since.

Only then did he call his driver and have himself taken to the offices of Fenton Rines Investigations, the secret headquarters of the Agency.

It was the only place he had that felt like home.

Chapter Two

March—Lucerne, Switzerland

The nurse was all bustle. She never smiled, and she gave orders like a printing-shop foreman, but she always made Regina feel better.

Right now, she bustled into the room with a glass contraption, thrust it at Regina, and said, "You must express now the milk. Your little one drink and drink while you sleep."

"I'm sorry," Regina said.

"Sh-sh-sh," the nurse told her. "It is not to be sorry. You had the difficult labor and the cesarean section, eh? That is major surgery. You must sleep. But little Alain must eat, no? So, you must express now the milk."

"Allan," Regina said.

"Alain, as I have said. The young nurses fight over who is to feed him. You will have to watch that one, Madame Hardin. Ring the bell when you are done."

The nurse bustled out. Regina smiled at her back as she went. They were very good here. They knew their business, and they asked no questions.

That was why she'd come to Switzerland—because the Swiss were famous for not asking questions.

Regina untied her nightgown, placed the pump over her breast, and began making sure her baby would be provided for. In the long run, that would be no problem. The sale of the Hudson Group had netted her enough to support a whole village for several lifetimes. She could have gotten even more if she'd sold it to that British publisher, but she was content to sell to a syndicate headed by Sean Murphy in a leveraged buyout.

For a while, when she'd first come overseas, she'd kept up with the international edition of *Worldwatch* just to see what Sean would print about the end of the Van Horns, considering how much he knew. He printed nothing the rest of the media didn't print. *Worldwatch* was a little more careful about calling Allan Trotter the *alleged* assassin than the others, but that was about it. The mysterious Congressman had probably wanted it that way. And to be fair, Regina had to admit that however much Sean knew, he had no evidence to back it up. As soon as she saw the item about Joe Albright's being released from the hospital and leaving the FBI to become vice president of Fenton Rines Investigations, she lost interest and stopped reading.

She had the baby to worry about. She often wondered just when the child had been conceived. She would always believe it was that last day, in that cold hotel room. If Allan had to leave her, at least he had left something behind.

Regina had known she had to leave the States as soon as she knew she was pregnant. It was too much. Her life had become a walking supermarket tabloid. RUSSIAN-SPY DAUGHTER MEDIA HEIRESS PREGNANT WITH VAN HORN ASSASSIN LOVE CHILD. She had dealt with a lot in the few years since Allan Trotter (I've never even known his real name, Regina thought) had come into her life, but she was damned if she was going to submit her baby to the ordeal of being fair game for the press. So the media heiress sold off her heritage and beat it before her condition became known.

She was going by the name of Ruth Hardin. Ruth because she also found herself husbandless in a foreign land, and Hardin because it was the first thing she could think of that started with "H." All her luggage was monogrammed.

Now she had the baby, a beautiful little boy, already curious about his world and these strange giant creatures who populated it. When the time came, she would tell him about his father—how he was strong and brave and very lonely, because he had been chosen to try to save the world from its own stupidities. She would tell him how during the time they had together, he had been happy for the first time in his life. How the idea of having a baby had scared and excited him. And how his love still existed, and would be shared between the two of them forever.

The container was full. Regina rang for the nurse. She came and took it away, gave Regina a shot, and told her to go to sleep. She dreamed, as she frequently did, of Allan. Happy dreams, this time, full of the things they'd planned to do, but never got around to.

The nurse came to see her when she woke up. The room was dark.

"Did you sleep well?"

"Very well," Regina said. She'd slept so well that she was still a little groggy.

"You had a visitor while you were asleep. Of course, I did not let him in."

Oh, no, Regina thought, they've found me, and I'm in no shape yet to run away.

"Who was he with?" Regina asked wearily.

"With? No, no, madame, he was alone."

"No, I mean—oh, never mind. What was his name?"

"That is somewhat confused. I asked him, and he said to me, 'Just say to her, "Bash."'"

"*Bash?*"

"Yes, madame. This Monsieur Bash also said he would come back if he were able."

"Why didn't you wake me up? For God's sake, why didn't you—"

"The doctor has ordered, madame. I do not understand—this Bash. It means something to you?"

Regina didn't know whether to laugh or cry. In the end, she did a little of both.

Watertown, Connecticut–Port Chester, New York
January 1988–February 1989